We are, by (

LIARS

ALL

Inspired by more than 10,000 polygraphs
conducted as a Phoenix police examiner

L. D. ZINGG

ISBN-13: 978-1975757403

ISBN-10: 1975757408

First Edition: 2018.01

Cover illustration by John Ingle

Edited by Donna Alward

Published by L. D. Zingg, LLC

LDZingg@gmail.com

FaceBook: LD Zingg

Available at Amazon.com

11-2-19

To Darryl
All the Best!

Luigi

Dedication

To Carl, my friend and mentor, whose quick wit and sage advice was always a welcome reminder to keep things in perspective and not take life too seriously. May he rest in peace. And to all dedicated polygraph examiners who are expected to determine truth from deception based on inexact science, and to always be right in their conclusions.

Acknowledgments

A special thanks to my family and friends for their encouragement and critiques. To my daughter, Jennifer Zingg, for urging me to continue writing, and to John Ingle, whose genius is matched only by his generosity. Their input was invaluable in developing and publishing this story.

Other books in this series

DESTINY OF A COP

THE LIGHT OF TRUTH

WHERE IT ALL BEGAN

Other works by this author

THE POETRY OF LIFE

Children's Books

BARNYARD FRIENDS

A ROBIN INVITED ME TO DINNER

I once worked with a very intelligent man who would often correct people when they started out with, "If I were you, I would do..." or, "If I were you, I would say..."

Those people always sounded so sure of themselves; so convinced that they were right. But he would tell them: "If you were me, then you would be me and you would, therefore, say and do what I would say and do." So I put it to verse.

IF I WERE YOU

I've often wondered how it'd be
If I were you, and you were me.
If I could live inside your skin
And know what's going on within.

If I could see things through your eyes,
I wonder, would I be as wise?
Would I be right and never wrong?
And always act like I belong?

Or would there be some lesser times
When things go wrong and nothing rhymes?
Would I be right, but sometimes wrong?
Sometimes weak, and sometimes strong?

The answer is as plain can be
When viewed in its reality.
We'd each be as we are, you see,
If I were you, and you were me.

L. D. Zingg

PART ONE - THE TRANSFER

"Be content with what you are, and wish not change;
nor dread your last day, nor long for it."
– Marcus Aurelius, Roman emperor (121-180)

CHAPTER ONE

Phoenix, Arizona
January 1971

Phoenix Police Sergeant, Luke Canfield, picked up his empty cup and ambled to the break room for a refill. As far as he was concerned, it was the only benefit of working administration–the coffee pot was always near.

He filled his cup, poured in some creamer, and took a few sips of the steaming liquid before returning slowly to his desk. A heavy sigh escaped him as he set the cup down and eased his lanky frame into his chair.

Nearly a month into his assignment as administrative sergeant for the Special Operations Bureau, and Luke was still wearing a path in the carpet between his desk and that of Brian Dill, the veteran administrative sergeant of the Field Operations Division.

Their shared space consisted of one large room on the ground floor of police headquarters in the heart of downtown Phoenix.

Even though SOB had less than 200 personnel, the bureau generated more paperwork than Luke was prepared to handle without direction from the division sergeant.

Brian Dill was tall and lean, with short sandy hair, quick wit, and a ready smile. His immaculate appearance, handsome features, and articulate command of the English language, made him the perfect choice to interact with other city employees and coddle city politicians. Luke had judged him to be in his late thirties, and was surprised to come across some administration that listed his age at forty-seven.

Dill oversaw the work of six secretaries and coordinated the internal paperwork generated by more than 1,200 uniformed officers and support personnel. He was a fixture in administration and well respected as a competent administrator.

Luke soon discovered he wasn't alone in his quest for help. Bureau sergeants throughout the department frequently sought Dill's advice on administrative matters.

It was comforting to have a ready source of help just a few steps away. But equally comforting was the fact that Luke's desk was in a far corner of the room, away from the center of activity, even though it was right outside the door of Captain Harvy's office.

Luke was relieved his boss had taken the day off. It normally didn't bother him if his supervisor watched him work, but today he was too agitated to accomplish much, and the captain would surely have called him on it.

Ever since walking into the office that morning, Luke had felt anxious. He had a hard time concentrating on his work. The memos and transfer requests that should have been immediately dealt with were still languishing in his inbox. He'd picked them up several times, but put them back without taking action. He'd also made several trips to the break room, and then the bathroom, after consuming a half-dozen cups of coffee while trying to figure out what was bothering him. He'd even called his wife to see if everything was all right with her and the kids. She assured him it was.

He glanced around the room. Everything appeared normal. Sergeant Dill, whose desk was purposely placed to intercept anyone coming into the room, was updating the personnel board behind his desk. It held the colorful array of magnetic name tags of everyone in the division. The color of tag denoted the status of each person: blue for sworn, green for probationer, white for clerical, purple for police aide, and black for special operations personnel.

All of the secretaries, except Shirley Frey, were either tapping away on their typewriters or filing papers. Shirley was helping

Sergeant Dill.

Although Dill & Frey appeared to be engrossed in their work, it was obvious to Luke that the two had something going on besides a working relationship. Shirley hung around Dill's desk so much that no one paid any attention to it anymore.

Even though there was nothing out of the ordinary, something bad was about to happen. Luke could sense it. Hell, he could even taste it: a metallic flavor that coated his tongue and lingered in his mouth even after consuming damn-near a whole pot of coffee.

He was still wracking his brain in an attempt to figure out what was eating him when out of the corner of his eye, he glimpsed a woman trudge into the room. No one else seemed to notice. Normally, he wouldn't have either. But his inability to concentrate on his work had kept him wary.

The visitor looked neither left nor right as people do when they enter an unfamiliar room. Her gaze was fixed on the back of Sergeant Dill who was still facing the personnel board.

The woman had obviously been here before. It was also obvious that Brian Dill was the person she came to see.

Under normal circumstances, Luke would have paid her no mind. There wasn't anything about her to command attention. She wasn't good looking by any stretch of the imagination, and a person would be hard-pressed to believe she ever was. People in the Midwest would call her big-boned. But in Phoenix, she was just plain overweight; the stereotype of a middle-age housewife.

She reminded Luke of a joke someone once told after he'd mentioned being from Iowa: "Do you know what they call a good looking woman in Iowa?" he was asked. "No," he'd gullibly replied. "A tourist," the jokester answered.

Thoughts, such as that, often came to him at the most inappropriate times. It was annoying. He needed to get back on track and concentrate on the matter at hand.

There was nothing visibly threatening about the woman. She was just another faceless person in a sea of faceless people. One of the invisibles: the waiters; the janitors; the grocery baggers; the people we interact with a dozen times a day and never give a second glance. But on this particular day–at this particular hour, and at this particular moment–she had Sergeant Luke Canfield's full attention.

It wasn't the lifeless stringy hair, and tortured, tear-stained face that drew his interest. After nearly ten years with the police department, he'd seen hundreds of people who fit that description. It wasn't even the stance she took as she planted herself in front of Sergeant Dill's desk. It was the shoebox under her left arm that triggered the silent alarm in his brain.

As shoeboxes go, it looked harmless enough. But it wasn't something a person normally carried into a police station, and

Luke was trained to notice things that were out of the ordinary.

The cautionary part of his brain wanted to shout, to warn the administrative sergeant. But another part warned him about jumping to conclusions without proof that something bad was about to happen.

From force of habit, he dropped his right hand to his gun. It wasn't there. For an instant, he panicked. *Where...?* He suddenly remembered. He hadn't been in a plain-clothes assignment long enough to get used to wearing civvies.

Without taking his eyes off the strange woman, Luke quietly reached for the desk drawer where he always placed his gun as soon as he got to work. There was no need to wear a sidearm in the office. The only danger he faced there came from paper cuts.

He discounted the idea of picking up the weapon. He would look pretty foolish brandishing a .38 S&W at a woman with nothing more threatening than a shoebox. Still, he'd better do something. Instinctively, he rose to his feet.

Before Luke could take a step, Sergeant Dill turned slowly around. A shocked expression came over him as he stood motionless, a bundle of name tags clasped tightly in his left hand.

Shirley Frey turned with him. Her face, which a few seconds ago was alight with the glow of a woman in love, had suddenly turned a ghostly white.

The visitor transferred the shoe box to her left hand. With

her right, she removed the lid and tossed it aside. Slowly and deliberately, she reached inside the box and withdrew an object that Luke was unable to see clearly. Holding the object close to her body, she dumped the contents of the box on the desk. A pile of photographs splayed across the desk and onto the floor.

Dill's right hand grasped the top of the chair he'd pushed under his desk while working on the personnel board. His face, always quick to smile, suddenly turned from chalky-white to sickly-gray. His jaw dropped and his knuckles whitened as he faced the menacing look of the woman standing before him.

Without saying a word, the woman suddenly thrust her right hand forward. The snub nose revolver she was holding spoke for her. Bang! Bang! Bang! Bang! Bang! Five times in rapid succession.

As soon as Luke saw the gun in the woman's hand, he jerked his desk drawer open and grabbed his weapon. He was too late.

The blasts sent shock waves cascading across the room as the projectiles tore into Dill's body.

Blood spurted from the left side of Dill's neck like a burst water hose. Wide-eyed, his mouth twisted into a grimace, he reeled back against the personnel board, sending name tags tumbling. Then, with a slight turn, his slender frame pitched forward and crumpled to the floor.

Shirley's eerie scream was cut short as she clawed at her chest and also tumbled to the floor.

As if in slow motion, the woman laid the gun on the desk and slumped to her knees with the shoe box still clutched tightly in her hand, her body wracked with sobs.

It took a few seconds for Luke to recuperate from the deafening sounds and get his bearings.

Acting on impulse and training, more than conscious thought, he rushed over and retrieved the gun, shoving it into his back pocket before turning his attention to the victims. Only then did he realize he was still holding his own weapon. He shoved it into his other back pocket.

Blood oozed from Dill's wounds and pooled on the floor under his head. An off-colored hole on the right side of his face where his eye and nose came together, marked the spot where one of the slugs had hit. That, along with the one that slashed open the artery in his neck, had ended his life. It was obvious to Luke that either one would have done the job. Brian Dill's life was over before his body hit the floor, a fistful of name tags still clutched tightly in his left hand.

The rainbow of name tags he'd knocked from the wall were now blood-red. It was as if someone had spray-painted the whole damned area.

Shirley had taken two slugs to the chest. One near the right shoulder and the other one right through the heart. She gasped for breath several times before becoming silent.

Luke took a mental inventory. Five shots fired and only four slugs accounted for. The other one must have gone wild. He would let the Dicks search for it. Luke had his hands full at the moment.

Major Larson, whose office was closest to the action, responded almost as quickly as Luke. He glanced at Luke, who slowly shook his head after checking on Dill and his secretary.

With help from the major, Luke wrested the empty shoebox from the woman's hand and guided her to a nearby chair. "Call an ambulance," he calmly ordered the nearest wide-eyed secretary who had jumped up from her desk and was huddled with the others.

His ears were still ringing from the sounds of the blasts and his voice sounded hollow. The acrid odor of gunpowder hung in the air, providing a dramatic reminder of the violence that had just taken place.

The secretary that Luke had addressed stood motionless, still staring at the woman who had just shot her sergeant.

"Hey! Call an ambulance right now," Luke barked.

The secretary picked up the phone as Luke turned his attention to one of the other women who'd also tried to distance herself from the commotion.

"Call the Dicks and tell them to get someone down here," he said.

The secretary slowly picked up the phone. "Who…should I call?" she haltingly asked.

"Call the Detective Bureau and tell them to get someone down here right away," Luke harshly repeated.

He glanced at the photos on the desk, and stared in disbelief as he recognized Sergeant Dill and Shirley Frey in a variety of sexual poses.

"Bring her into my office," the major directed as he also glanced at the photos.

After escorting the woman to the major's office, Luke returned to the scene and started to gather the photographs, but suddenly stopped. They were part of the crime scene and shouldn't be moved until the detectives finished processing the area.

He glanced at the secretaries who had apparently gotten over their initial shock and were trying to get a peek at the photos without appearing too obvious. "Oh, the hell with it," he muttered as he scraped the ones from the desktop into the shoebox. He'd already picked up the gun and screwed up the fingerprints on that piece of evidence, he may as well grab the photos too.

He removed the murder weapon from his pocket, placed it in the shoebox on top of the photographs, and secured the lid.

Normally, he would have been more careful not to touch anything. But it was a pretty open and shut case. There were a number of eye witnesses. A few photographs, more or less wouldn't detract from the facts of the case. And even though both parties were dead, leaving the photos out where everyone could see them wasn't right. The ones on the floor smeared in blood would be sufficient evidence to prove a motive for the shooting.

He took the box to the major's office and placed it on his desk before taking a seat next to the woman who had just committed murder.

"Get Mrs. Dill a glass of water," Major Larson directed.

Luke went to the break room and returned with a paper cup full of water.

The woman took a sip and set the cup on the major's desk. Her voice cracked as she spoke. "I was looking for something in our closet this morning when I found the photographs. He kept them in our bedroom closet. How could he do such a thing? How could he?"

Mrs. Dill glanced through the office window at the secretaries who were huddled around each other, while staring at the group of detectives who were examining the bodies of their dead co-workers. "These whores you got in here were all having sex with my husband. I should have shot them all," the woman snarled. "They…"

Her comment was interrupted by a detective who had just walked in.

"I'll talk with you outside," Luke said as he picked up the shoebox and guided the detective away from the major's office.

He explained what had happened and turned the shoebox over to the detective. "I'll write a supplement and get it to you as soon as possible," he said.

Both men returned to the major's office.

"Come with me please," the detective ordered as he helped Mrs. Dill to her feet and escorted her out.

Luke watched them leave with mixed emotions. He felt sorry for the two people lying dead behind the desk, but even sorrier for the woman who had shot them. Dill and his secretary's troubles were over. His wife's were just beginning. An awful lot of harm had been done over a careless act.

Who the hell would have an adulterous affair, take pictures of the act, and leave them in his wife's closet?

He shook his head in dismay. It didn't make any sense. But then, a lot of things in Luke's life didn't make sense. This was just one more thing to add to the pile.

Medical personnel hurried in, and after a quick examination of the bodies, pronounced Brian Dill and Shirley Frey officially dead.

After a quick exchange of paperwork with the lead detective, they left almost as quickly as they'd entered.

The bodies would remain where they were until the medical

examiner arrived and the detectives were finished processing the scene.

Luke returned to the major's office and slumped into a chair. Both he and the major watched the hubbub of activity as detectives were separating the secretaries in order to take statements. The popping flash from the camera of a crime scene tech made everything look surreal.

I knew something bad was going to happen. Why didn't I react sooner?

Luke always blamed himself the most when things went wrong, but it would take some time to get over this one.

It was only yesterday that both administrative sergeants were in the major's office when Luke mentioned how grateful he was to Sergeant Dill for his help.

"Brian," Major Larson said, "you'd better never retire. I doubt this place could function without you. I certainly rely on you, and a lot of others do too. I think the whole department would fold if you weren't here."

But that was yesterday. Today, Sergeant Dill, the glue that held the whole department together, was dead. Shot to death by a jealous wife.

Luke felt sorry for the poor bastard who would have to take Dill's place. He was extremely glad it wouldn't be him. He didn't have enough experience in administration to handle his own job, let alone that of someone who was irreplaceable.

Luke's reminisces were cut short by Major Larson. "Canfield," he quietly said. "As soon as they get the area cleaned up, move your stuff over to Dill's desk. You're going to have to take over Field Operations."

Luke started to chuckle. The major was obviously joking. But he looked serious.

"I..." Luke didn't know what to say. "I couldn't handle that job, Major. Hell, even after nearly a month, I still have to run to Dill a dozen times a day and ask him how to do something." He caught himself. "I should say I *used* to run to him. I guess it's past tense now."

"I don't have a choice. You're it," Larson said. "It took a while for Dill to become proficient, too. You'll catch on."

***

Take care of the little things. The big things will take care of themselves.

The words his father had spoken nearly thirty years ago were burned into Luke Canfield's brain like a brand on the rump of a steer. The words weren't harsh, nor were they accusatory. They were matter-of-fact, and one of many lessons a father teaches his child. But to a nine-year-old boy, they were a charter for life, indelibly etched into his psyche.

Those cautionary words had transformed a carefree Iowa farm boy into a man driven to pay attention to detail, to act responsibly, and to always do the right thing whether anyone watched or not. He accepted the fact that his father's advice made him *what* he was today. He just didn't like *where* he was.

It was barely eight-thirty, and Luke was already wading through the mountain of paperwork that always awaited his morning arrival. Even after two years in administration, he was still amazed at the river of correspondence that flowed through his office like the Amazon through South America. In his estimation, the volume was about the same, and they both carried a lot of crap.

How in the hell does all this stuff accumulate in just one night?

He reached across the desk for his coffee. He'd established a routine–a sip of coffee and then a file; coffee; file; coffee; file. Coffee always came first. That was the only way he could shuffle through a never ending barrage of written material day after day and still maintain some semblance of sanity.

How in the hell did I get here? It was a rhetorical question that he had often asked himself since transferring to Administration, even though he remembered very well the pathway that led him to his present role of Administrative Sergeant for the Division of Field Operations. He'd never forget the day Mrs. Dill walked in and pumped four slugs into her cheating husband and his secretary. The detectives had found the fifth slug in a wall near the ceiling. The one that tore through Dill's artery was embedded in the personnel board behind his desk.

Nothing in the office had changed much, except the personnel. Special Operations Sergeant Bill Franks' desk sat in the same corner of the room as it had when Luke occupied that position. But they might as well share the same desk, considering the number of times Franks had been over to ask for Luke's help with an administrative issue.

Luke grinned at the thought. It hadn't been that long ago since he'd beaten the same path in the carpet to ask Brian Dill how to do something. Besides an admin sergeant, a new secretary had been hired to replace Shirley Frey.

Not only was Luke plagued with the thought of two people being shot right before his eyes, and him unable to prevent it, but other thoughts were even more troubling.

He tried to keep his mind from wandering to the always painful memory of his little sister's near-drowning, but he couldn't help it. Another force dictated his thoughts. Other forces were always at work. They determined what he was *destined* to do, overriding what he *wanted* to do.

He credited his father for admonishing him to always pay attention to detail, and to do the best job he was capable of doing, whether he liked it or not.

The advice was as relevant today as it was then, and even though his father had passed away years ago, the voice in Luke's head was as clear as when the words were first spoken. Ironically, it was the ingrained obsession of paying attention to detail that drew the attention of his supervisor and prompted a transfer to administration.

Circumstances had always dictated a different direction in life than Luke consciously preferred. He loved farm life. He felt a kinship to the land, and to the rows of corn that stood like soldiers, shoulder to shoulder awaiting harvest. He loved the smell of newly-mown hay, and the song of the meadowlark as it swung back and forth on the tips of the oats that swayed like an ocean wave in the summer breeze.

But the land he loved, and the crops he'd poured his heart and soul into, had risen up against him. Allergies to the corn pollen that his wife, Emily, and son, Michael experienced, had worsened.

The girls, Rebecca and Amy, were unaffected, and like their father they loved the farm. But if one member of the family was in trouble, they all rallied. So Luke gave up the life he loved and moved to Arizona.

He had repeated the reason for leaving Iowa so many times, he almost believed it himself. It was partially true. His wife and son *did* have allergies, and a doctor *had* suggested a drier climate.

But there was a darker motive that prompted his departure from the land he'd sworn to never leave. He couldn't explain it to others. It was too painful to openly admit that his carelessness, his lack of attention to detail, his singular failure to latch a gate, had caused the entire family years of grief.

His father had often cautioned him to make sure the gate was latched that led from the house to the farmyard. Normally, he did. Until that fateful morning, when in his haste to reach the barn and help his pet cow give birth, he failed to properly close the gate. His three-year-old sister, Evelyn, had slipped through and fell into the stock tank that was always kept filled for the cattle and horses.

Even though he was in the barn, helping with the birth of a calf, a voice in his head had told him his little sister was in trouble. He'd run from the barn and pulled her limp body from the water.

He had rescued Evy from drowning—that much was in his favor. But he hadn't rescued her from brain damage by being under water too long, or from being totally dependent on others her whole life. And he hadn't been able to rescue his sister, Thelma, from devoting the best years of her life to the care of her baby sister, becoming a spinster in the process. Most of all, he couldn't escape the constant feeling of guilt for failing to act responsibly. He failed to latch the gate. He hadn't paid attention to detail.

Evelyn had died at the age of twenty-two. The doctor said her heart just gave out. He never said it was caused by near-drowning, but Luke was sure it was. A month after her death, he'd loaded up his family and moved to Arizona.

If someone had told me when I was picking corn in the snow, that one day I'd be a cop in Arizona, I'd have told them they were nuts. Administration! I'm a farmer, for Christ's sake. I should be in the field chasing down crooks, not sitting on my ass behind some desk. I'd have been better off if I'd stayed in the Army.

Luke gulped another mouthful of hot coffee. "Guess they won't get done by themselves," he grumbled, as he picked up a personnel folder and delved into another day of paperwork. "The major will soon be in, and he's going to wonder what the hell I've been doing. He'll probably ship me back to the field." He hoped.

Two years. I've been chained to this freaking desk for over two years. Hell, I've known armed robbers who weren't sentenced to that much time. The only thing lacking is a ball and chain. I'd better not mention it or they'll probably think it's a good idea and slap one on me. I've got to find a way out of here.

CHAPTER TWO

About mid-morning, Luke was still lamenting his woes and trying to figure a way out of his role as a paper shuffler when Major Lymon Garrison strolled in.

Garrison could have been a poster child for the police profession. He carried his 6' 3", 190 pound frame like a military man, with shoulders squared and head high. Yet, there was a relaxed air about him; like he was sure of himself without appearing arrogant. With his short black hair, with a hint of gray at the temples, his square jaw and high cheekbones, he looked like a throwback from the early days of lawmen. Luke visualized him in cowboy boots and Stetson with a six-gun strapped low on his thigh. He could have easily fit the profile of the Arizona Ranger in Marty Robbins' song, *Big Iron*.

"Sergeant Canfield, I have some good news for you," the

major casually announced. "Floyd Simmons is retiring from the polygraph section and they need a replacement. You're going to polygraph school."

"I don't want to go to polygraph school." The words exploded from Luke's mouth before he could stop them.

Major Garrison had started for his office as soon as he broke the news, but he stopped short and turned slowly around. His jaw moved as if to say something, but no words came. He kept looking at the sergeant as if trying to decipher a foreign language and couldn't quite find the right meaning.

"Are you kidding me?" Garrison growled, his brows raised and his eyes wide. "Everyone wants to go to a school of some kind, especially a technical school, and you didn't even have to ask. I handed you a plum on a silver platter, and you tell me you don't want to go?"

A deep frown spread across the major's face. His eyes narrowed as he continued in a slow, measured tone. "We went through the file of every sergeant on the department, and you were selected. I went to bat for you. Now you tell me you don't want to go?" The major's clenched teeth and unflinching stare unnerved Luke.

"I appreciate the consideration, but no, I don't want to go." Luke shuffled some papers, hoping the major would accept his refusal and move on.

Garrison stood motionless as he glared at his administrative sergeant. His face turned red, then white, and back to red again as he obviously struggled to keep his emotions in check.

It had been more than a year since Major Larson had transferred out and Major Garrison became commander of Field Operations. In all that time, Luke had never seen his boss this upset. He felt more uncomfortable by the minute. His gut clenched and his pulse raced. He needed a slug of coffee. He reached for his cup. It was empty.

Garrison stepped closer.

The major's countenance softened as he slowly and calmly said, "So you want me to go back up there and tell the chief that after all the trouble we went through to select the right man, you won't go?"

Disappointment in the major's voice sounded eerily similar to the tone Dan Canfield had used that day in the barn, after Luke's little sister nearly drowned. The thought made him wince. He didn't want to go to polygraph school. But neither did he want to disappoint his boss like he'd disappointed his father.

What am I going to say? If I agree to go, I'll be stuck in that job for the rest of my life. If I refuse, I may as well kiss a promotion goodbye. I'm backed into a corner.

He glanced up. Garrison hadn't moved. Luke felt like a bug under a microscope as the major continued his intimidating stare.

Luke had great respect for his boss, and he wouldn't deliberately do anything to make him look bad. But polygraph school? Hell no.

After a few more agonizing seconds, Luke heaved a sigh and said, "I have no desire to go to polygraph school. But I'll go if that's what the department wants."

"Good," Garrison said as he hurried to his office as though he wanted to get away before the sergeant changed his mind. "I figured you'd agree with the decision once you had time to think it over," he added as he cast a glance over his shoulder.

Luke had to bite his tongue to keep from lashing out. *A chance to think it over? I guess thirty seconds is considered enough time to think something over that may affect the rest of my career.*

His mind was in turmoil as he got up from his desk, picked up his empty cup, and shuffled to the break room. He felt vulnerable–exposed to the elements. Coffee was his security blanket, and he needed something to wrap around him at the moment.

He poured a cup of the piping-hot liquid, dumped in some creamer, and mulled over the conversation he'd just had with his boss.

I can see it all now. If I refuse, my career is in jeopardy. And if I go, I'm too valuable in that specialized assignment to get promoted. Something is definitely wrong with this picture.

He was still muttering to himself as he returned to his desk with the steaming cup of coffee. He settled down in his chair with Major Garrison's comments about the selection process still buzzing in his head.

Luke stared into space, his mind awhirl with thoughts of his situation. He'd worked administration long enough to know that the main reason he was selected was because he had no suspensions, reprimands, or other discipline in his file. That way, if something went haywire, the selection committee could say it was a complete surprise to them as his file hadn't indicated a problem.

Cover your ass above all else, that's the name of the game. Well, I guess it serves me right. Never wish for something. You just might get it. A few minutes ago, I was trying to figure a way out of here. Well, it looks like they figured it out for me. What in the hell am I going to do now?

***

On his drive home that evening, Luke's head was spinning. *I should have just said no, and stuck to my guns. So what if they send me back to the field. I don't want to work administration anyway. But neither do I like working nights. At least Emily will be happy with the news. If she had her way, I'd be working days forever.*

He drove slowly, staying in the far right lane so as not to impede others who were hurrying home. Normally, he hurried too. But not tonight. He had too many thoughts to sort out. One minute, his mind was on the interaction with Major Garrison, and the next minute he was thinking about the conversation he was going to have with his wife.

"I hope she didn't forget to take her meds," he muttered as an impatient driver whipped around him and sped on ahead, only to be stopped by the next traffic light. Luke hardly noticed. He was too deep in thought about his personal life to concern himself with the public.

I bet she wishes she'd married the banker. She could be living in a fancy house and driving a fancy car. That's never going to happen if she stays with me. Her mother was right. She should have married the banker.

***

Emily Canfield swallowed one of her "don't go crazy" pills as she often called them, and placed the empty glass in the sink. She felt a lot calmer since she started a daily regimen of the medication. Her panic attacks had lessened, and she could once again control her emotions, at least most of the time.

Luke supported her monthly visits to a psychiatrist. He

agreed with her decision to consult a mental health specialist after symptoms of a heart attack caused several frantic trips to the emergency room. Extensive tests revealed no physical problems, and the psychologist, recommended by the hospital couldn't prescribe medication. Only a medical doctor could do that. But their family physician was reluctant to prescribe a mind-altering drug, so she was referred to a psychiatrist.

She thought her mind had healed after several visits to a counselor, following the death of her father. The nightmares had ended, and she could get through an entire night without reliving his stinking breath, slurred speech and stinging blows. Guilt still haunted her, but until recently, she'd managed to keep it under control.

Her doctor couldn't explain why the emotional disruptions were happening when she was happily married and everything was stable. It would have made more sense if she'd had them when she was young, when every night was chaos. But panic attacks can occur anytime, even when life is good, her doctor told her.

Luke's family would never have understood the need for medication because of something that happened in the past. There was no time or patience for such stuff on the farm. They believed a person should tough it out, and not rely on "a bunch of pills" to get them through the day. But Luke never criticized her occasional outbursts. She was grateful for his considerate stance.

He frequently mentioned his happy childhood, but he never offered any details. She wondered about that. There were times when he would clam up and brood for no apparent reason. It always upset her. She thought it was something she had done. But he assured her it wasn't, saying his younger sister's death at an early age still bothered him.

It was shortly after Evelyn's funeral that Luke moved their family to Phoenix. But Emily felt guilty about leaving her mother with no other relatives or close friends. So guilty in fact, that she'd invited her mother to join them. After a few years, Eleanor Thurston accepted the invitation and moved to an area a few miles north of her daughter.

That didn't solve the nagging uneasiness Emily felt, but couldn't put into words. Luke had nothing to feel guilty about. Regardless of what happened when *he* was a child, it couldn't come close to the trauma she had suffered at the hands of her drunken father.

She'd tried several times to tell Luke about her childhood, but the words lodged in her throat. Luke's childhood had been stable. He couldn't relate, so she kept her past to herself.

When they first discussed marriage, Emily insisted on a large family. As an only child, she was envious that Luke had so many brothers and sisters to watch out for each other. She wanted the security and camaraderie she envisioned in large families.

Marriage to him would assure her of that.

It wasn't until Rebecca was born that she realized how naive she had been. Giving birth and raising a child was a lot of work and a tremendous responsibility. She was relieved the day Luke got a vasectomy.

Emily stared through the kitchen window to the carport. She found comfort in the passion vine that clung to the block wall along the west side of the driveway. It always made her feel better. Every time she glanced through the window, she was reminded that Luke had planted the flowers especially for her.

She sometimes wondered what her life would have been like if she had taken her mother's advice and married Max Gordon. Maybe he'd have treated her differently if she had agreed to marry him. Maybe he wouldn't have gotten so angry and aggressive and…

She refused to think about that night. It must have been her fault. She'd led him on.

She needed to think positive thoughts. Remember only the good things. Max had been a teller back then, but he probably *owned* a bank by now. Funny, no matter how hard she tried, she couldn't visualize sleeping with him and having his kids. Even the thought made her cringe. Of the men she'd known, Luke was the only one she could tolerate for more than a few dates.

She glanced at the clock. Four-thirty. Time to make fresh

coffee before Luke got home. She'd never seen anyone drink so much coffee. She didn't mind. Better coffee than booze.

She shuddered at the thought of Luke coming home drunk like her father. Her breath caught in her throat. It felt like her Buick was parked on her chest. The mere thought of her drunken, abusive father had triggered a panic attack. She grabbed the pill bottle, but realized she'd taken one less than two hours ago. She concentrated on her breathing, just as the doctor had taught her: take a deep breath and hold it; then exhale slowly, letting all of the muscles in the body relax. Three more breathing exercises, and a few minutes later she felt normal again.

The smell of meatloaf going dry jerked her back to the present. She poured a half-cup of water in the pan. She'd caught it in time. The meat was slightly singed, but that was the way Luke liked it.

Again her mind wandered. Her marriage seemed strong as steel one day and flimsy as wet newspaper the next, depending on her mood and whether or not she had taken her medication. Maybe Luke wouldn't keep his promises. Even after nearly twenty years of marriage, she still had doubts. He never missed a day of work. He appeared to favor his job more than his family, just as her father had with the bottle.

She'd sensed the good in Luke from the first. He hadn't struck her, at least not yet, but she couldn't be too sure that he wouldn't. She had taken a chance with him, realizing she couldn't go through life mistrusting everyone. But she wouldn't...she couldn't...let her guard down completely.

***

After a long and thought-filled ride, Luke finally pulled into his driveway. As he turned the knob and swung the door open, he half-expected his welcoming committee waiting to greet him. Whenever he had a difficult day at work, his mind compensated by taking him back to simpler times when the kids were little.

When she knew what time to expect him, Emily would have the children bathed, dressed, and standing in line to greet him as he came through the door. Even Skippy, the family dog, would be in the line-up, sitting on his haunches, waiting patiently for his master.

Skippy wasn't a very dignified name for a German Shepherd, but that's the name the kids had given him as a pup, and the dog didn't seem to mind. He would give Luke the usual two sniffs and walk away to do what dogs do when they're bored: sleep. On special occasions, such as when the kids felt like it, Skippy would even be wearing one of Luke's neckties.

"What's that dog doing wearing my tie?" he'd ask with faked indignation. They'd pulled a good joke on their dad and they always enjoyed that. But the old Skippy passed away years ago from distemper. They were determined never to get another dog. None could take the place of Skippy. But Luke had run across a puppy on one of his calls before being transferred to administration.

The owner had said if a home couldn't be found for the puppy, he would be taken to the Pound. So another German Shepherd became part of the Canfield family. When they couldn't decide on a better name for the new dog than the one they used to have, they named him Skippy, too.

But the kids were no longer of the age when they yearned for a dog, or eagerly awaited their father to come home. They were teenagers, and Rebecca was already of age. Teenagers always had more important things to do than play with the dog or wait by the door for their father.

"Hello," Luke called as he came in. "Anybody home?"

"Just me," Emily shouted from the kitchen.

She turned from the stove as he strolled in. He took her by the shoulders and gave her a quick peck on the forehead.

"Where're the kids?" he asked as he grabbed a cup of coffee and lingered near the stove to take in the pleasing aroma.

"Who knows?" Emily smirked. "If you didn't see them in a line-up, then I guess they're still out creating mayhem. I guess they take after their father...whoever *he* is."

Luke smiled. They often joked about the identity of the kids' father. One look and it was obvious. They were all spitting images of him.

"Meatloaf. It smells good and I'm hungry," Luke said as he peeked in the oven. "Do we have to wait for the little brats or can we eat now?" He rubbed his stomach and pretended to look frantically about as he whispered, "Maybe we can finish it before they get wise to the fact we have food?"

"Well you better hurry and get washed, then, because the *little brats* will soon be home," Emily mocked as she reached in the oven and pulled out the sizzling dish.

They joked about stuff like that, even in front of the kids, but everyone knew where they stood. They were a family, and nothing could dampen that

Emily finished setting the table and had pulled back her chair when Michael and Amy burst through the door. Each greeted their parents with a, "Hi Dad. Hi Mom."

They ran to the bathroom and washed up before flopping down in their usual place at the table. Rebecca had gotten a job at the State Lab as soon as she finished high school, and was also taking a science class at Arizona State. She went directly to ASU after work and would be late again tonight.

"Well, I see you've had another interesting day," Luke commented as he noticed the black eye Michael was sporting.

"What happened now?" Emily asked as she reached over and turned Michael's head to get a better look at the swollen eye. "Have you been fighting again? Why is it you can't get along in school? It's not enough I have to worry about your father getting maimed or killed. I also have to worry about you kids getting your eye knocked out at school."

Emily shoved her chair back and got up from the table. She got a cold washcloth and held it against Michael's swollen eye.

He jerked his head away. "Ouch! Not so hard. That hurts worse than when I got hit."

Luke stifled a laugh. He had occasionally come home with a shiner when he was Michael's age, and he'd survived. All boys went through that. It was part of being a boy.

"It's no big deal," Luke said as Emily continued to hover over her son. "It'll heal up before he's married."

Emily shot her husband a look of disapproval for making light of their son's injury before slowly resuming her seat at the table.

"At least you don't have to worry about *me*," Amy said as she heaped some mashed potatoes onto her plate. "I never get in fights. At least not physical ones. And I can beat all the other kids, and even the teacher, in a *mental* conflict."

Luke smiled to himself. He knew what she was saying was true. He didn't have to worry about her. But somehow, he always did. He worried about them all. Emily, Rebecca, Michael, and Amy. Life was too complicated, too chaotic, not to worry. It seemed there was always an obstacle in the pathway of life. Trouble was lurking right around the corner. One misstep and it may be too late. He must be prepared. But where would it come from, and whom would it target? He didn't know. He only knew trouble would come. It always had in one form or another.

***

After the kids were in their rooms and settled down for the night, Luke broke the news to Emily, who was in her usual position on the couch, legs tucked under her, leafing through the pages of Vogue.

He always felt guilty when he saw her gazing at images that illustrated the lifestyle she'd known before marriage. She never complained, but he was certain she yearned for those days when she could pick out what she wanted and her mother would buy it for her. She'd never be able to do that on a cop's pay.

"The department is sending me to polygraph school."

Emily kept her eyes on the page. She must not have heard him. "The depart..."

"Is that good...or bad?" Emily asked hesitantly, lowering her magazine, a look of confusion on her face.

"Well…I don't think it's good," he replied. "At least I don't want to go, but they selected me and I have no choice. The school is six-weeks long and it's in Chicago."

"Tell them you're not going," Emily said. She laid the magazine aside and rose to her feet, her lips compressed to a slit, her hands resting on her hips in one of her classic *like-hell-you-are* stances.

Her blue eyes took on a darker shade when she was angry. It fit her disposition at the moment. Luke had seen that look of *a thousand paper cuts* a number of times since they'd been married. It was painful. Lingering. A thing to be avoided.

"Don't you have some say in going to a school, especially one that's six weeks long and out of state? Do they know you have a family? Are you sure you didn't volunteer for this school? Did you…?" Her voice pitched higher and higher.

It reminded Luke of his high school days in Iowa, and the alarm that sounded in the little town of Denver each day at noon. It always started low and ended with an ear-shattering wail.

Her questions flew faster than he could answer. He broke in before she got too worked up. "I told them I didn't want to go, but they wouldn't listen. If I raise too much hell, I'll be working shift three for the rest of my life. I really don't have a choice." He got to his feet and extended his arms palms up, as if the display of empty hands would mollify his angry wife.

When she didn't respond, he continued, half-pleading, half-irritated. "I don't want to go any more than you want me to. The good thing about it is you won't have to worry about me working nights anymore. I'll probably work days from now on."

He eased back to his seat. His pulse raced as it usually did when they argued. He closed his eyes in an attempt to regain some composure. Sometimes it was difficult not to respond in similar fashion when Emily exploded. He had to keep reminding himself she couldn't help it. The doctor said it was important that he accept her emotional problems, and remain calm when she had one of her outbursts. But he couldn't understand how someone who'd been pampered all her life, could have *any* problems, emotional or otherwise.

When he opened his eyes, she was still glaring, hands on her hips. He braced himself for another tirade. He knew from past experience that it didn't take much to set her off.

But just as suddenly as she'd become angry, she'd calm down. He always marveled at her ability to change so rapidly from one disposition to another. When he got mad, it lasted for days, but she could get over it in seconds.

"Well, I guess we'll have to make the best of it," Emily said as she slowly headed for the bedroom.

She hesitated in the doorway and turned to face her husband once again. A coy smile crossed her lips. "But you'd better tell them you need some time off when you get back. Maybe we can take the kids to Disneyland." Her tone was lighter now, jocular.

Luke nodded in agreement. He knew she was pulling his chain. During the years the kids were growing up, it was either a Disney movie or Disneyland itself. *Disneyland!* His personal vacation-of-last-resort. The perfect punishment. But he'd agree to just about anything tonight. He didn't want his wife still angry when they went to bed. If she was awake, she made sure he was awake, and that made for a very long night.

He turned on the television. He usually stayed up until Becky got home, but after watching the news, he decided his time would be better spent in bed with Emily.

He turned off the set and washed up before climbing into bed. Emily was already curled into her sleep position, facing away from him. He scooted over and put his arm around her. He lay quietly until the warmth of her body, and the fragrance of her silky-smooth skin, calmed his senses and lulled him to sleep.

CHAPTER THREE

The following Monday, Luke began his assignment in Police Personnel, located on the 3rd floor of police headquarters. The same floor as the chief's office.

He had two weeks to familiarize himself with the workings of the bureau before going to Chicago for polygraph training. He glanced at his watch as he entered the office. Seven-thirty. He was a half-hour early.

He could tell his boss was in before he reached his office door. Cigarette smoke gave him away. It came boiling out of the open door like the whole damn place was on fire. The cloud of noxious gas made Luke wish he'd brought his brother's gas mask–the one Henry had brought home from the war.

Luke took a deep breath before entering the "smoke-house."

"Damn, I'm surprised the smoke alarm doesn't go off." The

words began as a thought, but ended up spilling out of his mouth.

Lieutenant Fred Sloan was in his early forties, with a full head of dark hair that always looked as if he'd just come from the barber. He was 5' 10" and 160 pounds of catalog-model fashion. His off-the-rack clothes fit his body as if they were tailor-made.

Sloan looked up from a stack of files as Luke entered. A hint of a smile tugged at the corners of his mouth as he gently laid his cigarette in the ashtray and leaned back in his chair.

"I see you haven't changed. Still saying what you think," Sloan said as he reached for the burning cigarette.

"Old habits are hard to break," Luke replied with a grin.

Luke felt comfortable with Sloan. The two had ridden together out of the old Sunnyslope station when they were both at the bottom rung of the ladder and Luke was still a probationer.

After a few minutes catching up, Lieutenant Sloan leaned forward and focused his attention on the sergeant. "I had a discussion with Merle about you coming in here prior to polygraph school. We both agreed you should stay out of the polygraph rooms. We don't want you picking up any bad habits or trying to figure out how the thing works before being taught the correct procedure."

Sloan leaned back in his chair and eyed his subordinate as if waiting for an argument. When none came, he continued. "Besides, I want you thoroughly familiar with the personnel and the administrative process before going to school so you'll be able to conduct polygraphs and perform supervisory duties as well. Do you have a problem with that?"

"I don't have a problem with *never* going into a polygraph room, even *after* going to school," Luke said.

Sloan ignored the facetious remark. "The city is annexing a big chunk of land on the north side, and we're hiring as fast as we can in order to keep up with the expansion. But Merle's health is poor. I don't know how long he'll be able to keep up the pace. I'm glad they finally agreed to send me another examiner."

Sloan took another drag, blowing the smoke skyward and watching it circle around the ceiling. "As you know, Floyd Simmons is retiring. He had to burn some vacation time or lose it, so he'll be gone for the next two weeks. I've farmed some polygraphs out to a private company. But we really don't trust the accuracy of other examiners, so as soon as you get back from school we'll do all tests in-house."

Luke remained silent. He wanted to get the meeting over as soon as possible so he could get the hell out of there. The smoke was making him woozy and nauseated.

"That's all I have. Unless you have any questions, I'd better get back to these files." Sloan took another drag from his cigarette before picking up a file from the stack on his desk.

Luke hurried out, thankful to be out of the smoke-filled

room. He'd quit breathing as long as he could, and then took shallow breaths. It didn't help much. His lungs felt like he'd inhaled the smoke from a whole damn forest.

"How the hell does he stand it?" he muttered as he strolled into the polygraph section.

***

Merle Broone was a wizened little man. His thinning gray hair and oversized glasses reminded Luke of a wise old owl. But unlike the owl, Merle was even wiser than he looked. He was a veteran polygraph examiner with a stellar reputation.

Luke had heard so much about Merle, he felt as if he already knew him. Nearly everyone on the department was familiar with the aging examiner. He had personally polygraphed many employees during the hiring process, and later during an internal investigation. He'd made a name for himself as an honest, capable, and intelligent individual. Anyone subjected to a test by Merle Broone was always assured of fair treatment. He looked up from his desk as Luke entered.

"You must be the new guy." Merle picked up a cup from his desk and headed for the break room. "I'll show you the most important thing first—the location of the coffee pot. Everything else that goes on around here is of much less importance."

"I'm certainly glad to hear that," Luke replied as he followed Merle and helped himself to a steaming cup of coffee. "I was afraid they might have sent me some place where I actually had to work."

Between sips of coffee, Merle carefully scrutinized the "new guy." His gaze traveled slowly from top to bottom as though measuring him for a new suit; or in Luke's opinion, a pine box.

"What made you decide you wanted to be a polygraph examiner?" Merle asked.

"I didn't," Luke grimaced. "The suits down the hall made the decision for me. I was drafted to replace Simmons, though I doubt I'll ever be able to replace anybody. That's pretty good coffee." He drained his cup and went for a refill.

When he returned, Merle scooted his chair closer and sat quietly for a while. "Do you know Floyd Simmons?" he asked in a hushed tone.

"Never met the man," Luke replied.

Merle took a sip of coffee and set his cup down before continuing. "As you've probably heard, Floyd is having a mental tug of war with the department. Anyone with half-a-brain knows the government always wins, but that doesn't stop people from trying. The best advice I can give you is always be on guard. Floyd considers you a threat to his position." His tone of voice didn't sound like a warning, but the words sure did. Before Luke could question Merle about his comment, Tom Kraft walked in.

Tom was an applicant background investigator who had been a detective longer than Luke had been on the department. He was a tall, balding, *old-school* detective. His fatherly appearance and easy-going demeanor put people at ease. Applicants opened up to him. Those who knew him said it was understandable why he was so successful with his interviews. He kept talking until they spilled their guts just to shut him up.

Everyone liked Tom. He was good at his job and he never pretended to be more important than he was. He often said he would never retire. He enjoyed the work so much he wanted to die at his desk.

Kraft shook hands and welcomed Luke to the bureau. He didn't waste time with small talk, he hurried to his desk.

Luke had a strange feeling as he watched the detective walk away. It was as though Tom was walking out of the present and into another dimension. He seemed to vaporize and then reappear as if his soul had left his body to take a look around before returning to its host.

Luke's pulse quickened. He resisted the urge to call the detective back and keep him talking a while longer so he wouldn't disappear. He stood silently as Tom sat down at his desk.

What are these feelings I'm getting? What are these thoughts I'm having? Am I losing my mind? I know damned well the man isn't going to disappear. He's made of flesh and blood just like me. I must be losing my mind.

CHAPTER FOUR

After his initial creepy thoughts about Tom Kraft on Monday, Luke was apprehensive about going to work. He was fearful Tom wouldn't be there. But each day he found the detective in apparently good health. After a few days, Luke dismissed his thoughts about Tom's demise as an overactive imagination.

Tom Kraft wasn't the only person on Luke's mind. Merle's cautioning remarks about Floyd Simmons required an explanation, but the time never seemed right to clarify his comments or find out more about Merle.

On Thursday morning, Luke sat silently by as Merle completed typing up the report on a pre-employment examination he'd just conducted. The applicant had been recently discharged after a four-year hitch in the Army.

Luke reviewed each report before passing it on to the Bureau

Commander. He was technically the supervisor in charge of the polygraph section and, therefore, responsible for the quality of work being done. He also needed to become familiar with the format as well as the type of information being reported.

"Boy, this guy is pretty clean, especially after spending four years in the Army," Luke commented as he finished reading the report. He placed it in the pile of acceptable applicants.

"Yes, he is," Merle replied. "He appreciated his tour in the Army almost as much as I did. In fact, if he doesn't get hired, he'll probably re-enlist."

"I had a good time in the military too, except for when we had to jump, but who the hell would make it a career?" Luke grinned as he glanced at Merle.

The two men had hit it off right from the start, and while they ribbed each other from time to time, there was no animosity in their comments.

"I thought the military was a life of luxury, compared to farming," Merle snorted as he turned his chair to confront the man who had made such an antagonistic inquiry. "After basic training, I didn't have to get up until five-thirty. I received three meals a day; a clean place to sleep; and I got paid regularly. That's more than I can say for my life on the farm. It beat getting up before the sun even thought about rising. And it sure as hell beat working all day without a break. As far as I was concerned, I had found my utopia."

A wistful smile broke across the veteran examiner's face as he leaned back in his chair and gazed into the distance. His reverie was interrupted by a ringing telephone. Merle picked it up as Luke headed for his office. He had some paperwork to catch up on.

***

The following morning, after Merle's explanation about his preference of the military over farming, Luke got his usual cup of cream-laden coffee, and assumed his reflective position. He leaned back in his chair, draped his long legs over a corner of the desk, and clasped his hands behind his head.

The calm and quiet of early mornings provided an opportunity to talk with Merle before being buried in paperwork. This was a time to learn and forge a solid bond.

After a few minutes, Merle broke the silence. "So you were in the paratroops," Merle said with all the half-joke, half-sarcasm he was known for. "Didn't anyone ever tell you the only thing that voluntarily falls out of the sky is bird shit?" He hoisted his cup and took a gulp of coffee, a look of self-satisfaction on his face as if he'd just told a joke no one had heard before.

A wry smile flickered at the corners of Luke's mouth as he

reflected on his decision to join the Army. "Seems I've always been a victim of situation and circumstance," he said quietly. "Some*one* or some*thing* is always pulling the strings, always dictating my life. I just wanted to live a quiet, obscure life on the farm. But things happened faster than I anticipated. I got married because my wife was pregnant. Her allergy to corn pollen prevented us from living on the farm, so we lived in town with her mother. I drove out to the farm each day."

Luke hesitated as he recalled the situation that thrust him into military service. "That didn't work out so well. My dad needed me on the farm more, and my wife wanted me home more. I felt like each leg was tied to a team of horses pulling in different directions. I finally joined the Army to keep from being torn apart."

Luke lost his train of thought for a few seconds as his mind raced back to the early days of his marriage. Merle cleared his throat. The raspy sound jerked Luke back to the present. He continued with his story.

"Then, I found that seventy-eight dollars a month wasn't enough to live on with a wife and baby, so I transferred to the airborne. They paid an additional fifty-five dollars a month for jumping out of airplanes. I was scared to death of heights, but I thought I could kill two birds with one stone. I'd make enough money to support my family, and I would get over my fear of heights.

"Neither turned out to be very successful. We barely scraped by, and even after fifteen parachute jumps, I'm still afraid of heights." Luke chuckled softly at the thought.

"After my discharge, I returned to Waterloo and drove a truck distributing petroleum products. But farming was still in my blood. My father needed help so I returned to the farm. Things happened, however, that convinced me to finally give up and move to Phoenix." With his head bowed as if in prayer, Luke whispered, "Situation and circumstance is still dictating my life."

Luke looked up to see Merle staring at him. He'd blurted out his entire life story without even realizing it. He needed to lighten things up. "I wonder if I was in the Army now, if I'd have to jump with a polygraph strapped to my back. Of course *you* weren't brave enough to jump from an airplane," he chided, "but did you carry a polygraph everywhere you went?"

"Well...I'll tell you what," Merle's nostrils flared as he shook his head in mock disgust. "The thing is, it's not that I wasn't *brave* enough to jump out of a perfectly good airplane in flight, it's that I wasn't *stupid* enough. Anyway, I did carry a polygraph regularly, and I was really kept busy. Here, we have the luxury of conducting examinations in a stable environment. It's a lot more difficult when things aren't so stable."

Merle looked away and stared into space. When he spoke

again, his voice was barely audible. "I was often ferried from base to base by helicopter. Many times I'd have to set up in a makeshift office or tent. South Korea was infiltrated with North Korean spies. Since I didn't speak the language, an interpreter was used during a polygraph. In cases where I found the subject deceptive, he'd be taken out of the building and executed. I heard the gunshots."

Merle hesitated. His face turned pale as the memories of such a stressful time in his life came flooding back. Luke strained to hear his next words.

"What if I was wrong in my assessment? What if the interpreter didn't ask the question correctly? What if I was sending innocent people to their deaths? What if…? What if…?"

Merle gazed at the floor and slowly moved his hand to his mouth as if to wipe away the thoughts that were so obviously painful. "This went on day after day. Sleep became impossible. I couldn't block out the gunshots. I became physically ill and lost control of my bowels. After a brief hospital stay, I was sent back out to do the same thing all over again."

The look on Merle's face–pain written in every furrow of his brow–told the story even before the words came out. It was the strained and tired face of a man who had endured more than his share of stress. A face that detailed his darkest hours while being mentally transported back to a time in his life that was best forgotten.

Luke felt like an intruder, an eavesdropper and a voyeur who had sneaked up to a window in the middle of the night. What he was seeing and hearing was too personal, and yet he was mesmerized by the transformation taking place right before his eyes. He couldn't move if he wanted to, and he definitely didn't want to.

"I'm very glad to have that part of my life over," Merle concluded as he dropped his head to his chest.

Luke was emotionally drained. A faint feeling of nausea hung around his shoulders like an old blanket. He struggled for perspective, for relief from the overpowering embarrassment of having listened to what were obviously some very personal thoughts of a very private individual. He avoided eye contact, as if that would somehow lighten the situation and make everything right again.

Only after Merle broke the spell of the moment by going for another cup of coffee, did Luke feel confident enough to move. He walked to the restroom, not out of need to go, but of the need to get away and give his mentor some privacy.

When he returned, Merle was pounding away on his typewriter as if the revealing conversation had never taken place.

Luke quietly retreated to his office. His in-basket was full, but it would have to wait. He settled down in his chair, draped his legs over a corner of the desk, clasped his hands behind his head, leaned back and closed his eyes. He thought back on what Merle had said, and how he looked while saying it.

God! I hope I never get like that. There must be some way out of this nightmare assignment.

CHAPTER FIVE

Two weeks in Police Personnel passed swiftly, and the day came for Luke to leave for Chicago sooner than he wanted. But then, *anytime* was sooner than he wanted. He was glad Emily had finally accepted his leaving without further argument.

As Luke carried his suitcase to the door, Emily took his arm. "It's going to be cold in Chicago and you don't have a very heavy jacket, so I packed some flannel shirts. You wouldn't want to get sick that far away from home. Who'd take care of you?" Her voice cracked as she spoke.

Concern was evident in her azure-blue eyes. She was looking out for her man, and that always made Luke feel good. Moisture was already beginning to form in the corners of her eyes. It wouldn't take much for the tears to start.

"I'll be all right," Luke said as he wrapped her in his arms and pressed his lips against her forehead. "I'm tough. I can take it," he added with a smile.

He wanted to keep things light so she wouldn't cry. It hurt him too much when she cried, and he was afraid he might succumb to the temptation and refuse to go.

He'd said goodbye to Becky before she left for work, and to Michael and Amy before they went to school, so at least that part was over. He fought to keep from saying anything that would make things more difficult. He would rather see her mad than sad, but hopefully, he could avoid both.

The sound of a horn tore Luke from his challenge to keep things emotionally stable. "Sounds like my ride is here. I'd better go."

After a long hug and a quick kiss, Luke picked up his suitcase and walked to the door. Skippy seemed to sense something unusual was happening. He stood close, his tail wagging, looking intently at his master.

"Take good care of things, Skip. You're the man of the house now," Luke called over his shoulder as he walked out to the airport shuttle and climbed aboard without looking back.

***

Luke arrived at Sky Harbor with an hour to kill before

boarding. For a few minutes, while getting his ticket and checking his luggage, he almost forgot about his trip. The interaction with the airline employees was a welcome, though brief, respite from the nagging thoughts of going to polygraph school. But as he wandered around the terminal, the negative thoughts intensified as if they'd gotten their second wind.

He felt like a muskrat caught in a trap. The difference was, an animal could chew its leg off and escape. Luke had a feeling that even if he accomplished such a feat, they would send him anyway.

His favorite expression was coming back to haunt him: *Sometimes you eat the bear, and sometimes the bear eats you.* Those words rolled around and around in his head like a loop tape stuck on play, and he couldn't seem to find the stop button.

He had long forgotten where he'd picked up the expression about the bear, or when he decided to apply it to police work, but it had been the perfect fit when making an arrest. Especially after seeing the shocked look on the perp's face as he slapped on the cuffs. It was clever back then. But now, since he was the one being *eaten*, it had lost its appeal.

CHAPTER SIX

Luke's flight to Chicago had started out smoothly, but the closer they got to their destination, the more turbulence they encountered. He had his seat-belt buckled as tightly as it would go and he still found himself dangling in the aisle, the belt wedged in his armpits.

"Damn. I should have brought my parachute," he mumbled as the plane shook and groaned as if trying to free itself from the passengers who were clinging like possums to their seats as well as to each other.

As if I wasn't apprehensive enough. Maybe I won't have to worry about polygraph school. I probably won't live long enough to see it.

It was a sobering thought, and one that remained until the plane touched down at O'Hare. Luke breathed a sigh of relief as they pulled up to the gate.

It wasn't until he was walking through the terminal that he realized he was short of breath. He sat down and rested until his breathing returned to normal. "Well, that was a perfect start to a miserable six weeks," he said aloud before he even realized it. He quickly glanced around to see if anyone had heard, but others appeared too busy with their own problems to pay attention to him.

This was his first trip to Chicago and February wasn't a good time to visit, especially since he'd just come from Arizona. It had been sixty degrees in Phoenix when he boarded the plane. It was four-above zero when he landed in Chicago–a staggering temperature swing of fifty-six degrees in just a few hours.

Luke took a taxi to the hotel, checked in, and after leaving directions for a 6 a.m. wake-up call, went directly to his room. He spotted a restaurant off the hotel lobby on his way to the elevator, but decided to wait until morning to pay it a visit.

He was scheduled to report to The Diogenes Polygraph Institute the following morning for written tests and a polygraph examination. Training would officially start Monday. At least it would if he passed all the tests on Saturday. If not, he'd be heading home the following day.

He called Emily as soon as he got to his room. He told himself she'd be worried if he didn't call. What it boiled down to, however, was that he already missed his wife and family. Coming home to a hot meal and a warm greeting at the end of a busy and stressful day was always something he looked forward to.

"Hello," Emily said in her usual sultry tone.

Talking to her on the phone always excited him. She had a sexy telephone voice.

"Hi," he said. "How is everything there?"

"We're OK, considering our husband and father is halfway across the country when he should be at home," Emily replied. "I assume you're in Chicago, and not secretly meeting another woman," she added, in a tone she often used to tease.

"I'm in my hotel room in Chicago and it's colder than a well-digger's butt. I'd almost forgotten how miserable winter can be," Luke said, ignoring her remarks about another woman. "I wasn't sure I was going to make it."

He shuddered as he thought back on the terrifying plane ride. "The plane was bucking and heaving like a rodeo bronc. I may take the bus back. I don't want another trip like that."

Emily's tone softened. "I still think you could have gotten out of going if you had wanted to, but I'm glad you made it there safe and sound. I worry about you even when you're in the same town, and now that you're two thousand miles away, I worry even more." The resignation in her voice was evident. She had finally accepted his absence.

"I'm always careful," he replied. "How are the kids?"

"How would I know? They're out doing what teenagers do. They said they were going to a friend's house, but who knows?" Emily chuckled.

Luke forced a grin. She always knew exactly where the kids were and what they were up to.

"Well, at least you'll have some peace and quiet so you can read," Luke countered. He wanted to ask if she was taking her medication. But she always resented that question and he didn't want to upset her.

After a few more exchanges, Emily said she had to go pick up the kids and wished him a good night.

Luke attempted to analyze their conversation. He often did that. He couldn't help it. Their thought processes were as different as their backgrounds. Emily was an only child, used to all the attention, while Luke was the eleventh of thirteen kids. That was too many for individual attention. He was also practical. It was a required trait for a farmer.

Emily didn't have a practical bone in her body. Even though they barely scraped by payday to payday, she couldn't understand why Luke worked so much. She expected an easier life with more time together.

The Banker could have fulfilled her expectations. The thought flashed through Luke's mind. She probably thinks about that a lot. Maybe Luke was just selfish, thinking only of himself and what he wanted, rather than what was best for the woman he loved. The banker could surely have provided a lot better life for Emily than a cop. Maybe that was the real meaning of love: *selfishness*. People always want what's best for them at the expense of someone else.

It was too early for bed, so Luke remained fully dressed except for his shoes. He always judged the cleanliness of a hotel room by whether he felt comfortable walking across the carpet in his bare feet. One look around and he made an early determination to keep his socks on. It looked old, and with the familiar smell of carpet that saw a lot of use and little maintenance.

He flipped on the television and made himself as comfortable as he could, while watching *Chicago's Very Own, WGN News*.

He had felt better while talking with Emily. The sound of her voice lifted him out of his doldrums for a few minutes. But the feeling of optimism soon left. He felt even worse than before. Depressed.

He couldn't concentrate on the television. His mind was too busy feeling sorry for himself and still trying to find a way out. One minute he was in Phoenix, and the next minute he was two-thousand miles away.

He needed to focus on something. He glanced around the room, hoping something would catch his eye and stop the turmoil in his brain. His gaze carried him across the walls, stopping briefly to examine a framed print of Van Gogh's, *Sunflowers*, before returning to the television perched on top of a battered chest of drawers.

A low rent room in a rundown hotel was the perfect setting to try to figure out what had gone wrong. Before today, he had only been in the dumps emotionally. But now, he was there physically as well.

He couldn't understand why he always ended up doing something he didn't want to do. Everything happened too fast. The driving force that propelled him to his present situation could no more have been stopped than a train hurtling down a mountain. He may have been the engineer, but he wasn't in charge. *They* were at the controls. *They.* Those nameless, faceless administrators of failed policy and bad news. He was merely along for the ride, left to wonder if he would come to a safe stop or a career-ending crash. He wouldn't know until tomorrow. Until then, all he could do was try to understand how the hell he'd ended up in Chicago.

He shivered. The miserably-cold weather was enough to send a chill through his bones, but this was a different kind of cold. It started from the inside, as if he had swallowed an ice cube and it lay in his stomach, freezing his gut and spreading icy tentacles that wrapped around his brain like frost on a water pipe.

Was this a message or a warning? Either way, he must be on guard. From all indications there was a treacherous road ahead.

He wouldn't know until tomorrow whether he'd made the first curve or come to a career-ending halt.

***

The night dragged by with Luke tossing and turning in a strange bed, fearful he would oversleep and be late for school, even though he'd requested a wake-up call.

When the call finally jangled through the room, he woke with relief. He hurriedly dressed and went downstairs for breakfast.

The restaurant was busy with only one booth available. It had been nearly eighteen hours since he'd eaten anything except a bag of airline peanuts. The aroma of fresh coffee and fried bacon spurred his appetite.

He joined three others who had checked into the hotel the same time the night before. A brief conversation with them during check-in revealed they were headed for the same class. They all crowded into the lone booth and waited to be served. The waitress ignored them.

After several unsuccessful attempts to get her attention, a man in the next booth leaned over and whispered, "If you want to get waited on you have to hold up a dollar bill."

The group thought he was joking. But after they continued to be ignored, one of them did as suggested and the waitress hurried over. She snatched the dollar from the raised hand like a seal snatching a fish from its trainer.

"What'll it be?" she snapped.

They ordered breakfast and watched as the waitress hurried off to the kitchen.

After she was out of earshot, the patron in the next booth explained the restaurant ritual. "You boys are obviously not from around here. In this place, you only get waited on if you tip first. Then if you don't leave at least a ten percent tip when you finish eating, you won't get waited on again until you make up for it. Welcome to Chicago, boys."

PART TWO – THE EXAMINATION

"Oh the nerves, the nerves; the mysteries of this machine called man! Oh the little that unhinges it, poor creatures that we are!" – Charles Dickens, English novelist (1812-1870)

CHAPTER SEVEN

Luke stepped out of the hotel and into a blast of freezing air that took his breath away. "Now I understand why they call this place the *Windy City,*" he muttered as he braced himself against the gale-force wind.

He wasn't used to harsh weather anymore. Iowa winters had been brutal too, but he'd lived in Phoenix for the past eleven years and had become acclimated to warmer weather. Even in winter, temperatures seldom reached the freezing point.

The two blocks to the school seemed like two miles. His thin coat fit the winters in Phoenix much better than the ones in Chicago. He pulled it tighter and turned the collar up around his ears to ward off the cold, damp, wind blasting across Lake Michigan.

Miniature tornadoes created a swirling pattern of snow that

danced ahead of him as he made his way down a walkway lined with splotches of dirty snow and an occasional heap that was still white

The tree-lined route took him past large, steep-roofed houses intermingled with an occasional business office. But his thoughts weren't on the landscape. He wasn't even thinking about the polygraph he had to face. His immediate concern was getting to his destination without freezing to death.

He was chilled to the bone and shivering uncontrollably by the time he ducked inside the office building that housed the school. His face and hands stung and his feet felt like two chunks of ice. The warm building was a welcome relief from the piercing wind.

A large group of men milled about the lobby. Luke counted twenty-five, including himself. All were in government work of some kind, according to the letter of acceptance he had received from the Institute.

Several displayed the "I'm in charge" attitude most cops demonstrate, especially to each other. One man didn't fit that mold. He kept to himself and seemed unconcerned with the activity in the room. *Gotta be a spook,* Luke guessed. It made sense that the CIA would send a student. *They probably rely heavily on the polygraph to verify information.*

The group appeared nervous and apprehensive. Each man

stood quietly for a few minutes, and then several attempted to talk at the same time. They were obviously trying to keep up the typical cop-on-the-beat front to let everyone know they were in control.

They reminded Luke of a herd of wildebeests preparing to cross a crocodile infested stream. They knew some would be eaten, but they went anyway. They had no choice. There was no turning back. Luke understood their predicament. It was exactly the way he felt.

I wonder what they're most concerned with, the written tests or the polygraph. The question ran through Luke's mind as he continued to survey the room. *I'd bet their biggest concern is the polygraph. I'd also bet the herd will be thinned considerably by the time testing is over.*

No women, he noticed, glancing around the room. *Maybe they don't have female polygraph examiners.*

His analysis of the group was interrupted when a man entered and directed them to an elevator. Luke caught only a brief glimpse of him, but he felt a sense of discomfort similar to the one he had in the barn the day his little sister nearly drowned. The man disappeared as readily as he appeared. Luke's strange feeling vanished with him.

The elevator could only hold eight people at a time, so Luke waited for the last batch. As his turn came and he stepped inside, the odor he encountered triggered a flashback to the basement of the old farmhouse in Iowa. It was a damp, musty smell that never went away, even in the summer.

The elevator creaked and groaned as it made its way to the top floor. After a jerky stop, the men stepped out directly into the office of the Diogenes Polygraph Institute.

It was a typical business office with a reception desk, a half-dozen chairs, and some file cabinets. A middle-aged woman with a chubby face and brown hair sat behind the desk. She adjusted the gold-rimmed glasses perched at the tip of her stubby nose as she motioned to a door leading to a large classroom. Everyone entered and sat down.

The windowless room was stark, with bare white walls and desks with chairs attached, similar to those Luke experienced in grade school. All were lined up in evenly-spaced rows across the room. A business desk was positioned a few feet behind the lectern.

There was a subdued air about the place. No one spoke. Each man appeared preoccupied with his own thoughts.

One of the men in the front row took off his coat and hung it on the back of his chair. Others followed his lead.

Even as Luke removed his own coat and draped it over the back of his chair, he couldn't help comparing the activity to a flock of sheep.

He'd often seen sheep walking single file across a field. Each one jumped at the same spot, just as their leader had done. There was no logical reason why, they just did.

That's us...a flock of sheep being led to slaughter.

A packet of papers lay face down on each desk. A note on the packet contained a warning in red ink: "FAILURE TO FOLLOW DIRECTIONS WILL RESULT IN DISMISSAL."

Luke's heart pounded. It was already racing before he arrived, but now, it felt like it was going to jump right out of his chest. He sensed a difficult time ahead.

While awaiting further instructions, he glanced around the room. Seated to his right was a giant of a man with hands the size of baseball mitts. His long-sleeved flannel shirt came down to the heels of his enormous hands. He looked miserable squeezed into such a small space. The edge of the desk cut into his belly, but he paid it no mind. He looked neither right nor left. He kept his eyes glued to the front.

Luke pegged him as a boxer. Facial scars gave him away. Or maybe he'd been in a car accident. It was hard to tell with a casual glance.

I bet officers on his department are glad to see him coming when they call for a backup.

The man wore a forest-green jacket he'd taken off and placed on the back of his chair. It hung like a huge tent, too big for the poles intended to hold it up. The sleeves collapsed on themselves and lay in a heap on the floor. Luke labeled him "The Jolly Green Giant."

A few rows up, and to Luke's right, sat another man who stood out from the crowd. He looked like he'd stepped right out of the Dick Tracy comic strip, square jaw and all. His long black hair swept back on his head made him look as if he was ready for trouble. Several others appeared to have just gotten out of boot camp with their short hair and military bearing.

Luke was still taking stock of the group when a female staff member strode to the front of the room. She was tall and slender, with long blond hair flowing over her shoulders. She wasn't bad looking, but there was something about her that didn't appeal to Luke. Too tough. Too hard.

She never identified herself, but simply told the group that a number of written tests would be administered while the students were waiting for their polygraph test. She directed them to follow the instructions in their packet and begin taking the tests, then turned on her heel and left the room without as much as a backward glance.

Luke noticed the tests covered honesty, intelligence, aptitude and everything in between. There was even a portion in which the students were required to select their favorite color in order of preference.

After he completed the General Aptitude section, Luke stopped long enough to take stock of the room. As stressed as he was, he had to smile after seeing three of his fellow students pop their heads up from their papers and eyeball the door that led to the polygraph rooms. The smile rapidly disappeared when he realized he was one of them.

He kept working on the tests, but each time he glanced up, it seemed another man was missing. He counted at least five empty seats. The "Jolly Green Giant" returned from the polygraph room, lumbered to his desk, grabbed his jacket and made a beeline for the door.

I wouldn't want to be the one to tell that man he failed a polygraph and was being kicked out. He looks like he could crush a man's skull as easily as a piece of bubble wrap.

A military-looking man, clean-cut and well-built, also made a hasty retreat after coming from the polygraph room.

Apparently those attributes weren't sufficient to get him past the polygraph, Luke mused. He noticed at least two more come from the polygraph room and quickly leave. *What the hell is going on in there?* He was still mulling over the rejection rate when his name was called.

Luke was ushered into a small room with barren walls except for a large window behind the chair where he was told to sit. He recognized it immediately as one-way-glass. Observers could see in, but those in the room couldn't see out.

The chair reminded him of pictures he'd seen of an electric-chair, with long wooden arms curved up on the sides forming a shallow trough. A cold shiver snaked its way down his back. He had the strange feeling that if he took a seat in that chair, he would be transformed in some way, molded into something he didn't want to become. It wasn't too late. He could still walk out. He steeled himself and eased into the chair.

He glanced at the silver-colored machine embedded in the desktop. It had four pens with curved tips that rested on a length of chart paper. Black knobs were located near the base of the pens. It looked intimidating and complicated.

The woman who directed Luke into the room was the same long-haired blonde he'd seen earlier. She followed him in and closed the door. Without a word of greeting, she took a seat on the opposite side of the desk and immediately began asking questions.

"Have you ever taken a polygraph before?"

"Yes," Luke replied.

"When and what for?" Her tone was reminiscent of a bingo caller.

"In 1962, when I joined the Phoenix Police Department." He tried to mimic her tone.

"Any problems with the test?" she asked.

"No," he replied.

The examiner quickly went down a list of questions, barely giving him time to think before answering. They covered every aspect of human frailty, from theft to sexual habits.

He denied stealing anything from a place where he'd worked. Those questions were easy. The ones about sex were a little more complicated.

"Did you ever engage in an abnormal sex act?" the examiner asked as calmly as if she was inquiring about the time of day.

The question caught him off guard. He started to panic. He had instant flashbacks. *What about the time in first grade when Yvonne put my hand down her pants behind the coal-house? Does what happened at six years old count? What about Emily? She was only seventeen when she got pregnant. And that other time...*

Luke looked up to find the examiner staring at him. He finally realized she was waiting for an answer. "What...do you mean...abnormal sex?" He hesitantly asked, glancing first at the woman behind the desk, then at the paper she was writing his answers on.

"Whatever is abnormal to you," she responded in a slightly exasperated tone.

"In that case no," Luke said as he breathed a sigh of relief.

After clarifying all of his answers to the numerous questions, the examiner got up and came around to Luke's side of the desk.

"Lean forward," she commanded as she stepped behind his chair. "I'm going to place two rubber tubes around your body.

"This one measures your lower breathing, in case you're a belly breather," she explained as she placed one of the tubes low on his stomach. "And this one goes higher, in case you're a chest breather," she explained as she placed the other tube under his armpits. "Some people are chest breathers and some are belly breathers, so we have both areas covered." She seemed to be in a controlled-hurry, slinging the tubes around his waist and deftly catching and fastening the ends.

He'd noticed a bunch of wires and tubes coming from the polygraph and hanging off the front of the desk. He was finding out, firsthand, the purpose of each.

After the tubes which measured changes in respiration were attached, the examiner lifted Luke's left arm. "This is a standard medical blood pressure cuff," she said, as she wrapped it around his upper arm, pulled it tight and smoothed out the wrinkles. "It will be inflated and may get uncomfortable. It will only be inflated about two or three minutes. It measures relative changes in blood pressure and pulse rate." She was halfway through each step before she finished her explanation.

Luke expected a feminine touch, like when the nurse in Doctor Brady's office took his blood pressure. But there was nothing feminine about the hand that hoisted his arm. It was all business. She had the same dour expression as a hangman in a western movie as he slipped a noose over the head of a cattle rustler. Considering the atmosphere of the place, it wouldn't have surprised him much if she had whipped out a rope.

The last item placed on Luke were two electrodes that went on the first and third fingers of his left hand.

"These measure the skin's resistance to electricity," the examiner explained, as she wrapped the Velcro straps with metal plates around his fingers.

"Any chance of getting electrocuted?" he asked with a forced grin.

"Not if you're truthful," said the examiner, matter-of-factly.

He assumed she was joking, but he wasn't quite sure as she never changed expressions.

Guess I'd better be completely truthful, he cautioned himself as he positioned his body to face the front and made himself a little more comfortable.

He wasn't worried so much about the polygraph. He'd lived a pretty simple life. He was more concerned about the future. There were dark days ahead. He could feel it in his bones.

Swish. Swish. Swish. Swish. The rhythmic cadence of the cardio pen was barely audible. As the chart paper rolled, the pens moved up and down, keeping time with the ebb and flow of the circulatory system. Red ink created an abstract painting of the physiological changes taking place in his body.

Luke experienced considerable discomfort from the blood pressure cuff. He was certain it was inflated too high. His arm hurt like hell. *Maybe she made a mistake and the over-inflated cuff is going to injure my arm.* He argued with himself over whether to say something or continue to suffer in silence.

His concern about the cuff was interrupted by the sudden, cold, and detached voice behind the desk. It sounded like a ventriloquist speaking through a dummy. The cadence was slow and deliberate. Each word was enunciated clearly and distinctly.

"I am going to begin," the examiner said. "I am going to be asking you some questions. Just answer the questions by yes or by no. Don't do any other talking. Do not move throughout the test, and...don't shake your head when you answer."

The mechanical activity of the slowly moving chart, recording the pen movements, was lost on Luke. All he could concentrate on at the moment was the pounding in his head and the pain in his arm, interrupted momentarily by intermittent questions from the examiner.

"Is your first name Luke?"

"Yes." He barely got the answer out.

"Are you a citizen of the United States?"

"Yes." He heard his response, but he didn't recognize the voice. It sounded distant, like an echo.

"Do you intend to try to lie during this test?"

"No." He tried to sound more confident.

"Have you told me the whole truth here today?"

"Yes." He had calmed down. His voice sounded more normal.

"Are you wearing a watch?"

Luke didn't know what to say. He always wore a watch, but he couldn't feel it on his wrist. Did he lose it? Did he leave it in his hotel room? He resisted the urge to move his head to see if his watch was on his wrist. He'd been given strict orders not to move.

"Are you wearing a watch?" the voice asked again, more forcefully.

"Yes," Luke answered.

He still didn't know if he was wearing a watch, but decided to answer just to get it over with. He would explain once the test was over.

"Do you drink...water?" she asked, briefly hesitating between the words "drink" and "water."

"Yes," he answered, still trying to determine if he had his watch on or not.

"Have you ever stolen any property from a place where you worked?"

"No." That question helped distract him from the watch as well as the pain in his arm. He wanted to make sure the machine didn't register anything other than a truthful response.

"Have you ever stolen any money from a place where you worked?" the examiner asked in the same, cold, emotionless voice.

"No." Luke responded emphatically.

"Remain still," the examiner said. "I'll release the pressure on your arm in just a few seconds."

As the cuff pressure eased, Luke looked at his left arm to see if he was wearing a watch, but more importantly, to see if there was visible injury to his arm. It was painful and numb at the same time.

"That was very uncomfortable," he said, relieved to find his arm still intact. "Does the cuff have to be that tight?"

The examiner ignored the question as she tore off a length of chart and studied it intently. "What came to your mind when I asked if you were telling me the whole truth?"

"I don't know. Nothing I can think of," Luke replied.

"Well you obviously thought of something. The chart shows something came to your mind. How about when I asked if you were wearing a watch?"

Her accusatory tone caused Luke to shoot a quick glance at his left wrist before responding. He wanted to make sure the watch was actually there. His arm was still trying to catch up with the prolonged period of restricted blood flow, and he still couldn't tell if the watch was there without looking.

"I couldn't feel my arm and I couldn't tell if my watch was

there or not," he said, rubbing his left arm vigorously.

"But you answered yes when I asked you a second time. Why is that?" She leaned towards him, her eyebrows raised in an "I gotcha" moment.

"Because I always wear a watch, so I thought I must have it on even though my arm was too numb to feel it. The only thing I felt was the pain." His explanation sounded lame, even to himself.

After a lengthy series of questions resembling an inquisition more than an interview, the examiner seemed to accept Luke's explanation. She quit asking about the watch and turned her attention to thefts from an employer. "What items have you taken from a place where you've worked?" she asked, in a manner reminiscent of Perry Mason or Hamilton Berger.

Luke scrambled to remember. He knew he must have taken something. Maybe the pens, pencils, and other minor office supplies that ended up on his dresser bothered him more than he realized.

"I guess I took some pencils and pens. I never really thought of it as stealing, but I guess it was," he sheepishly admitted.

"How about money? Did you ever take any money? Maybe borrowed some and forgot to put it back?"

There go the eyebrows again. Luke couldn't help but notice as she raised her eyebrows to a height that rivaled the Sears Tower.

"No," he said emphatically as he tried to look the examiner

in the eyes. He was unable to do so as she seldom looked up long enough from her examination of the chart. All he could see were her eyebrows arched to her hairline.

"I never took any money," he added, his voice sharper and stronger by his character being called into question.

After studying the chart intently, the examiner asked, "Why do you think the question about taking money bothered you? Have you ever taken any money that didn't belong to you?"

"No," Luke said more forcefully as he turned to face the person he perceived as his accuser.

The examiner got up from her chair and with the chart in hand, headed for the door. "I'll be right back," she said, as she left the room, closing the door behind her.

Luke began feeling sorry for himself again. *Why me? I was happy in the field. This can't be happening. I didn't want to work administration, and I sure as hell didn't want to come here. What in the hell have I gotten myself into?*

He recalled his time as a field sergeant with a uniformed patrol squad. He enjoyed going to work every day. He felt confident that he could handle anything that came up in the field. *So, what the hell am I doing here?* His rumination was interrupted by the return of the examiner.

As soon as she was seated, she asked, "Did you remember anything else while I was gone?"

"No!"

"You said you had taken minor office items. So if I ask you, other than what you've told me, have you taken anything else from a place where you worked, can you truthfully say you haven't?" Her voice sounded doubtful, like she knew he was a damned liar and would trip him up on the next test.

"That's right," Luke said.

"What can you tell me about your reaction to taking money? Have...?"

"I've never taken any money. In fact, I was once reprimanded for putting more money in a coffee fund than required," he sharply replied.

The examiner glared at Luke, obviously irritated by his sudden interruption. Red-faced and narrow-eyed, she opened her mouth to respond, but apparently thought better of it and sat quietly until she regained her composure.

"Tell me about it," she calmly directed.

Luke told about the time he worked for Major Garrison. "Everyone in the office was required to put fifty cents a week in the coffee fund. I felt guilty about drinking more coffee than anyone else so I put in a dollar. The major found out and called me into his office. He asked if I thought I was better than the rest who only put in fifty cents. Without waiting for a reply, he cautioned me not to do it again. After that, I made sure I put no more than fifty cents a week in the coffee fund."

The cuff was re-inflated and the examination continued. After each set of questions, the examiner took the chart and left the room, only to return and resume the interrogation. Her main focus was on Luke's involvement in criminal activity. Not just minor thefts, but robberies, burglaries, and even murder. She seemed to be as frustrated with his answers as he was with her questions. Each time she left the room, she took the charts with her and stayed longer.

After what seemed like hours, the ordeal was over, and Luke was sent back to the classroom to resume written tests.

As he glanced around the room, he noticed that besides the "Jolly Green Giant," another man he had dubbed "Dick Tracy," as well as several others who he'd categorized as "clean cut," were no longer in the room. The papers they had worked on were the only reminder that anyone had ever occupied their seat.

Here today. Gone today. Guess they're right. You can't judge a book by its cover, or as dad used to say, 'You never know if an ear of corn has a worm in it until you peel back the husk.'

He noticed that one of the men he suspected of being CIA, as well as two others who fit the stereotype of federal agents with their white shirts and dark ties, were still in their seats.

This should be an interesting class, he thought, as his breathing returned to normal and he resumed working on the written portion of the testing process. He had managed to jump another hurdle, but the way he felt now, it was doubtful he would have enough emotional strength left to reach the finish line.

I wonder if the worst part is over or if it's yet to come? I've got a hunch I haven't seen anything yet.

***

After what seemed a lifetime, according to the ache in his back and his butt, Luke turned in his completed tests to the secretary in the front office. He stood quietly as she carefully placed a template over each sheet of paper and scanned the results. He half-hoped she would tell him he failed so he could get the hell out of Chicago and back to a warmer climate.

After a few minutes, she glanced up and announced in a non-committal tone, "You can go. School starts at eight Monday morning."

That's it? Luke couldn't help the thought as he slowly ambled to the elevator. Surviving the testing process should have been worth a "Congratulations" at the very least.

He reluctantly left the warm building and hurried to the hotel, not only because it was bitter cold, but because he wanted to tell Emily he'd passed everything. He still didn't like the idea of staying in Chicago for six weeks, but failing the tests, especially the polygraph, would have been much worse.

As soon as he reached his room, he hurried to the radiator. Warming his hands first was a must. They were too numb to have dialed the phone. When they thawed out, he called his wife.

"Hello," Emily answered in her classic telephone voice.

"That's a voice I always like to hear. Damn. You still sound sexy after all these years," Luke said.

"Well, I'm glad you think so," Emily chuckled. "You're in a good mood. You must have found someone there to keep you warm."

"Yes, I did," Luke replied. "She's a nice warm radiator and she sits just below the window. It's two blocks to school and I had to warm my hands before they would thaw out enough to dial the phone. It's miserable out there."

"So...how did all the tests go?" Emily sounded more sympathetic, caring.

"You probably won't believe this, but I passed them all, including my polygraph," he bragged.

"Well, I would think so. You had *better* pass your polygraph or you may be looking for a new wife," she joked.

The banter continued for a few more minutes. Nothing more was said about Luke being gone. He was relieved.

***

After Saturday's testing, Luke had the rest of the weekend to recuperate before starting what he suspected would be a rigorous six weeks of school.

Sunday morning, he went to the restaurant early to get a jump on the crowd. He was pleasantly surprised to find it not nearly as crowded as the day before. He got seated and held up the obligatory dollar. A waitress he hadn't seen before strolled over and snatched the bill from his hand before he realized what had happened.

Wow. She's good, Luke thought as he recovered from her sudden action sufficiently enough to place his order.

After a leisurely breakfast of eggs, crispy bacon, toast, hash browns, and coffee–lots of coffee with lots of cream–he returned to his room. The wind-whipped snow was enough of a warning not to venture out, so he spent the day sleeping and watching television. He called his wife before going to bed. Even considering the time difference, she should still be up.

"Hello," a sleepy voice answered.

"Hi. I'm sorry to disturb you. I didn't think you'd be in bed this early. One of your migraines again?" He recalled how devastating her headaches could become.

"Yes, I've been fighting one all day. But it's better now that you called. What time is it there?"

"I think it's around ten," he replied.

"How are things going?" She still sounded groggy.

"I guess all the testing yesterday, especially the polygraph, wore me out. I slept nearly all day. I'm relieved that I passed everything. At least I guess I did. They told me to be at school on Monday."

"I never doubted you would," Emily said. "Although I kind of hoped you wouldn't so you'd come home. I don't mind you being gone in the daytime, but I hate sleeping alone."

"I hate sleeping alone too," Luke said. "I'd better go and let you get to sleep. Sorry to hear about your headache. Hope it gets better. Tell the kids I miss them. Miss you too," he hurriedly added.

He felt even lonelier after speaking with his wife. It only served to remind him that he had to face another distasteful episode of his life alone. Throughout his life, he'd often felt alone, even in the company of others. He felt different. Like a stalk of corn in a bean field. Out of place and out of step with everyone and everything around him. He often wondered if others felt the same.

Unique, just like everyone else. He shook his head and berated himself for thinking he was different.

"Yeah, you're an idiot for thinking you're different than all the other idiots," he said aloud as he turned out the light and curled into his sleeping position. "Guess we'll soon find out."

PART THREE - EXPECT THE UNEXPECTED

"There are more things, Lucilius, that frighten us than injure us,
and we suffer more in imagination than in reality."
– Seneca, Roman dramatist, philosopher & politician.
(5BC-65AD)

CHAPTER EIGHT

Monday morning, while brushing his teeth and mentally preparing for the first day of class, Luke studied himself in the mirror.

He had only been in Chicago since Friday night, but it seemed a lifetime. He didn't look any different, but he felt different. Like he'd slipped through a time warp that had aged him ten years in two days. He brushed the feeling aside and reminded himself to think positive. *Positive thoughts produce positive results.* He repeated it like a mantra.

He went to the hotel restaurant early. The smell of fried bacon and hot coffee put him in a better mood. "Maybe this trip won't be so bad after all," he murmured.

Two other students joined him, and after waiting for a booth to be cleared, they got seated. Luke remembered to hold up a dollar bill. The attention-getter worked. Brenda rushed over and took their orders.

"What the hell is going on?" asked Joe Bailey, a police sergeant from Montana. Bailey was a broad-shouldered man that Luke judged to be about, 6'3" and 240 pounds. He could easily have passed for a movie star with his coal-black hair, even white teeth and rugged good looks. "Why is it so damned crowded? Is this the only freaking restaurant in town?"

"It must be the excellent service," quipped Mel Murtaugh, a lieutenant from Las Vegas. Mel was nearly as big as Joe, but with the beginning of a pot belly that Luke associated with years of sitting behind a desk. He looked to be in his early fifties and slightly balding. He had that confident air about him usually associated with those of higher rank. Mel had obviously been around the block, and coming from Vegas, there probably wasn't much he hadn't seen.

"And who the hell is Die-O-Jeans?" asked Joe.

Luke recognized the name immediately from stories he'd read. "Diogenes was a Greek philosopher known for always carrying a lantern in a symbolic search of one honest man," he explained. "So I guess it's an appropriate name for a polygraph school. It's pronounced Die-odd-jun-ease."

Joe squinted as he glanced around the room. "Well, it's a good thing that Die-O-Jeans isn't here today looking for one honest man in *this* shit hole. He'd never find one. By the way," he added between sips of hot coffee, "what the hell was going on with your polygraph? You must have been in there a good two hours."

Joe set his cup down and gave the room another scan as if looking for someone before turning his attention back to Luke. "Did you notice all the empty seats after the polygraphs? It looked like they'd emptied half the room. Since you were in there so long, I expected yours to be one of them."

"You *were* in there a long time," Mel added, a quizzical expression on his face. "*I* expected your seat to be empty too. What happened in there?"

"I don't know," Luke replied. "I'm not sure the operator knew what the hell she was doing. She kept hammering away on questions about my involvement in organized crime. Hell, I'm not sure I even know what organized crime is."

Luke slowly sipped his coffee. He needed a minute to gather his thoughts before continuing with his explanation. "I guess it could be considered organized crime when several other farm boys and I stole watermelons out of the neighbor's patch. We had plenty of our own, but stolen melons always tasted better."

He sighed and stared into his cup as he recalled the difficult time in the polygraph room. "I guess I was reacting to just about everything. Probably because in the back of my mind, I kept thinking it was a crime that I had to be there when I really didn't want to be." Both men nodded agreement.

As an afterthought, Luke said, "When she asked if I had ever engaged in abnormal sex, I was going to tell her, hell yes. When you've been married as long as I have, any sex is abnormal." Appreciative laughter came from his companions. "I didn't think she had a sense of humor so I thought I'd better not try to make a joke," he quickly added. "Besides, I wanted to get the hell out of there, and any unnecessary talking would have prolonged the misery."

Joe and Mel slowly nodded, seeming to reflect back on their own test experience as they quietly sipped their coffee.

"I came damn near telling her to go to hell and walking out," Luke continued. "She left the room after every bunch of questions and let me sit there for what seemed like an hour. Then she'd come back and start with the questions all over again." He rubbed the back of his neck, which ached at the memory.

"I was in there less than an hour and I thought that was a lifetime, so I can only imagine what you were going through," said Joe.

"I was in there about an hour too," Mel added, "and that was plenty long enough for me."

"Well, I'm glad it's over. I wouldn't want to go through another one. I'm not sure I could do that to some poor bastard, brow-beat him into submission. Gentlemen, I don't think I'm cut out to be a polygraph operator," Luke said resignedly as he finished his coffee, tossed down tip money, and got up to leave.

He made his way to the register and waited patiently in line to pay his bill, quietly thankful to have made it past the first hurdle, but wondering about the next one.

CHAPTER NINE

After breakfast, Luke returned to his room and prepared for the freezing walk to school. He put on his white dress shirt and a flannel shirt over top of that, before pulling on his jacket. The thought of facing the Chicago winter made him consider adding another shirt, but the layers he had on were already too tight, so he resigned himself to staying with what he had.

He took the elevator to the ground floor and headed out the door. The wind wasn't blowing as hard as it was on Saturday and it had quit snowing, but the temperature hadn't eased much. It still felt like he was in a giant freezer.

He walked as quickly as he could, dodging ice patches and small drifts of snow, wondering what to expect from the next six weeks. "I guess it never hurts to have more training under my belt, regardless of what it is. *Think* positive and things will *be* positive," he muttered.

The slight improvement in the weather made the distance to school seem shorter than before, and he wasn't nearly as cold as he entered the building and punched the elevator button for the top floor. Maybe he was already getting used to the weather, but he doubted he would ever get used to Chicago with their "tip first" waitresses. He heaved a sigh as he entered the elevator and prepared himself for another creaky ride.

After a jarring halt, he stepped out and into the office. Several students were already there, including Joe and Mel, who had apparently headed for school directly from the restaurant.

The men were huddled together like they were on Saturday. But today, they seemed more at ease. He understood how they felt. He had the same relieved feeling. The initial weeding-out process was over and he had survived. He exchanged the normal greetings, but didn't feel like participating in small talk.

While waiting for class to start, Luke busied himself reading the certificates and letters that lined the walls. Whenever he visited the office of a medical doctor, or any professional, he always examined documents that were displayed. He was curious to know as much as he could about the people he was dealing with.

Hmm. The written material I received was signed by Doctor Hardison. I don't see anything that says he's a doctor.

He was still going over the items when several students arrived and filed into the classroom. He followed them in and grabbed the same chair he had on Saturday. His chosen location was lucky enough to get him past the testing process; maybe it would see him through the next six weeks.

I've got to get a grip on myself and think more positive. I don't know how long I'm going to last, but I'm here now, and I have to make the best of it.

Luke settled into his chair and tried to take his mind off his personal plight by concentrating on his surroundings. There was a different feeling in the room than there had been on Saturday. Everyone seemed more relaxed. Many of the seats that had been filled with apprehensive faces prior to their polygraph, were now vacant. He missed seeing the "Jolly Green Giant" and his bright-green coat. The man's presence had given him comfort somehow. A smaller, more dignified man, was the current occupant of the chair. Luke gave a quick count. Twelve, including himself.

Damn! More than a fifty percent reduction. Unbelievable! And the guys who got bounced were cops somewhere. I wonder what they did that was bad enough to get them kicked out.

He was still trying to remember who was missing from the Saturday testing when the sudden appearance of Doctor Nathan Hardison caught his attention. The man seemed to materialize out of nowhere. After careful scrutiny, Luke noticed a side door partially concealed by a drape.

The instructor wasn't a particularly big man, just shy of six feet with a slim build, but he radiated an intimidating aura. His gray-flecked black hair was curled at the ends. A pair of horn-rimmed glasses straddled a long, hooked nose. He had the pale complexion of someone who saw little sunlight.

Maybe he's a vampire. Luke quickly dismissed the thought in irrational fear that the doctor would know what he was thinking. He couldn't shake the fact however, that the man shared the same washed-out look as alcoholics, the morning after being booked for drunk and disorderly. But he didn't discount the vampire idea altogether. *They probably look the same when their blood supply runs low.*

A hush fell over the group. Everyone seemed to stop breathing. The doctor's mere presence created an atmosphere of tension. He seemed to suck the air out of the room as soon as he entered. Maybe it was the fact that he wielded so much power over his students. After all, he had their polygraph report. He knew everything about them, even more than they knew about themselves. Or maybe it was the way Hardison carried himself, with a self-confidence that seemed to say he not only knew who *he* was, he knew who each student was, as well as what they were thinking.

Luke couldn't put his finger on it, but there was something

about the man that was different from anyone he'd ever met. It was like the doctor had some mysterious power. A Svengali.

Luke developed the same weird feeling as he had when he'd first spotted Hardison on Saturday. That deep-down defensive feeling that comes with facing something your mind is rebelling against. Like going to the dentist. You know the drill is going to hurt like hell, but the alternative would be worse. Every part of his being urged him to bolt for the exit. But going home in disgrace was not an option–at least for the present.

He remembered Merle had briefly mentioned Hardison during the two weeks Luke spent in Police Personnel prior to his trip to Chicago. He showed Merle the Letter of Acceptance signed by Doctor Nathan Hardison.

"Doctor of what?" Luke quipped.

"It doesn't matter," Merle replied. "The title of Doctor may be self-anointed, but it's never questioned, because he has the ability to open up a person's mind and extract information. His theory is, people think they have information securely locked in their mental vault, but everyone will talk if you find the right key."

Luke wanted to run away, and yet he felt drawn to the man. It was as if they shared the same brainwaves and were connected on a higher level than verbal communication. They were hardwired to each other like the power lines that ran past the farm. The problem was, the power on the farm could be regulated by anyone flipping a switch. At the Diogenes Polygraph Institute, there was only one man at the controls–Doctor Nathan Hardison.

What the hell is the matter with me? We have nothing in common. The guy is spooky. Luke tore his gaze away and tried to concentrate on the pen he was holding. He hoped it would somehow take notes without too much effort from its master. He flipped open the blank notebook that each student was given.

Without a word of greeting or so much as a glance at the students, Doctor Hardison strode to the podium and began reading from the course book.

All were listening intently when the instructor suddenly stopped and looked up. His eyes swept back and forth across the room like an eagle searching for a rabbit. Tension hung like a pall, stifling any last bit of optimism Luke had prior to the doctor entering the room.

Luke was feeling more uncomfortable with the man. In fact, he was uncomfortable with the whole situation. He felt like he should be doing something or saying something. But he remained silent, staring at the instructor like everyone else. His mind raced. *What have I missed? What are we supposed to do?*

After what seemed an eternity, Hardison said, with a cold, hard, stare and accusatory tone, "You people must have awfully good memories as I don't see anyone taking notes. I want everything I say in class, taken down verbatim, typed up, and presented on my desk in notebook form every Monday morning."

He hesitated for some time, fixing his gaze on one area of the room and then on the other, before zeroing in on Luke. His eyes narrowed as if ready to cast a death ray that would render the hapless student to dust before turning slowly away.

Suddenly fatigued, Luke could hardly hold his head up. All of the energy drained from his body, yet his mind remained crystal clear as Doctor Hardison continued with his directions.

"There will be a considerable number of written tests. If anyone gets less than seventy percent on any test, he is automatically expelled and we keep the tuition. There are no exceptions. Your notebook is included in the grading process. My secretary will fill you in on the details. See her before leaving here today."

Everyone scrambled to take notes. Several students asked him to start over, which he did without comment. As he continued to read from the material before him, there were frequent requests to repeat. He never appeared impatient with anyone's request.

After what seemed long enough to be the entire six weeks, the first day of class was finally over. Luke gathered up his numerous pages of notes and hurried out. He had obtained a typewriter from the hotel, and a binder for his notes, as well as other necessary items from the secretary during lunch break. He decided to get the jump on things by typing up his notes before dinner.

He would grab a sandwich later.

During his walk back to the hotel, Luke's mind was more on the day's events than on the freezing temperature. The same question kept playing over and over in his mind: *What in the hell have I gotten myself into?*

CHAPTER TEN

The days crawled by with agonizing slowness. Luke's wrists were sore from copious amounts of handwriting followed by hours of typing.

Just when he thought he was getting the hang of things and able to keep up, Hardison would stop reading from the lesson plan. Each time, he stared out at the group, and each time, his stare settled on Luke.

What the hell does he keep looking at me for? Why doesn't he look at someone else for a change?

The man's attention unnerved him. The doctor was trying to get inside Luke's head. Figure him out. Luke knew it. He could feel it. But why him? He had no special qualities. It would make more sense if Hardison concentrated on one of the government workers, like the CIA guy. Surely, he was the smartest one in the class.

Luke continued to argue with himself until another thought struck him. *Maybe the man is cross-eyed, and I only think he's looking at me.* The rationalization for Hardison's stare caused a smile to creep across Luke's face. But the intimidating gaze of the instructor quickly wiped it away. His thoughts returned to his original comparison of Doctor Nathan Hardison.

He once reminded Luke of an eagle in search of rabbits, but on second thought, he looked more like an owl, with his horn-rimmed glasses and hooked nose. *I guess it doesn't matter,* Luke sighed. *Both are birds of prey, and we're the rodents unlucky enough to be in his field of vision. Wish I had some tall grass to hide in right now.*

CHAPTER ELEVEN

On Friday morning of the first week, Doctor Hardison came in as usual, ignoring the group and walking briskly to the podium. Also, as usual, everyone was poised to take notes.

Instead of reading, however, the instructor remained silent. His eyes swept the room with a gaze as penetrating as the relentless Chicago wind.

After a few minutes, he moved the lectern to the side of the room and took a seat on the desk. He'd done that on several occasions recently. When he seemed to be in a more reflective mood, he'd sit on the edge of the desk at the rear of the podium while he explained a point. Luke thought it was an odd arrangement, but it seemed to work, as everyone appeared even more attentive than usual.

"This is normally a six month course," the instructor began, "but since most agencies cannot afford to pay for student attendance and lose a body for that length of time, it has been condensed into six weeks. The reason for writing down verbatim what I say...is...to get you used to being accurate in taking notes."

He stopped talking long enough to let his words sink in. When he continued, his voice dripped with sarcasm. "That is, I might add, on the outside chance that you graduate from this Institute, and are able to conduct polygraph examinations."

Hardison focused his attention on the written material for several minutes before once again glancing around the room. His gaze always rested on Luke, and the reluctant student was always the one who looked away.

After degrading the class with his sarcastic comment, Hardison continued in a more normal tone. But as far as Luke was concerned, nothing was normal about the man, especially his tone of voice.

As the instructor continued addressing the group, his voice softened. "I am also trying to prepare you for an unexpected event. Something out of the ordinary."

He leaned forward. "There will be many lessons in the art of anticipation and interpretation; figure out the next move of your opponent and prepare to overcome denials. Interrogation is like a game of chess, only far more serious. You must always expect, and be prepared for, the unexpected. You must also accept the fact that, given the right set of circumstances, everyone lies. There are no exceptions.

"We learn at an early age that telling the truth results in punishment. It doesn't matter if the punishment is physical or emotional, it is still painful in one form or another, and it is inherent in all creatures to avoid pain. So we lie about breaking our mother's favorite vase, or putting the cat in the toilet and closing the lid. As we get older the lies get bigger, because there is more at stake than being grounded or sent to bed without supper. Telling the truth could send us to prison or...to the morgue."

Hardison removed his glasses, rubbed his eyes, and replaced them. He slowly pushed them up the bridge of his nose before continuing.

"Some of you might think that your best friend would never lie to you. That your parents would never lie to you. That your spouse would never lie to you. Do not be fooled by preconceived notions. Do you think your best friend is going to tell you how insignificant he thinks your troubles are, when he is faced with some far greater? How about your parents? Do you think they are being truthful when they tell you how handsome and intelligent you are? How about your wife? Do you think she is being truthful when she says she doesn't mind if you have a night out with the boys?

"We justify our lies by telling ourselves that it was for the best. We didn't want to hurt another person's feelings. But lies are still lies, regardless of the motive.

"Most lies of the type I have mentioned, are insignificant in the overall scheme of things. The ones most harmful…are those we tell to ourselves. If you believe the flattery, it is time you looked into a mirror and come to terms with the person you really are? We are, by our very nature…liars all."

For the first time since he'd been told he was going to polygraph school, Luke found himself interested in the subject matter. He listened intently, waiting for the doctor to continue. He was disappointed when the man stopped talking.

Hardison sat quietly for a few seconds before suddenly getting to his feet. He moved the lectern back to the center of the room and resumed reading from the lesson plan.

The students picked up their pens and hurried to catch up with what he was saying.

Either I'm nuts or he is. Luke reluctantly followed the actions of the other students, and hurriedly began jotting down notes.

CHAPTER TWELVE

On Wednesday morning of week two, Hardison broke tradition by walking slowly and quietly into the room. It looked so effortless, he appeared to be floating. His usual entrance was more hurried and aggressive. He went directly to the podium. But instead of reading from the lesson plan, he remained silent, his gaze fixed on everyone, and on no one.

What the hell now? Luke waited with the others in the uncomfortable silence.

Something doesn't look right. Am I seeing things or is this guy wearing the same clothes every day?

He gave his instructor the once-over. He was certain Hardison was wearing the same gray dress pants with the light-blue shirt and dark-blue socks that he wore on Monday and Tuesday.

You'd think he'd shine his shoes, or at least wipe them off. I don't think they've seen any polish since he bought them.

Luke was so intent on trying to decide if the doctor did, indeed, have the same clothes on that he failed to notice the eyes boring into him until he looked up. He found himself locked eyeball to eyeball with the man. He tried to turn away, but an irresistible force kept their eyes glued. He felt the pull of Hardison's gaze as it seemed to turn him inside out, revealing his inner thoughts, and leaving him naked in the Chicago winter.

Luke dropped his head to his chest. He had tried to throw up a mental barrier, but it was too little, too late. All of his energy had been siphoned. He was bone-tired. His body felt like a warm, wet washcloth, thoroughly used and wrung out to dry.

Just as he had done the Friday before, the instructor slowly slid the lectern off to the side of the room and took his customary seat on the edge of the desk, one foot on the floor, the other dangling.

His tone was always different when he came out from behind the lectern. This time it was softer and more reflective as if he had become kinder and gentler. The darkness that seemed to always surround him had lifted.

When he spoke, he was no longer intimidating. His features had softened. He looked like a harmless old man. Even his hooked nose seemed to straighten. He reminded Luke of a chameleon that could change appearance to fit the occasion. The man Luke saw before him had just morphed from a scary, merciless monster, into a gentle and helpful soul.

Luke was linked to this man. He didn't know how or why, but his strength and feeling of wellbeing ebbed and flowed with the energy displayed by Doctor Nathan Hardison. And right now, he was feeling stronger and more confident.

How in the hell does he do that? Even as the thought filled his mind, Luke relaxed his guard and prepared for the flow of information.

Hardison waved his hand. "I want you to put down your writing instruments and pay attention to what I am about to tell you. This will not be on any test, so do not worry about it. Just remember what I say, because it is important that you do."

When everyone's pen was down, he continued. "You will hear many times during your training, to always expect the unexpected. Since most of you are in the front line of law enforcement, you undoubtedly have implemented that protocol or you would not be alive today. But until now, you have applied that lesson only to the street...and only to physical confrontations." His voice was calm, and yet there was a hint of suspense, like when a secret is about to be told.

Hardison shifted his position and swept the room with his gaze. "As a polygraph examiner, you are now about to enter the realm of psychological confrontations. The unexpected will confront you with nearly every polygraph examination you conduct. You will have a psychological tug-of-war with the subject. It is a battle of wills. You must always win that battle, or your career as a polygraph examiner will be short-lived."

Luke sat enthralled, lost in the moment. Hardison's words embedded themselves in his brain. They became a permanent part of him as securely as the oak pegs that held the barn together. He felt comfortable with his situation, and fortunate to be a part of the process. He no longer had to strain to comprehend what was being taught. It was easy. For the first time since he arrived, he was leaning forward physically, as well as mentally, in order to absorb as much information as possible.

"In addition to expecting the unexpected," Hardison continued, "many confessions will be obtained during a polygraph examination. It is important that you write down exactly what is said, and…in the exact order it is said." Hardison's face was expressionless as he stopped to take a few breaths.

Luke didn't want him to stop. *Damn it. Why does he do that just when things get really interesting?*

As if reading Luke's thoughts, Hardison continued his presentation. "Another requirement is to ask the test questions exactly as written, and pen the answers exactly as presented… in order to certify that an examination was properly conducted. There should be no question about that. It is common sense."

Having finished his comments, the instructor rose slowly to his feet and moved the lectern back to its normal position.

Luke sank back in his seat, disappointed the intimate lesson was over.

The next hour was spent with brief starts and stops. Sometimes in the middle of a sentence, Hardison would appear to think of something that wasn't on the lesson plan and immediately share that thought with the students.

The procedure caught some off guard, and first one and then another asked him to start over. He honored each request and repeated himself several times without sounding annoyed.

Luke struggled to keep up with note-taking and watching the instructor too. *The guy is an enigma. When I think he'll be upset, he isn't, and when I think he won't be, he is. Maybe he's trying to reinforce the need to always expect the unexpected. I guess I need the training. The atmosphere here was sure as hell unexpected, and I definitely wasn't prepared.*

The conflict brewing in Luke's head between the negative aspects of his predicament and the desire to obtain more interesting information continued. He rode a roller coaster of emotions. One minute he was high with his new-found knowledge, and the next he was in the depths of despair.

He sensed a lighter side of polygraph. The times when people were cleared of wrong-doing and gained their lives back, or proved to be victims instead of suspects. But it was the darker side that always muscled its way in: admissions and confessions wrenched from individuals as aggressively as gutting a hog. Those thoughts lingered, because reflecting on the negative was something Luke could do with ease. Maybe it was habit. Something he'd picked up at the age of nine.

***

From the moment Luke had walked into the building that first Monday morning, he had a strange feeling about the place. It felt as if ice-cold hands had a stranglehold on his gut. He felt a heavy darkness, as though he was stepping into a dimension from which there was no return. The farther he ventured into the abyss, the more difficult it would be to find his way back. As the days passed, he would revisit those thoughts time and time again.

He couldn't put his finger on the reason for feeling so stressed. He'd been through situations in the paratroops, and as a patrol officer, where he didn't know if he would live or die. He never felt undue stress with any of them. But here, with no apparent physical danger, he was constantly feeling apprehensive, like something terrible was about to happen–or already had. He shrugged it off as just his imagination. He tried to think more positive thoughts.

Think positive and things will be positive. Yeah, right. If only he could believe that. His mind kept repeating the mantra, but his body wanted to get the hell out of there.

CHAPTER THIRTEEN

The days progressed, each much like the one before. The students were constantly threatened with expulsion, sometimes subtly and sometimes overtly. By the end of the second week, everyone seemed to be caught up in a psychological nightmare.

There was minimal interaction with each other. Rumors were rampant that a spy was among them who reported their negative comments to the instructor. Everyone believed they were being watched, and their conversation monitored for clues as to their true nature. No one wanted to go back to his respective department and explain why he was too dishonest, too dumb, or too emotionally unstable to pass the course.

After one particularly hectic day, Luke walked back to the hotel with Mel and Joe. The men strode briskly without speaking until Joe blurted out, "This is the damnedest training class I've ever been in. Why the hell am I so nervous about everything? Hell, I once faced a bear in Montana with nothing more than a hatchet, and it didn't scare me half as much as walking into that classroom every day."

When neither Luke nor Mel responded, he continued. "From watching the reactions of others, and the comments I've overheard, I'd say everyone else feels the same. It seems like we're constantly being watched. I swear I could feel someone's eyes on the back of my neck today, but when I turned around, no one was there."

"Aw, you're just paranoid," Mel said with a grin. "I kind of enjoy it. I keep looking to see who'll crack up first."

"Yeah. Bullshit," Joe shot back. "You're just as screwed up as the rest of us. Or maybe more so, since you say it doesn't bother you."

"Nah. I think everyone wishes they were somewhere else," Mel chuckled. "I know I do. But I sure as hell don't want to go home early, so I guess I'll just have to tough it out."

As they reached the hotel and quickly ducked inside, thankful to be out of the freezing cold, Luke looked at Joe and managed to grin. He could have grabbed the big guy and hugged him. Until now, Luke had the impression that he was the only one who was stressed or weak. Hell, it wasn't just him. Everyone was in the same boat. He felt like celebrating.

"Like they say, just because you're paranoid doesn't mean someone isn't watching you." He rubbed his hands together to get the blood circulating. "I'm not happy to be here either," he continued as Joe and Mel stood listening, "but I'm relieved I wasn't one of the group who had to go back to their department and admit they failed the polygraph."

"You got that right," Joe said as the trio entered the elevator that would take them to their respective rooms.

Mel chipped in with his agreement also. "Every day is difficult. But not as difficult as facing my boss after failing a polygraph, or being too dumb or too emotionally unstable to pass this course." The elevator stopped at his floor and he stepped out.

Joe held the elevator door open. "I asked the female polygraph examiner–whose name by the way, I still don't know– why the psychological torture." He seemed to relish what he was about to say. Luke and Mel gave him their full attention.

After a few bounces of the elevator doors trying to close, and Joe blocking them with his foot, he continued. "She explained that the thinking of school officials is to place each student under severe emotional stress to see how they handle it. Their rationale is that if you're going to crack up, they would rather you do it here than in front of some poor slob during a polygraph examination."

Joe's face held a self-satisfied look after having delivered what he obviously considered to be an important piece of information.

He slowly pulled his foot back and continued the climb to his room.

Luke always thought of himself as emotionally strong. He was confident he could handle anything that came his way. But several times during his self-described "incarceration in a psychological torture chamber," he considered walking out and returning to Phoenix, more than happy to be on shift three in patrol.

He was still leaving that option open. Like the elevator doors that kept slamming shut on Joe's foot, the decision to step out or stay in school continued to bang on his mind.

CHAPTER FOURTEEN

A variety of instructors rotated through the course, depending on the topic. There were medical doctors, lawyers, psychiatrists, psychologists, interview and interrogation specialists, and others, telling the students more than Luke was capable of digesting in such a short span of time. He perked up instantly, however, when he barely passed a Physiology and Anatomy test. He missed the question: "What is the location and function of the mitral valve?" He'd placed it on the wrong side of the heart.

When Doctor Hardison handed Luke his graded paper, he glared at him with that cold, hard stare the group had come to expect when they did or said something the instructor found objectionable.

"You have apparently been attending the wrong class, or you have not been paying attention." He looked at Luke as if he had just committed a felony. "You would have a pretty screwed-up heart if you had one like you described."

Hardison frowned, then pointed to the answer Luke had given to the test question. "But maybe you do, and that may be the reason why you almost failed this test. What do you think your department will say when you go home and tell them you were not paying attention in class and got kicked out? So far, you have failed to live up to expectations."

He moved away, but stopped suddenly and turned back. "Not *my* expectations," he said with a sneer. "*Your* expectations. You set a pretty high standard for yourself. But so far, you have failed to live up to it. So...you have two choices: you can quit now and save yourself some time and effort, or...you can get your head out of your ass and learn the material. The choice is yours." The disappointment in his voice was similar to the way Luke's father had sounded when he corrected the children.

"I'll do better next time," Luke murmured, in a feeble attempt to appease the man–or whatever he was–standing before him. The instructor walked away to confront another student.

Luke breathed a sigh of relief. He didn't like the man standing that close. It gave him bad vibes. Hardison wore the misery and tears from confessors like an invisible cloak. Luke had glimpsed an insight into the everyday life of a polygraph examiner.

That will never happen again, even if I have to study day and night, Luke promised himself. He placed the corrected test paper in a folder and prepared for more note taking. *Never again.*

CHAPTER FIFTEEN

After the confrontation with Doctor Hardison over the mitral valve, it was as if someone had turned on a light in Luke's brain. He was confident he could correctly answer all future questions on physiology and anatomy.

His optimism was challenged by a question that appeared on a test the very next day: "Trace a drop of blood from the left ventricle to the right foot and back using major pathways."

Luke glanced around the room after he'd read the question. The look on the faces of his fellow classmates provided an indication of the turmoil taking place in their minds.

As he picked up his pen, Luke felt more at ease about the test. He had made up his mind after the mitral valve encounter, to quit worrying and just do the best he could.

***

The following day, an equally difficult test was administered. It included the following question: "An elderly man is straining to have a bowel movement and passes out. What is the process taking place in the body that may contribute to the cause of the man losing consciousness?" The question covered not only the nervous system, but the respiratory and circulatory systems as well.

That night, Joe, Mel and several others gathered in Luke's room to discuss the tests.

"Those were some tough questions on that test today," Joe said as he opened the discussion. "That miserable bastard hit us with a hellish test two days in a row. You'd think he'd give us a chance to catch our breath before slamming us with another."

Some of the students nodded in agreement, but no one responded verbally.

"What answer did anyone give for the one about the old man passing out while taking a crap? Hell, I've almost done that myself," Joe said, to subdued laughter. "I think they may have forgotten that we're cops, not doctors," he added. "Who gives a damn what the process is for the man losing consciousness? It's not like we're gonna test someone while they're on the shitter." His comment drew another chuckle from the group.

When no one spoke up with an answer, Luke glanced up to see everyone looking at him. He explained his response with a disclaimer.

"My answer on paper was more detailed and drawn out to make them think I knew what I was talking about, but here is basically the answer I gave. Straining as he did caused the man to hold his breath. That prevented a sufficient amount of oxygen from getting to his lungs. The blood vessels were also restricted by continued straining. The combination of a drop in blood pressure, and a decrease of oxygen to the brain, caused the man to lose consciousness."

Everyone agreed they'd answered essentially the same way.

"Well," Mel chipped in. "I guess we'll eventually know if it was the right answer or not. The doc is not the least bit shy in telling us we're wrong. I think I'd better prepare myself for a confrontation like Luke went through on the mitral valve question. I'm not sure I answered as completely as I should have."

"At least I'll never forget where the mitral valve is located," Luke said as he rubbed the back of his neck. "In case the rest of you don't know, it's the valve between the left atrium and the left ventricle of the heart. I wonder if whoever grades these papers really pays attention to the answers. There was one yesterday about tracing a drop of blood through the body. I don't recall exactly what I put down, but no one ever called me on it, so it was either right or else no one checked the answer."

"Well, if it wasn't correct, Hardison would have jumped down your throat," Joe said. "What the hell is going on with you two? He never misses a chance to slam you for something. I'm not complaining. When he's picking on you, he's leaving the rest of us alone. I was just wondering why he has it in for you."

Several others agreed. "Yeah," Mel said. "I noticed it too. For some reason, he seems to give you more attention than anyone else."

"I have no idea why he concentrates on me," Luke said. "Somehow, I don't get the feeling he specifically dislikes me. I don't know what to make of it. But I wish he'd get off my ass and target someone else for a change. He gives me a strange feeling, like maybe he's from another planet or something."

"He is kind of an alien-looking son of a bitch," Joe chipped in. "I'd be glad if he went back to his own planet."

"Yeah," a detective from Houston, chimed in. "Do you notice that he always talks with a slow deliberation, and enunciates every word carefully? I've never heard him abbreviate anything, like saying we're, or they're. He always says *we are* or *they are,* like he has us hooked up to a polygraph and wants to make sure we understand the question."

Luke felt uneasy talking about Hardison. Maybe he had the room bugged. He wouldn't put it past him.

He was glad when the group left his room. He was tired and he still had a handful of notes to type. He promised himself to never get caught short again. It was unnerving to interact with Nathan Hardison on a personal level. In some respects, it felt like he was the doctor's reflection, talking with himself. The thought disgusted him.

CHAPTER SIXTEEN

On Monday morning of week four, Doctor Hardison walked in slowly, looking neither left nor right. When he got to the podium, he scanned the room as usual, but this time, his gaze didn't settle on Luke. In fact, he never even glanced his way. Luke was surprised and relieved.

Maybe he's going to leave me alone for a change and intimidate some other poor bastard.

After a few minutes, Hardison addressed the class in a low, calm voice, "During the past week or so, you have been introduced to the nervous system. I would like one of you to tell us about the body's nervous system. I wonder how many of you have been paying attention. Is there anyone here capable of explaining the nervous system to the rest of the class?"

Each student lowered his eyes as the instructor's gaze passed over him.

Luke sensed what was coming. Electricity flowed in the other direction now. The power and energy that had been siphoned from him on prior occasions had returned. He could feel the force getting stronger as Doctor Hardison turned his attention to him.

This time there was no feeling of anxiety, no wishing the man would go away and leave him alone. For the first time since he stepped into the classroom, Luke was in sync with his instructor and at ease with his surroundings. He knew what was coming, and he knew how to address it.

"I know who can tell us about the nervous system, because he was paying attention. Mr. Canfield, will you please stand and explain the nervous system to the rest of the class?" It sounded like a request, but Luke knew better.

Luke slowly rose to his feet. He'd studied extra hard on the nervous system because he'd known this day was coming. The information had parked itself in his brain like a cop on a stakeout.

"The Central Nervous System," Luke began, unable to recognize his own voice, "is composed of the brain and spinal cord. Everything outside of that is the Peripheral. Under the Central Nervous System are two sub-systems: The Somatic and the Autonomic. The Somatic controls voluntary movements, such as the decision to raise my arm. The Autonomic is basically involuntary. It regulates bodily functions such as heartbeat and breathing."

Luke knew he was talking, but he felt like a human tape player regurgitating the words that had been programmed into it. He continued with his explanation. "Under the Autonomic is the Sympathetic and Parasympathetic systems. The Sympathetic acts like the foot-feed on a car. It kicks in during times of need, such as when you're faced with the decision to stand and fight or run. That is called the Fight or Flight mechanism. The Parasympathetic acts like the brakes on a car. It slows things down so you won't blow a gasket, so to speak. Sometimes, it overcompensates, shuts the body down too fast and too hard, and you lose consciousness. Like when your car stalls if you slam the brakes on too hard."

Luke slumped into his seat, too exhausted to see or even care if his answer met with the approval of his instructor. The drumbeat of his heart and the samba dance of his pulse blocked out all other emotions, except relief.

The room became hushed as everyone waited in anticipation of either a negative or positive response from the man in charge.

Luke regained sufficient strength to steal a quick glance at his instructor. He didn't know what to make of what he saw. He must have been mistaken. He blinked hard and looked again. For the first time since he'd met the man, he witnessed something he didn't think possible. For a brief second, Doctor Nathan Hardison had smiled.

CHAPTER SEVENTEEN

As the weeks progressed, the class spent almost every evening in a restaurant, a hotel lobby, or a bar where Hardison took them for training in psychology. He pointed out different people and instructed the students to watch their mannerisms, and how they reacted to different stimuli, such as people bumping into them or speaking with them. He often mentioned that the comfort zone for men was about arm's length from each other while with women, it was a little closer.

Hardison explained to the group what type of person someone was, and then asked that person to come over and verify his observations. He identified himself as Doctor Hardison, and introduced the group as his students. When asked to interact with the group, most people did so without hesitation.

On Friday night, the fourth week of school, class reconvened at the Rainbow Bar.

It was a seedy-looking place in a rundown neighborhood. Above the entrance hung an arch of various colored neon tubes with the bottom one burned out.

Even before the door to the establishment was fully open, the rancid odor of cigarette smoke and stale beer gushed out like air escaping from a blown tire. The prospects of getting in from the bitter cold, however, dispelled any thought of hesitating before stepping inside.

As he entered, Luke noticed a bar stretching nearly the length of the room. Its color and condition matched the atmosphere–dark and scarred. Cigarette smoke hung like a cloud of noxious gas, assaulting his lungs and adding to the dinginess of the place. It reminded Luke of a smoggy day in Phoenix on a "don't burn" day.

A quick survey of the room revealed the typical bar scene. Liquor bottles lined the counter in front of a large mirror that backed the bar. Two bartenders were busy drawing glasses of Hamm's, Pabst Blue Ribbon, and Schlitz. A variety of beer signs were lit up around the room.

Obviously the place to be if all a person wants to do is get drunk.

The thought intensified when a customer brushed past the group and bellied up to the bar.

It's probably not the place to be if you just want to socialize–too many people, too little room, and too damned noisy.

The Wurlitzer at the end of the bar blared out the Hank Williams classic, *Cold, Cold, Heart,* making it difficult to carry on a normal conversation. Luke wished he had some cotton to stuff in his ears. It wasn't that he didn't like country music; far from it. He'd been raised on the stuff, and he still listened to it whenever possible. He just didn't like it to be deafening.

He was surprised to see so many people. All of the bar stools were occupied as were the booths that lined the wall and the tables in the middle. In spite of the noise level, patrons talked and drank, each holding a glass or a bottle.

What a dive. The thought came to Luke as he watched a woman who'd obviously had too much to drink, slosh beer from the nearly full glass she carried while tottering her way between the tables.

"Are these people all nuts? What in the hell are they doing here? I sure as hell wouldn't hang out in a place like this if I could be somewhere else," he muttered under his breath as the group followed their instructor.

It was apparent that arrangements had been made to accommodate the class. Two large tables were pushed together in a far corner, and Hardison headed directly to them.

They were barely seated when one of the bartenders hurried over and began taking drink orders.

"A double Jack Daniels," the doctor ordered.

Several students ordered a glass of beer, but Luke, Mel and Joe ordered soft drinks. Luke didn't think it was a good idea to have an alcoholic drink; it might be a test. At any rate, he wasn't taking any chances. He wanted root beer, but he ordered a Coke. He didn't want to attract attention by ordering something that the bar probably didn't even have.

After a few drinks, Hardison began pointing out various people. One man had a drink in one hand and his other hand on another man's shoulder. He was obviously trying to make a point, but the man he was trying to convince appeared to be uncomfortable with the contact. He kept backing away until the hand slipped from his shoulder.

The doctor's psychoanalysis of people wasn't restricted to outsiders. He also pointed out things about members of the class. Joe was running his fingers up and down the dew that had formed on his Coke glass.

Hardison watched him for some time. When he spoke, his voice carried not only to the recipient of the comment, but to all of the students. "People who do what you are doing with their glass, subconsciously consider it a phallic symbol. They are masturbating."

Even after his comment, Hardison continued to skewer the embarrassed student with his glare.

Luke was relieved when the ordeal was over and the

instructor's attention shifted to ordering another drink.

Joe didn't touch his glass again except to pick it up to drink. This also gave notice to the group to be more careful of their actions.

What a miserable son of a bitch. Anything to embarrass us. Luke quickly tried to think of something else. Hardison could probably read his mind. He concentrated on the Hamm's beer sign of the bear diving into a lake of sky-blue water. He'd always liked that commercial.

After mentioning another social *faux pas* of a patron, Hardison pointed to a group by the bar. "Watch that woman over there. See how she's acting?"

The woman that the doctor pointed out was in her forties, Luke guessed. She was tall and thin with medium-length brown hair. Her heavy sweater and corduroy pants blended in with the rest of the crowd. She didn't stay long in one place before moving on, first talking with one man and then another.

"That woman has never had a climax," Hardison said as nonchalantly as if he were ordering another drink.

Luke cast a quick glance at Hardison before turning to others at the table. *What the hell was that about? How could he know such a thing?*

As he examined the faces of the other students, they appeared to be of the same mindset. Some stifled grins. Most kept their heads down, and only looked up when Hardison summoned the bartender.

Hardison waved his hand in the direction of the woman. "Give that lady over there a drink on me and ask her to come over here."

The woman accepted the drink and acknowledged the offer with a wave of her glass as she made her way to the table.

Attractive, but not overly so, Luke thought, as the woman flashed a quick smile. Even with her pale complexion, her uneven front teeth were noticeable.

"Thanks for the drink," she said as she lifted her glass in salute to the man who'd bought it for her.

"You are quite welcome," Hardison replied, his voice ingratiating as he returned the gesture with a wave of his own glass.

"What can I do for you fellas?" she asked.

"I am Doctor Hardison and these are my students," he responded. "I am teaching them personal psychology." He took a drink of Jack Daniels and waited as the lady mimicked his actions and took a sip of her own drink.

"Would you mind if I asked you a few personal questions?"

"Not at all," the woman replied as she took another sip. "Fire away."

"We are interested in the interaction that one person has with another," Hardison continued. "Are you married?"

The woman threw her head back and gave a short laugh. "Not at the present. Why? Are you offering?" Her voice turned sultry, inviting. She seemed to get a kick out of her own comment as she continued to chuckle, though none of the students even cracked a smile.

"Do you have a boyfriend?" Hardison asked.

"I have lots of boyfriends," the woman responded, "but none I'd take home to mother." She again let out a short laugh and tossed her head back, exposing a pasty-white neck.

"I hope you will not be offended by this next question," Hardison said as he lowered his glass. "I assure you it is purely clinical and is not meant to embarrass or offend in any way. Would you tell the class if you have ever experienced an orgasm?"

Luke was embarrassed by the question. He could feel the heat rise from his neck to his face. For the first time since he'd arrived in Chicago, he needed some cold air. He lowered his head and looked away in an attempt to emotionally, if not physically, escape. Several others in the group did the same.

When there was no immediate response, Luke looked up to see how the woman was reacting. A pained expression spread across her face. Her brow wrinkled as though she was having a severe migraine. She opened her mouth as if to say something, but closed it again and said nothing.

Silence reigned for an uncomfortable moment, her sad eyes piercing the man who'd asked her such a personal question. The confident and attractive qualities that she'd displayed when she walked up to the table had disappeared, leaving an empty shell of her former self.

Luke was waiting for her to slap Hardison's face, or at least tell him to go to hell. In fact, he wanted to do it himself.

She finally spoke, her strained voice cracking with emotion, "No...Is it that obvious?"

She didn't wait for a response, but slowly turned and walked away. She looked smaller than when she'd first approached the table. Luke followed her with his eyes, but lost her in the crowd. He didn't see her the rest of the night.

Hardison resumed his drinking, but the incident had put a damper on everyone's mood. Joe and Mel stood up and pulled on the coats they had shed when they first sat down. Luke followed suit.

As if he understood, Doctor Hardison ended his lesson and got up from the table. The group left the bar and piled into taxis. Luke watched Hardison stumble into a cab and drive away.

As they left the curb, Luke glanced back at the Rainbow Bar, his mind filled with the events of the evening and the lessons they had learned. Everyone has bones buried somewhere. The woman they'd met was just one of many trying to keep theirs from being uncovered, even by themselves. Liquor seemed to be the common grave for their buried secrets.

The neon sign over the entrance of the Rainbow Bar could never come close to painting the picture of what the interior held, or capture the heart-breaking personal stories of those who sought its sanctuary. It would take something larger than a billboard to do that.

As the lights of the bar faded from view, Luke wondered what Hardison still had in store for them. One of the questions he'd asked himself on several occasions since he got to Chicago surfaced again: *Could things possibly get any more bizarre?*

CHAPTER EIGHTEEN

After several evening psychology classes, it became apparent to Luke that Nathan Hardison was at home in a bar. Each night, the instructor would drink steadily until it was time to pour him into his car where his wife waited to take him home. Other than the night at the Rainbow Bar, Mrs. Hardison always showed up at eleven o'clock, just as her husband dismissed class and headed for the door.

I guess they must have an arrangement, but she acts more like a servant than a wife.

Greta Hardison was short and thin, with thick black hair that bobbed up and down on her shoulders when she walked. She was always neatly dressed and pleasant to the students and staff during her infrequent visits to the Institute. Luke couldn't help but wonder what she saw in her husband. They seemed an unlikely pair. He snickered as he suddenly realized that he and Emily fit the same mold. *I guess whoever said opposites attract was right. We're as different as day and night. Maybe that's what keeps us together.*

***

Even with only two weeks to go, Luke felt insecure. He still had serious doubts about completing the course. Several times recently, he was sure he was being watched in class, maybe from the polygraph room with the large window. But that was impossible. It was a one-way glass. Still, someone was watching from somewhere. He could feel their eyes burning into him. Maybe it wasn't a one-way glass. Maybe he was hallucinating. Maybe he was losing his mind.

Monday night, following a particularly difficult day, and a late night visit to a restaurant for another psychology lesson, he quickly typed up his classroom notes and readied for bed. But something didn't seem right. He still felt as though he was under surveillance.

From his perch on the edge of the bed, he glanced around the room. Maybe he could spot a hidden camera or something that would account for the feeling that Doctor Hardison was aware of every move he made. He examined every inch of the room. He was a trained observer. He could tell if his room was bugged. Nothing caught his eye. Still, he felt uneasy.

He rose from the bed, strolled to the window, and scanned the street below. Maybe someone was keeping track of his study hours. He saw the shadow of a man behind a row of cars. Binoculars might help to identify the man, but his were at home in the closet. A lot of good they did him now.

He turned away and started for the bed, trying to ignore his suspicions. He chalked it up to unreasonable paranoia. But the hair on the back of his neck stood up. Someone was at the window. He whipped around to confront the shadowy figure. The man's face was pressed against the pane, pale and gaunt, with a twisted mouth and hollow eyes...Hardison. But how did he get there? It was nine stories up.

Luke backed slowly to the bed and sat down. He buried his face in his hands while massaging his eyes slowly and methodically. He was a rational person, pragmatic to a fault. He didn't believe in unexplained occurrences or coincidence. Everything happened in order, as it was supposed to. Everything had a reason for being–even hallucinations.

He rose to his feet and walked slowly to the window. The face was gone, and there was nothing on the street below except snow-covered cars and a lot of cold. His mind had played tricks on him.

Maybe it was a self-defense mechanism. The fight or flight part of the autonomic nervous system was looking out for him, always protecting him without his conscious effort. It was cautioning him to be careful, to pay attention to detail, and to always do the right thing, whether anyone watched or not.

He returned to the bed and got undressed, then heaved a sigh as he turned out the light and crawled into bed. His father's voice echoed in his ears as he buried his head in his pillow: *Always do the right thing. Take care of the little things. The big things will take care of themselves.*

CHAPTER NINETEEN

Besides being a school, the Diogenes Polygraph Institute was an active business.

Tuesday morning of the fifth week, Doctor Hardison was scheduled to conduct a polygraph examination. He'd been out with the class Monday night and drank himself into a stupor. None of the students expected to see him up and about the next day, but here he was, business as usual, with no noticeable effects of the night before.

Luke recalled his father being like that. He could be falling down drunk the night before, but the next day he would be up early, working in the field alongside his sons.

The person to be tested was a small man in his forties accused of setting fire to the building that housed his business in order to collect the insurance money.

The students were invited to watch the examination through the large one-way window of the polygraph room. Instead of a window behind the subject's chair as Luke had noticed when he was tested, the window in this room covered the wall behind the examiner, so the subject could easily be observed by those peering in. In addition, an outside speaker with subdued volume, provided an audible account of what was being said.

Doctor Hardison led the man into the polygraph room. He seated himself behind the desk, took out a fountain pen and a form from a drawer, and placed the items on the desk. While he prepared to conduct the examination, the doctor ignored the man in the chair across from him.

He finally pushed a form over to the subject and said in a matter-of-fact tone, "I need your written consent to give you this test. Read it and sign at the bottom." The subject did as directed.

Hardison appeared to busy himself with forms and pens which he took out of the desk and then put back as though he'd changed his mind. Finally, he began asking pertinent questions: name, address, phone number, birth date, and recent medication the subject had taken.

After writing down the response to each question, he looked directly at the man and asked, "Why are you here today?"

"I was told to come and take a lie detector test by a detective." The man's voice was high-pitched and too loud for the little room.

He shifted uncomfortably in his seat.

Hardison leaned toward the subject and stared at him through his owl-eye glasses. "Why did the detective ask you to do that?"

"I don't know. I guess he thought I might have had something to do with the fire," the man said. The volume of his voice was reduced, but still louder than necessary.

"Why would he think that?" asked Hardison, his voice soft and low.

"That's what I'd like to know," the subject quickly responded.

The instructor stopped talking and began formulating the questions he would ask during the polygraph test.

During the silence, the subject crossed and uncrossed his legs. He looked up at the ceiling and down at the floor. The right corner of his mouth twitched, making him look as if he was trying to smile, but couldn't quite make it happen.

"I'm very nervous," the subject blurted as the silence continued. "I'm concerned that my nervousness will cause a problem with the machine." His voice rose again.

The doctor never looked up from the paper. "That is a good sign," he said. "If you were not nervous, I would be. The only people who are not nervous when they take a polygraph examination, are people with serious mental problems...and then *I* get nervous. So, I am happy to see that you are nervous. That means you are normal."

The questions Hardison constructed were read aloud to the subject. He was asked if he understood them and could answer each one truthfully by yes or by no. The man said he could.

Doctor Hardison placed the attachments on the man as had been done to Luke when he was tested. With each attachment came an explanation of what each component measured.

After placing the attachments on the subject, Hardison resumed his seat behind the desk. He sat quietly for a moment as he seemed to take on a different persona. No longer the doctor. No longer the instructor. He was now the *examiner.*

He inflated the blood pressure cuff and flipped a toggle switch on the instrument that set the chart paper in motion. The four pens trailed red ink as they traced the changes in blood pressure, pulse rate, respiration, and galvanic skin response. After some preliminary adjustments, the test began.

"Is your first name George?"

"Yes," the man responded in a barely audible tone.

"Are you wearing a shirt?"

"Yes."

Strange, Luke thought. Before the test, the man was practically yelling, but now, during the crucial time, he didn't give out much more than a whisper.

"Do you intend to try to lie during this test?"

"No." The answer was louder, emphatic.

Luke tried to watch the chart and the subject at the same time to see if he could determine the man's truthfulness. As he continued to stare at the man, a sudden insight rushed through him; an understanding of the man without even knowing him.

"Damn! He did it!" Luke said to himself. "He did it!" He had no idea how he knew. He just knew. Like that day in the barn, when he sensed his little sister was in trouble. Just as he rushed to the water tank and saved her from drowning, he felt the same urge to barge into the polygraph room, tell the subject to confess, and end his misery.

He curbed his impulse and watched quietly and intently as the questions were asked and answered and the chart continued to roll.

"Have you told the detective the whole truth about this matter?"

"Yes."

"Do you drink beer?"

"Yes."

"Do you suspect anyone of setting fire to your building?"

"No."

"Do you know who set fire to your building?"

"No," the subject squeaked.

Luke was mesmerized. He could have truthfully answered

for the man. He sensed which questions bothered him and which ones didn't, even without the voice inflection.

"Have you ever been drunk?"

"Yes."

"Did you set the fire?"

"No."

"Are you attempting to withhold any information about this matter?"

"No."

"Remain still. I will release the pressure on your arm in just a few seconds."

After writing the time and cuff pressure on the chart, the examiner turned the cardio knob and pressure was released from the cuff.

"You can relax now," he said as he also turned the knobs that regulated breathing and galvanic skin response. He tore off a section of chart paper and peered intently at the tracings.

The subject glanced at his left arm before turning his head toward the examiner. The corner of his mouth flickered again. He licked his lips and remained silent.

After a short while, the examiner put down the chart and moved his chair around to the end of the desk, closer to the subject. Nothing was said for several minutes.

"The polygraph tells me you set the fire." The examiner's voice was calm, matter of fact.

The subject faced his accuser, an obvious denial on his lips.

Before he could say anything, the examiner held up his hand, palm out. "I do not want you to say something you are going to be sorry for later. You do not need that on your conscience, too." The examiner's voice was empathetic, understanding. "You know, people do things when they have been drinking that they would not consider doing when they are sober. I am sure you realize that." The subject looked away without responding.

After repeated questioning, some accusatory and some cajoling, the subject looked down at the floor and quietly said, "I did set the fire, but it wasn't anything deliberate. I…It was an accident," he hurriedly added. "I thought the insurance company might not pay up if I told them what actually happened."

The examiner sat silent for a few minutes and then softened his tone and his demeanor. "Do you have a family?" he asked.

"I have a wife and two children. A boy and a girl," the subject hurriedly answered, obviously relieved that the conversation had shifted to one less threatening. The corner of his mouth that appeared so desperate to smile, had finally succeeded.

"That sounds like a very nice family," the examiner said. "Are they healthy?"

"Oh yes. They are healthy," came the reply. The subject sat upright and straightened his shoulders. "Each child is a treasure, and I would do anything for them." The smile was gone, his lips drawn tightly against his teeth.

"It sounds like you have a very good relationship with your family," the examiner said. "It is admirable for a man to love his family so much he would do anything for them."

Suddenly, the examiner became very quiet, he looked at the little man for some time before saying, "I am sure you are familiar with cancer and how it attacks the body. If an operation fails to get every cancerous cell, it continues to grow and becomes even more dangerous because a little portion was neglected by the surgeon. The entire body is at risk because the surgeon was not careful to remove all of the poisonous tissue that…if even a small portion is left, can create a devastating effect."

The examiner's voice and the cadence of his words were hypnotic. Luke could feel it. If his efforts were that evident outside the room, he could only imagine how effective they were on the man across the desk. The subject's face grew pale. His lip curled up at the corner. The twitch was back.

"You know you can never tell about something as devastating as cancer. Even the tiniest bit cannot be ignored, or it continues to eat away at the body until there is nothing left." The examiner inched a little closer.

The subject remained silent. The pinched expression on his face showed that he didn't understand what cancer had to do with arson. He slowly eased his body as far back as the chair would permit, as though sensing the conversation was leading to a more dangerous situation that he was helpless to prevent.

Luke knew what the man was going through. It hadn't been that long ago since he sat in a similar chair, getting grilled over something as insignificant as whether he was wearing a watch. "You poor bastard," Luke mumbled, as he watched the scene play out before him. "I know how you feel."

The examiner continued, his tone soft and understanding. "Now, I have no doubt that you love your family and would sacrifice yourself for any one of them. But let us say that one of your children is stricken with cancer."

The subject recoiled as though dodging a physical blow. His eyebrows arched as the examiner continued with slow, evenly paced words that pounded on the door of the subject's mind.

"Heaven forbid that ever happens, but it is possible…and we must face possibilities," the examiner continued. "If the amount of your child's cancer was removed according to your truthfulness, would you tell a partial truth, and take a chance on your child's health by just removing a portion of the cancerous tissue…or would you tell the whole truth, regardless of the consequences… and make sure all of the cancerous tissue is removed…so your child can have a happy and healthy life?"

The examiner's voice was sharper than when he started. His

words seemed to cut into the man, to bleed the truth out of him if need be. Without giving the subject a chance to respond, Hardison continued. "Lies are like cancer. They start out small, just like a cancer cell. And like a cancer cell, they continue to grow until they not only take over the mind, they ravage the body and tarnish the soul. Truth is the only remedy for a happy, healthy life."

Sometimes the volume of the examiner's voice would increase and decrease several times in the same sentence. The subject seemed confused. Luke understood. He could empathize with the man. His fight or flight mechanism was in conflict. It was a force of wills. Part of him wanted to continue denials while the other part wanted to confess and end the battle.

"From what I know about you," the examiner continued, "I have no doubt that you would gladly sacrifice yourself for any member of your family. Am I right?" His tone suddenly became more menacing. "Or am I completely wrong about you, and you are really a selfish man who thinks of himself first and doesn't care what happens to his family? Which kind of man are you?" The examiner's eyes had narrowed to slits as he thrust his head forward and stared the subject full in the face as if daring him to utter anything but the truth.

The subject moved his head back, his lips pulled into a grimace as the interrogation continued.

"I believe you are a good man who did something in the spur of the moment that you thought was helpful to your family, but now realize it will do irreparable harm if not corrected. You are the kind of man who can carry a physical burden, but an emotional one will break you down. It will break your family down. It starts out being tolerable for a while, and then...all sorts of emotional and even physical problems develop. If you want to stay healthy, if you want your wife and children to stay healthy, you need to clear your mind and start over."

Luke felt uneasy with the interrogation. He fought the urge to go in there and tell the man to fess up and be done with it instead of subjecting himself to the relentless assault on his psyche that, in the end, would result in a confession anyway. "Just get it over with," he kept saying under his breath.

The examiner continued to pour it on, his eyes focused intently on the little man in the polygraph chair. "Do not let your family suffer for something you thought was going to help, and now find it will hurt them if it is not corrected. Get all of that negative stuff out of your mind. Analyze your feelings. Surely you feel better just by telling me you started the fire."

Without waiting for a response or giving the man a chance to catch his breath, the examiner continued to psychologically hammer away at him. "Even though you did not tell me the whole truth, what little you did say had to make you feel better emotionally. You have an opportunity here today to make yourself whole, to make your family whole, to protect them from harm. Clear your mind. Get all of that cancerous material out in the open." He stopped talking and relaxed his posture, backing away a few inches.

Each man sat quietly.

Luke sensed what the subject was going through. The man's head was in a vice and the examiner kept twisting the handle. Talk or be crushed. The face of the examiner–stern, confident, in control–contrasted sharply with that of the subject–pale, confused, frightened and bewildered.

Luke was surprised when the examiner backed off. *Maybe he does have compassion.*

The respite was short-lived. The examiner suddenly moved in again, his eyes narrowed, his voice harsh. "Do you know how mold develops?" he asked, and then quickly answered his own question. "Mold grows in the dark, and if it isn't stopped, it continues to grow. It disappears only when exposed to light. Open up your mind, and get rid of the mold that is taking over your life. Make room for goodness to grow. Your family will appreciate the chance to live normal, healthy lives, and you will feel better about yourself because you gave them that chance." The examiner gave the long-winded speech without taking a breath; without giving the subject a chance to deny.

The situation reminded Luke of wash day on the farm. He often turned the crank on the clothes wringer that wrung every last drop of water from a heavy wash load, just like his instructor was doing with the subject. He was squeezing the little man's mind until it had nothing left to give, except the truth.

"I did it for my family," the subject blurted. "I was going to lose my business. I thought they would benefit from the insurance money. I'm sorry for putting them at risk. I guess I wasn't thinking clearly," he sobbed.

The examiner continued asking questions, not giving the man an opportunity to compose himself. "Start from the beginning. You need to explain the details. Everything you were thinking and everything you did. Get every detail out of your mind. Start with a clean slate."

Between blubbering gasps, and occasional deep breaths, the subject blurted out details of the crime. It was several minutes before he stopped crying.

"Now, don't you feel better after getting all of that out of your system?" the examiner asked confidently.

"I do. Yes. I feel much better," the subject said, his eyes wide. The tick at the corner of his mouth was gone, replaced by a genuine smile.

After getting the necessary details, the examiner unhooked the attachments and extended his hand. The subject stood and clasped it, holding on for several seconds before letting go and turning to the door.

"Thank you," he said. "Thank you very much for helping me realize I was headed down the wrong path. Thank you very much. I do feel much better. And thank you for your patience. You've been very kind. Thank you for helping me see the light. I promise to do the right thing from now on."

The subject left the room, still sporting a smile. He seemed lighter on his feet. Elated. He looked as if he'd just been handed a gift. In a sense, maybe he had. A man he didn't even know had pointed him in the right direction, and he was grateful.

Luke couldn't help feeling conflicted about the results of the interrogation. The little man's mind may be free of an emotional burden, but he now faces arrest and imprisonment as a result of his confession.

The class had stood transfixed as the master surgeon cleverly and precisely opened up the subject's mind and extracted the necessary information. Nathan Hardison might be a drunk at night, but in the daytime, he was definitely a surgeon.

CHAPTER TWENTY

That afternoon, Hardison strolled leisurely into the classroom, which was a departure from his usual aggressive entrance. Still, though, there was no greeting. Nothing indicated that he even knew a class was there. He sauntered to the podium and opened a folder he'd brought with him. He stood quietly as he scanned the room as if counting heads. When he spoke, his voice was soft, but left no doubt as to who was in charge.

"During the remaining time you are here, you will be watching a number of examinations like the one you witnessed this morning. I recently overheard one of you refer to the polygraph as a *machine,* and another one called it a *lie detector.*"

He cleared his throat, adjusted his owl-eye glasses and completed his usual eyeball sweep of the room. Regardless of what he was talking about, and no matter how many times he looked around the room, his gaze always came to rest on Luke.

"I must remind you that the polygraph is an instrument. It is designed to record physiological changes in response to verbal stimuli. It is no more a lie detector than it is a truth detector. *I* am the lie detector and the truth detector and each of *you* will become lie detectors and truth detectors. *If* you complete the training, and *if* you are sufficiently competent."

Luke kept his head down, pretending to concentrate on his note-taking. He could feel Hardison's beady eyes on him. Why were they always on him? He stole a glance. The instructor was looking away. Thank God.

"Some of you may have felt sorry for the subject when he began to cry." The instructor hesitated, scanning the group for what Luke concluded was to see if there were signs of sympathy. Apparently seeing none, he continued.

"It is important to understand that once they are in the polygraph chair, they are no longer an individual. They are a subject. It is necessary to think of them as such so there will be no feeling of sympathy, no like or dislike, no young or old, no male or female, but merely a subject. Getting the truth is the only thing that matters. You must detach yourself from all emotions. Because...if you like them...they are probably lying to you."

His features had softened, and his gaze wasn't as intimidating as it had been a few minutes earlier. He slowly continued. "Some of you may have noticed that I repeated myself during the interrogation. It is often necessary to be repetitious. That is because a guilty person is often unable to process what the interrogator is saying. The words do not register because his blood pressure is up, his head is pounding, and his brain is confused. His fight or flight mechanism is in overdrive. But his body reveals what his mind attempts to conceal."

There goes the chameleon again. The thought came to Luke even as he seemed to inhale the words that Hardison had spoken. They had become a part of him as effortlessly as the air that filled his lungs. Maybe it was because he experienced the same heart-pounding, brain-numbing symptoms during his own polygraph when the examiner had asked if he was wearing a watch. She'd had to repeat the question before the words registered.

That night as Luke lay in bed, the day's events played through his mind, especially the polygraph examination he had witnessed.

I knew the guy did it. How the hell did I know that? It was like I could read his mind. That was really weird. He was still mulling over his unexpected ability when he fell asleep.

***

The following morning at breakfast, Joe, Mel and Luke discussed the prior day's events. "Can you believe that guy?" asked Joe. "How the hell can you tell a man his kid is going to get cancer if he doesn't tell the truth?"

"And who would fall for such a thing?" asked Mel.

Luke made no comment. He understood the metaphor of linking cancer to lying, but the whole interrogation thing was unsettling, especially the fact that he knew the outcome of the test before it was finished. He pushed that thought to the back of his mind. *It was a fluke. An aberration. I'll never be able to do that again.*

CHAPTER TWENTY-ONE

Even on nights when the students were required to accompany Hardison out in public to learn more about psychology, they returned to their hotel rooms to type the notes for the day. That required working late, sometimes past midnight. Luke was thankful he could type. Those who couldn't, were forced to hire a typist from the hotel.

As they learned more about the polygraph, they were required to practice conducting polygraph examinations on Sundays. It was the only day without a formal class, and the only day where the students had the place to themselves with no staff. A student would be given some information known only to him, and the group would attempt to elicit that information. Even this process had its pitfalls.

Situations were set up where the students were required to use

Hardison's desk. Among the papers on his desk were the questions and answers for some of the tests. It was rumored that during a previous class, five students had been expelled for obtaining answers from Hardison's desk. Fortunately, no one in Luke's class succumbed to that trap.

Luke felt uncomfortable even going near the desk. Foreboding hung in the air as though something tragic had happened there. His body sensed a repellant force, similar to a polar opposite. Luke figured Hardison had to be the negative charge. At least he radiated negative vibes whenever he was close.

He found enough courage to mention his mood to Judy, the woman who'd polygraphed him, when they happened to ride the elevator together.

She eyed Luke intently. "The final week," she said in her usual sarcastic manner. "Do you think you can last another week?"

"Not sure," Luke retorted. "Depends on whether I can hold up to the gloomy atmosphere. I don't know if it's the climate outside or the one in the building that's so depressing." He hadn't meant to say all that. It just slipped out.

"Well, don't do like a previous student," she cautioned. "He jumped off the roof of the adjoining building and crashed right through the ceiling. He landed on Doctor Hardison's desk. It was quite a sight. Blood and guts everywhere."

She smiled, seeming to take delight in the look of disgust

spread across Luke's face. The elevator came to a halt at the institute and Judy walked away without further explanation.

The closing elevator doors prompted Luke to hurriedly step out. He stood silently as the doors banged shut. It seemed doubtful that such a thing could happen, but he didn't close his mind to it altogether.

This is Chicago, he mused. *I guess anything is possible here.* It did give him an explanation as to why he experienced such negative feelings whenever he ventured near the desk.

Suicide by desk. I guess that answers my question whether things could get any more bizarre.

CHAPTER TWENTY-TWO

On Wednesday night, the last week of school, Luke finished recording his notes for the day and was preparing for bed when the phone rang. He expected it to be one of the other students who needed help with a question on physiology.

"Hi, this is Brenda, the waitress from the hotel restaurant." The voice was soft, sultry. Not like the woman who waited tables with her clipped "What'll ya have?" attitude.

"What's going on?" Luke asked, wondering why she would be calling him, especially at such a late hour.

"What are you doing?" Brenda asked.

"Getting ready for bed," he replied.

"Do you want some company?" Her voice was low, sexy, with a come-hither quality that caught him off guard.

His mind raced. *Either Mel or Joe put her up to this. Or maybe it's just another test.*

"No thanks," Luke said coldly. He left no room for doubt.

He was about to hang up when Brenda said, "I'll be right up. I want to show you something."

"It'll have to wait 'til tomorrow. I'm going to bed. I'm half asleep already," Luke hurriedly said.

"I'll be right up," Brenda repeated.

When at home, Luke went to bed wearing shorts and T-shirt. But since the first night in Chicago, he wore flannel pajamas. He hurriedly slipped his trousers on over them.

He still thought it was a joke, but he wasn't taking any chances of being half dressed, just in case Brenda arrived. He couldn't imagine why she would call him. He hadn't spoken a dozen words to her since they'd met, and then, only to order breakfast. "This has got to be a setup," he said aloud. "She probably isn't even going to show."

He barely got his pants on when there was a knock at the door. He opened it to find Brenda holding a large cake.

"I wanted to show you the cake that I baked for Jim Teller," she said with a grin.

Luke was aware that Teller was one of several students who had hired Brenda to do some typing.

"It's his birthday tomorrow, and I baked him a cake," she added.

"Well, that was very nice of you," Luke said as he stood uncomfortably in the doorway. He wasn't about to let her in the room, but she appeared to be unwilling to accept his refusal.

"Are you sure you don't want me to stay a while?" she asked coyly as she tried to squeeze past him.

"I don't think my wife would appreciate me entertaining another woman in my hotel room," Luke said, hoping that mentioning his wife would be reason enough for her to leave. "That's a beautiful cake, and I'm sure Jim is going to be pleasantly surprised, but right now, I have to get some sleep. Thanks for showing me the cake. Have a good night."

He slowly began closing the door, forcing Brenda to retreat. She reluctantly backed up and finally said, "OK, well...good night." She turned with the cake and left.

Luke stood inside the door for a few minutes, half expecting her to return. He finally decided she had gone, so he removed his trousers and got into bed. As tired as he was, he had trouble going to sleep. He kept playing the evening's events over in his mind, trying to figure out if he was being set up. He couldn't imagine Brenda making advances like that. He hadn't given her any indication he was interested in her.

I'm not sexy and I'm not good looking. It has to be a setup, or... maybe I was reading more into the situation than was actually there.

***

The next morning, Luke joined Mel and Joe for breakfast as usual. Luke kept looking at the two friends in an attempt to get a read on them. He suspected one or both of sending the waitress to his room.

Brenda took their breakfast orders and acted no differently than she always had: friendly, but not overly so. Luke felt like he was in the twilight zone. Maybe he just dreamed it. He could finally stand the suspense no longer.

"Did one of you guys send Brenda up to my room last night?" He watched the men to see if their facial expressions would give them away. Both looked surprised.

"What are you talking about?" asked Mel.

Luke blurted out his story, ending with, "I figured it was either a setup by the school staff, or a joke by one of you guys."

Both men denied sending Brenda to Luke's room.

"Maybe it was a test and they plan on giving us another polygraph at the end of training," Joe said nervously. "If that's the case, we may be next."

"Aw, maybe the poor girl was just lonely," suggested Mel. "She sure didn't act any different when she took our orders this morning. I wonder if she tried that with anyone else...and if anyone took her up on it."

The trio finished their breakfast and headed for the door, after leaving the usual tip, of course.

CHAPTER TWENTY-THREE

Six weeks of polygraph school seemed to Luke like six years in San Quentin, with every day as miserable as the day before. Three students dropped out along the way, but at long last, the final day of school arrived.

All tests were completed and no polygraphs were administered to the students. A celebration dinner was hosted in the back room of a local restaurant. Certificates of completion were handed out to the remaining nine survivors.

Each graduating student was asked to stand and give his personal assessment of the past six weeks. Most muttered something about their ability to survive such a difficult ordeal.

When it was Luke's turn to speak, he didn't know quite what to say. How could he explain the dark, foreboding feeling that he'd carried with him every day for the past six weeks? How could he put into words, the feeling of depression and isolation since arriving in this city, even among the group? Should he admit that he hadn't gained sufficient knowledge to conduct polygraphs?

He felt as ignorant about the process as before he started school. And how could he explain that in spite of his dislike for his instructor, he understood the man far more than he wanted? Their minds were connected in some way. He knew the arsonist that Hardison tested had committed the crime, and he knew that Hardison had also known.

Luke felt like a different man than when he'd first arrived in Chicago. He was more attuned to the interaction of people. He might not be able to read charts as well as the instructor, but he could read people. There was nothing tangible he could say had caused this ability. It just seemed to come through the air like radio waves. He was afraid that he was slowly, but inevitably becoming another Nathan Hardison. The thought scared the hell out of him.

Luke stood to address the group, just as others had done before him. He remained still for a few seconds, trying to organize his thoughts. When he finally began to speak, he didn't recognize his own voice. It sounded as if it was coming from someone else, like a ventriloquist with a dummy. It was similar to the way the examiner had sounded during his polygraph test.

"This has been an experience like no other," Luke said

as he took a sip of water. His throat was already dry and he'd just started. "The emotional strain was beyond anything I had previously experienced, and even beyond what I could have imagined. I have been in situations where I didn't know if I would live or die. I once stood in one-hundred-fifteen degree heat of the Arizona sun with a shotgun pointed at my belly, and the crazed man behind it ready to pull the trigger. When I was in the military, I survived fifteen parachute jumps, two of which involved chute malfunctions, but I managed to reach the ground with no serious injury."

Luke stopped to take another sip of water and clear his throat. It was dry again. Everyone seemed to sit breathlessly as he continued.

"Neither of those incidents came close to the emotional strain that I have experienced in the past six weeks. I don't know why that was. Does anyone know? Maybe Doctor Hardison can explain why he found it necessary to create such an atmosphere. Maybe there's a reason I'm not smart enough to understand. It seems unreasonable and unnecessary."

The group remained silent as Luke took his seat.

Hardison finished his drink of Jack Daniels, set the empty glass down, and rose from the table. "Who in their right mind would jump out of a perfectly good airplane in flight? It sounds like you were screwed up in the head long before you got here."

Luke stared back. The class was over and he had passed. There was nothing more to be concerned with. But he still found it difficult to maintain eye contact with Hardison. There was no doubt that the man had some extraordinary power which enabled him to know what was going on in Luke's mind. Luke dropped his gaze as the instructor continued with his explanation.

"I do not know if any of you will ever be able to conduct a competent polygraph examination. We can only teach you the basics. We cannot teach intelligence or ability. If you do not have those traits, you will not succeed. Do not blame us for your shortcomings. We had nothing to do with your heritage."

Just as he had done many times in the classroom, Hardison stopped to examine his manicured fingernails. He drew his hand across his mouth, glancing briefly at his empty glass before continuing. "I will try to explain our procedure in the simplest possible terms. Building emotional strength, much like physical strength, takes time and effort. Six weeks is a short amount of time to prepare you for what you are going to face in that polygraph room. Subjects will cry. They will vomit. They may even wet themselves or defecate in their pants. They will tell you in gory detail of how they cut up a body and ate the flesh; how they tortured and maimed; how they raped and murdered a child. While these are all loathsome acts, you must remain emotionally neutral. You must not loathe or find them contemptible. No feeling sorry for either the victim or the perpetrator. The person you are testing is a subject, nothing more, and nothing less. Your personal feelings are not to get in the way of a confession. We…"

Hardison stopped midsentence and passed his gaze over the group as though he was counting heads. After a while, he continued where he had left off. "We attempted to bolster your emotional defenses by creating an emotionally-charged atmosphere. One where you either fall apart here, or acquire sufficient emotional strength to conduct a polygraph and an interrogation in a manner that befits your graduation from the Diogenes Polygraph Institute."

Hardison reached for his glass and took a drink of Jack Daniels that the waiter had just delivered. "After you have conducted a few examinations, you may begin to understand what you have learned during the past six weeks. Anyone can turn on the instrument and watch the chart roll and the pens make their marks. Psychologically speaking, people can only do to you what you allow them to do. Any feelings of psychological torture, as some of you have described, was self-induced. Once you stop to analyze the situation, you will understand what I mean."

There was another pause as the instructor raised his glass and took another sip. He glanced casually at the group. "You now have a certificate saying you have successfully completed the training course to conduct polygraph examinations. Unfortunately, that piece of paper does not magically give you the ability to do so. That is something we attempt to define in our testing process. Sometimes it works...and sometimes it does not. What you do with the information we have taught is up to you. Good luck to all of you. Some of you are going to need it." With those final words, Doctor Nathan Hardison got up from the table, took one last drink from his glass, and walked out of the room, much like he used to walk into the classroom: confident and arrogant.

As he was leaving, Joe rose to his feet, calling out in a loud voice, "You know that log chain I told you about during my polygraph? The one I found in the woods and took home? I forgot to tell you there was a logging truck attached to the other end of it."

Laughter sprang up from the group; a soft chuckle at first, and then more raucous, followed by clapping. Hardison left without acknowledging the comment.

Luke had mixed feelings. He was glad the ordeal was over and he had managed to survive. What the instructor said about strengthening the student's emotional defenses made sense in some respects. But the explanation was too simple. Stress was something a police officer knew only too well. He lived with it every minute he was on duty. There had to be more to what Luke had experienced than that. He felt different, as if he'd had a complete makeover. The problem was, his makeover was on the inside. He felt like he'd gone to the hospital for a migraine and emerged with a new mind. One that was filled with graph-paper, pens, and red ink. One that was destined to write a new chapter in his life. Had Doctor Hardison planted something in his mind, or had it been there all the time and had just been awakened?

Polygraph and interrogation? Is this my destiny? Is this what I've been programmed to do? He had a lot of questions, but no credible answers.

At least he would never have to deal with that son of a bitch again. He was grateful he lived so far away. If he *never* saw Hardison again, it would be too soon. He was never coming back to Chicago.

CHAPTER TWENTY-FOUR

The plane touched down at Sky Harbor shortly after 9 p.m. Luke gathered his bag from the overhead compartment and waited impatiently for the door of the plane to open, releasing him from the final vestige of his Midwest bondage.

He hailed a taxi, and as they left the airport, the tension he'd lived with for the past six weeks melted away. It was a relief to be back in Phoenix. He gloried in the warm air. He was feeling even better as the taxi pulled into his driveway. It was nearing eleven o'clock.

He stepped out of the vehicle and gathered his belongings. He gave the driver a substantial tip, as though it was the cabby who'd put an official end to the misery he'd endured for the past six weeks.

Before he could put his key in the lock, the door opened and

Emily greeted him with an affectionate hug and a kiss. He clung to her, reluctant to let go. He was afraid it was a dream and he would wake up back in Chicago.

After several minutes, they broke apart and walked hand-in-hand to the kitchen. The aroma of turkey and dressing filled his nostrils and overwhelmed him with a sense of well-being. It was good to be home. The kids were asleep, but Skippy was up and nuzzling his leg.

"Hi Skip. Did you miss me?" He knelt and massaged the dog's ears and stroked his head. "I missed you." A few wags of his tail and Skippy retreated to his favorite corner and flopped down.

Luke washed up and took his usual seat at the table. He ate a few bites, but he could hardly choke it down. The cranberries didn't even help. He saw Emily glance questionably at his lack of appetite, but she said nothing. Her silence was a relief. Luke would talk tomorrow. Tonight, he just wanted to relax. Maybe a few minutes of television would help. He needed to unwind. Emily cleared the table and left the room.

He'd missed her desperately when he was in Chicago. He couldn't wait to be in bed with her. It was always heaven to feel her soft body pressed against his, and inhale the pleasing fragrance of her skin; to feel her warm lips caress his neck and know the delicate touch of her hands. That's what he'd looked forward to. But that was when he was away. Now that he was home, he felt awkward. He was jumpy. He couldn't relax. He couldn't explain to his own satisfaction what was going on in his head. How could he expect his wife to understand?

"Are you coming to bed?"

Luke recognized that seductive tone. It still stirred passion after nearly twenty years.

He glanced away from the television long enough to see Emily standing in the doorway of the family room. Her silky-pink nightgown clung to her slender frame. He had the desire. If only he had the ability. He'd lost that somewhere in the past six weeks. He would wait until he was sure he could perform. It was too embarrassing to fail.

"Are you coming to bed?" she repeated, this time with more urgency.

Under normal circumstances, he would have hastily followed her to the bedroom. But things were no longer normal because he was no longer normal. He felt shaky. Insecure. His head buzzed like a hive of bees. He turned back to the television. "You go ahead," he replied. "I'll be along shortly." After a few minutes of silence, he looked up to find her gone.

He watched the late news, and after that, he sat and stared at the television screen. Emily was asleep by the time he stealthily crawled into bed. He breathed a sigh of relief. He couldn't be intimate tonight. His mind wouldn't stand still long enough for him to concentrate on making love. It was filled with too much extraneous information. He'd make up for it tomorrow night. By then, he'd be back to his old self.

***

The following day wasn't much better. He'd missed the family when he was away, but he felt self-conscious around them now. He kept waiting for someone to correct his manners: the way he sat, the way he talked, the way he ate. The fact that no one did made him even more wary.

He grabbed a pair of pruning shears and trimmed some citrus trees in the front yard. They didn't need the attention, but it was relaxing and something he liked to do. It also kept his mind occupied so he wouldn't dwell on the six-week nightmare he had just endured, or the work ahead that he dreaded facing. He tried to explain the school to Emily, but he knew she didn't understand.

She doesn't have a clue. How could she? She's been protected all her life. She's too fragile to be exposed to the real world. Her mother was right. She should have married the banker.

Saturday passed without Luke remembering much about it. His mind was still in a fog. He never considered what was going on in Emily's mind. There wasn't room in his brain for that. It was still filled to the brim with: "If you get less than seventy percent on a test, you are automatically expelled." And...the *look*. He couldn't get over the *look* that Hardison handed out like a judge handing down a death sentence. Luke was barely able to function on his own, let alone consider how someone else was doing.

Time for bed. Emily was already there, propped against the headboard reading a magazine. She put it down when he crawled in, but he turned away and shifted to his sleep position. He still pretended sleep when she turned out the light.

***

Sunday morning. One day closer to Monday, the day his failure would be revealed. The day he would have to admit he wasn't nearly as intelligent as the department thought.

He had managed to fool the staff at the Diogenes Polygraph Institute into thinking he'd learned how to conduct polygraph examinations. They even gave him a certificate that said so. But Monday morning, the truth would come out. He hadn't learned a damned thing. He managed to complete the course without being kicked out, but he would never be able to conduct a polygraph.

He forced himself to accompany the family to church, though he would rather have stayed in bed. He was drained emotionally and physically. The rest of the day was spent sleeping and watching television. Interaction with the family was minimal.

The evening went a little easier than the night before, but still, he watched television, washed up, climbed into bed, and went to sleep. They used to make love nearly every night, but the weekend passed without either initiating the act. They hadn't been intimate since before he left for polygraph training, and the way things were going, it wasn't going to happen any time soon. He was thankful Emily never pressed him when he wasn't in the mood.

Their relationship wasn't the same because *he* wasn't the same. Doctor Hardison had seen to that. He'd taken a mild-mannered, self-confident police sergeant, and turned him into a doubtful, self-conscious wreck; a shell of his former self. Not only had he lost his sense of well-being, but more importantly, his ability to integrate back into the special relationship with his family. He had to get his mind focused on the present and get back on track. He couldn't let the past six weeks dictate his life. He was stronger than that. Wasn't he?

PART FOUR – GETTING HIS FEET WET

"More potent than wine, women, or temporary fame, as a corrosive element on the character of a man, is the glitter of a police badge. To hang a badge on the wrong man, often produces from nothing, an arrogant and dangerous fool."

– Author Unknown

CHAPTER TWENTY-FIVE

By Monday morning, Luke was more apprehensive than ever about his transfer to the personnel bureau. He'd had the whole weekend to conjure up some self-confidence, but he still felt ill-prepared for his new assignment.

If it was simply administration, hell, he could handle that. He'd been doing it for the past two years. The name of the bureau didn't matter either. Paperwork was paperwork, regardless of the heading. What did matter, and mattered a lot, was the fact that he was no longer just a paper shuffler, he was a qualified polygraph examiner. He had a certificate that proved it–an official looking document with a gold seal and a red, white and blue ribbon. The signature of Doctor Nathan Hardison certified its authenticity.

But words on paper didn't mean a damned thing without the ability to back it up, and he was certain he lacked that ability. If only he had the same feeling of confidence as when he'd worked the streets. What was he going to do?

He started for work earlier than usual, joining the steady stream of traffic heading downtown. There was no need to consciously consider where and when to turn. His mind was on autopilot, programmed from years of repetition. Besides, he was too busy trying to imagine himself conducting polygraph examinations to think about anything else. No matter how hard he tried, his mind refused to accept the image. He finally gave up and concentrated on his driving after nearly rear-ending a car stopped for a pedestrian. Getting to work in one piece through the heavy traffic was a feat in itself.

He found a parking space several blocks from the station. The building's parking lot was reserved for the upper echelon. Luke didn't mind. He enjoyed the walk. It gave him time to think.

March was one of Luke's favorite months, not only because his oldest daughter, Rebecca, was born that month, but because it was a beautiful time of year. He'd spent the first half of March damned near freezing to death in Chicago. But at least he'd made it back to Phoenix for the last half.

Daytime temperatures hovered around the low seventies. The desert was coming alive. A colorful array of cactus flowers had awakened from their winter slumber and timidly poked their heads out of their prickly hosts. The sweet fragrance of orange blossoms filled the air.

The natural beauty that Luke usually admired during the early morning stroll from his car to the police station, was insufficient to shake him from his doldrums. He paid no mind to the mourning doves and their wistful serenade, or the wispy clouds floating high above. On most days they made him feel optimistic. But today, he trudged along with his head down as if marching to the gallows.

His walk carried him past the railroad tracks and produce area where large warehouses were once filled with products from the local farmers. Docks that were once laden with crates of fruit and vegetables were now sitting empty. A group of homeless men lined the wall under one of the docks. Some nodded as he passed by.

I would gladly trade places right now with any of you men. The thought brought a wistful smile to his lips. He found himself envying their lifestyle. Nothing was expected of them, and they were responsible to no one but themselves. He brushed the thought aside and continued his trudge to the station.

As he entered the building, a dual feeling of apprehension and excitement swept through him. It was always good to have additional training under his belt, regardless of what it was. On the other hand, more would be expected of him after completion of a training course. In this case, the certainty that he would never live up to expectations gripped his gut.

He was glad for the time spent with his new boss before leaving for polygraph school, and thankful that Lieutenant Fred Sloan was in charge of Personnel. They got along well and Luke had great respect for Sloan's ability. But he knew their friendship wouldn't prevent his boss from dropping the hammer on him if he didn't perform as expected. Merle might understand his apprehension, but that wouldn't save him if he couldn't do the job.

Luke hesitated before entering the polygraph section. The thought of being responsible for another person's future, and in some cases his liberty, was overwhelming. He had no problem making those decisions on the street. But there, he had something tangible to go on: external evidence; something physical; an eyewitness; the suspect's explanation or lack thereof. But as a polygraph examiner, he'd have to base his opinion on something intangible–markings on a chart that may or may not be a deceptive response.

Who, in their right mind would put me in a position to make those decisions? I don't have a clue as to what the hell I'm doing.

The situation was reminiscent of when he made his first parachute jump. He'd thought he was going to die, but he jumped anyway. Throughout his life, he'd made himself do what scared him the most, and somehow, he'd always made it through.

"And this too, shall pass. What can't be cured must be

endured," he murmured as he entered the polygraph office.

Merle Broone was seated at his desk when Luke reluctantly sidled in. Merle rose to his feet, greeted the freshly-minted examiner with a firm handshake, and acted genuinely pleased to see him. A broad smile only served to deepen the lines in his craggy face.

"Congratulations," he said. "I'm very happy to see you made it through school."

His warm greeting helped reduce the apprehension roiling through Luke's brain, but it would take a hell of a lot more than Merle's greeting to instill a sense of confidence.

Luke normally met a person eye-to-eye and toe-to-toe, but that was before polygraph school. That was before Nathan Hardison gutted his confidence and warped his mind. He looked away. He couldn't let Merle see how utterly helpless he felt. "I'm not sure I learned anything," he said, dejectedly. "I don't think I'll ever be able to conduct a polygraph."

Merle scrutinized him almost as thoroughly as when they first met, the day Luke began his two-week assignment in Police Personnel prior to polygraph school. This time, however, the look was one of surprised relief, like the cavalry had arrived in time to save the wagon train. He broke into a wide grin. His eyes sparkled through his horn-rims. "That is very good to hear," he said. "Now I know you've learned something. The ones who don't know what they're doing claim to know everything. You'll be fine."

Doubt still filled Luke's mind, but he did feel a little better after hearing Merle's observation. It helped to know that a veteran examiner would be standing by to bail him out when he couldn't read his charts. But first things first. He headed for the break room. He needed coffee.

Luke returned to his desk with the steaming-hot elixir and was about to take a seat when Lieutenant Sloan poked his head in. "Good, you're back," he said. "I'd like to see you in my office before you get started in here. I'm going to be gone most of the day, and I need you to take care of some things for me."

Luke took a sip of coffee and placed his cup on the desk. "Where's Simmons? He here yet?" he asked.

"He had one more vacation day to burn. He'll be back tomorrow," Sloan replied.

As he followed Sloan to his office, the question that dogged Luke since he was tapped for polygraph training was demanding an answer he was still unable to provide. *How in the hell am I going to get out of this one?*

***

The day flew by. Luke kept busy going over his duties with Lieutenant Sloan, discussing procedure with his subordinates, and reviewing applicant files. He planned to sit in with Merle during a polygraph test, but time didn't permit. That was alright with him. The longer he could stay out of the polygraph rooms, the better.

He worked late in an attempt to finish everything. It was nearly seven-thirty when he pulled into his driveway. He walked through the door as Emily was preparing to leave.

She stopped short and gave him a hard stare. "Good. You're finally home. I thought you might have forgotten Michael had a game tonight. We're already late, so I was going by myself. I'll wait if you want to grab a bite first." She sounded relieved and agitated at the same time.

"It's been a hectic day," Luke replied. "You go ahead. I'll meet you there. I have to wash up first."

Her features softened as she placed a hand on his arm. "You look tired. Why don't you rest a few minutes? There's some chicken and dumplings in the fridge." She gently withdrew her hand from his arm and turned to go. "I hope this isn't going to be a regular thing with you getting home so late." It sounded more like a warning than a statement.

The game had completely slipped Luke's mind. He quickly washed, grabbed a bite to eat, and headed for school. He never missed any of the kids' activities if he could help it.

He joined Emily, who was seated alone at the far end of the bleachers. They often sat apart from others at a school function.

Not that they didn't want to socialize with other parents, it was just something they had always done. Sometimes, they would sit through an entire game with hardly a word. He waved at Amy, seated on the top tier surrounded by friends. She appeared to be having a good time. Seeing his kids enjoying themselves always put a smile on his face.

They sat silently through an entire inning, and watched with dismay as Michael struck out. As the other team came up to bat, Emily placed her hand on Luke's arm. "So, how did your day go?" she asked.

"I was so busy, the day was over before I knew it. There was still a ton of paperwork I never even got to. If every day is like that, I'm going to be burned out before I do my first test," he replied, his head hanging.

"You mean you didn't do any polygraphs?" Emily asked. Her eyes widened under a wrinkled brow. "I thought that's why they sent you to school. Why would they have you do something else after they trained you for polygraphs?"

Luke was tired. He didn't feel like trying to explain something he didn't understand himself. "They expect more from me because I'm a sergeant," he reluctantly replied. "I have to supervise, do paperwork, and eventually run polygraphs, although if every day is like today, I don't see how the hell I'm going to do that."

"That seems pretty dumb to me," Emily said, a puzzled

expression on her face. "You need to remind them..."

"Thank God," Luke murmured as Michael caught a long fly ball that ended the inning. The home team cheering section erupted and by the time things settled down, so had Emily. She had apparently forgotten what she was going to say, or thought better of it. The remainder of the game was watched in silence.

"I'll wait and give the kids a ride home," Emily said as she gazed into the eyes of her frazzled husband. "You look awfully tired. Why don't you go on home, get washed up and unwind? I'll be along shortly."

"That's the best advice I've had all day." Luke managed a weak smile. He kissed her lightly on the forehead and stumbled to his truck.

It was nearly ten o'clock when he walked through the door. He normally watched television. It helped relax him before going to bed. But tonight there was barely enough energy left in his body to take a shower. He fell into bed and was immediately sound asleep.

***

"Are you asleep already, or are you just playing possum?" Emily stood by the bed, looking down at her motionless husband. She was used to him watching the news before going to bed.

"I hope you're not getting sick," she whispered as she lightly placed the back of her hand against his forehead. *He doesn't feel hot. I guess he was just tired and fell asleep.* His steady breathing confirmed her assessment.

He had been acting strangely since Friday night when he got home from Chicago. He was withdrawn, uninterested in everything, including her. She'd spent hours preparing a turkey dinner with mashed potatoes and gravy. She even had cranberries. He couldn't eat turkey without cranberries. But he hardly touched his supper, and he never even asked about her or the kids.

He'd blamed his demeanor on polygraph school. He was still reeling from the stress. She considered that a poor excuse. He'd have to come up with a better one than that.

She tried to rationalize his behavior. Maybe he'd just had a bad trip. He probably got airsick and didn't want to admit it. He sometimes failed to tell her when he was sick. She blamed his country upbringing for his stoic attitude. There was so much to do on the farm, one of the kids could have gotten his arm cut off, and his dad would have just smeared the stump with axle grease, slapped a piece of burlap around it, and sent him back to the field. At least that was her assessment of farm life.

Six weeks was a long time for them to be apart, and she'd expected Luke to act like he'd missed her as much as she'd missed him. She was dressed in her flimsiest nightgown Friday night when she invited him to bed, but he waved her off in favor of the television. She pretended to be asleep when he came to bed. She wanted to see how eager he was to hold her again, but she was deeply disappointed when he quietly crawled into bed and turned to his sleep position.

She'd watched him mope around the house all weekend, spending most of the daylight hours trimming trees that didn't need trimming. She and the kids had given him space. They'd gone about their daily activities as if he was still in Chicago. He may have been with them physically, but emotionally he was still 2,000 miles away.

When Monday finally came, she breathed a sigh of relief. Getting back to his old routine would snap him out of it. She'd planned all day for the evening's event. Luke would get home early. They would eat a leisurely supper before attending the ball game. After the game, they would come home. The kids would go to bed. She would take a shower—maybe he would join her. They would go to bed and make love. It would be the perfect end to a perfect day.

But it hadn't worked out the way she'd planned. Things seldom did. She wondered why. Maybe she expected too much. After all, she was a Leo. They always had an idealistic view of everything.

She had half a mind to wake him. She'd waited patiently all

weekend for him to act like a husband, happy to be home with his wife. But he'd practically ignored her.

Maybe he'd met someone new in Chicago. That would explain his reticence. Six weeks was a long time. When the cat's away, the mice... She quickly dismissed the thought. He was an Iowa farm boy. Once they said "I do," they seldom strayed. No, it wasn't another woman. Of that, she was sure.

Still...there *was* something different about him. He used to be rock-solid. Laid back. Unfazed. Nothing bothered him. He was so self-confident he thought he could fix anything, even Emily's emotional problems.

That was it...her emotional problems. Maybe he'd finally gotten tired of them—and her. It wasn't that he had a problem with *himself*—he had a problem with *her*. That's why he was acting strangely. He was trying to figure out how to tell her she no longer appealed to him.

I guess I'm not attractive enough anymore. He didn't have any trouble staying awake before we were married. He'd spend half the night at my house, drive back to the farm, work in the fields all day, and be back the next night with only a couple of hours sleep. But that was when I was young, and my body wasn't all messed up from having three kids.

Emily retreated to the bathroom and studied herself in the mirror, turning side to side, trying to get a look at her butt. She contorted her body and stood on her tiptoes to get a better view. It still looked pretty good. "Oh well," she sighed. "I guess we're all getting older. Maybe Luke was just tired."

She took a quick sponge bath, slipped into her nightgown, and turned out the light. As she snuggled up against him, she wondered what was really going on with her husband. He acted like he was completely worn out. But she couldn't understand how he could be so tired from just sitting in an office all day. *Maybe he's just tired of me.* She put the thought out of her mind and concentrated on her breathing. Tomorrow was another day. Things always looked better in the daylight.

CHAPTER TWENTY-SIX

Tuesday morning, Luke got to work before seven. He hoped things wouldn't be as hectic as the day before. He wanted an opportunity to talk with Merle before the other employees arrived. Any knowledge he could pick up might help overcome his concern about conducting polygraphs.

Merle looked up from his desk as Luke entered. The broad smile he'd displayed with his greeting the day before was gone. A look of dissatisfaction had replaced it.

"I thought maybe you took the day off after working so hard yesterday." The sarcasm in Merle's voice was more biting than usual. He glared at the sergeant with smoldering gray eyes, his glasses riding the tip of his nose. "What happened to you? I thought you were here to conduct polygraphs?"

Canfield got his usual cup of coffee loaded with cream before responding to Merle's comments. "I'm just trying to put them off as long as possible," he said, easing into his chair.

Merle took a sip of coffee before turning his full attention to his reluctant protégé. His disapproving scowl was something Luke had previously witnessed, but was never directed at him–until now.

"I hope your absence isn't going to be a regular thing," he growled. "If you're filling the position of polygraph examiner, then by God, you should be conducting polygraphs. By the time Simmons leaves, you need to be trained. You can't learn how to conduct polygraphs by doing administrative duties." Merle jabbed his finger in the direction of the polygraph rooms. His eyes narrowed, his lips drawn. "You need to be there–in that room–every day. That's the only way you're going to gain sufficient knowledge and confidence. I *cannot* and I *will not* continue to face this workload alone."

Luke remained silent. That was the longest string of sentences Merle had directed at him since they'd met. His first impulse was to laugh it off. But it was a serious matter. Merle was right. He should be doing polygraphs. His wife was right. He should be getting home earlier. He was in the middle of a tug-of-war, each side pulling him apart. He hadn't even started yet and he was already feeling the stress of the job.

As Luke was draining his second cup of coffee, Detective

Floyd Simmons, the examiner he was replacing, walked in.

Simmons easily carried his 190 pounds on a 6' frame. His bald head, broad shoulders and slim waist projected an air of superiority. He'd been hired twenty-five years ago, when the pay was low, the hours long, and recruitment difficult. Back then, it had been hard to find people who wanted to be a cop when there was a good chance of getting maimed or killed for less than three hundred dollars a month. Because of the difficulty in attracting applicants, hiring criteria had been less stringent.

Simmons was smart enough, but he lacked the personality critical for a successful interrogator. He looked like a detective and acted the part even more, with a smug, authoritative attitude that some cops develop after years on the job. He was from the old school of threats and intimidation. Those weren't desirable traits for coaxing a person to give up information against his own best interests. Yet, here he was, a polygraph examiner, getting ready to retire in another two months. He had secured his pension by putting in the minimum twenty five years of employment with the police department, the last four as polygraph examiner.

Luke was aware that Simmons lacked confidence in his own ability to read the charts. Hell, everyone knew that. It was all over the department. But Floyd didn't seem to know or care what his coworkers thought. Since he was often unable to determine truth from deception, many of his tests were inconclusive. Subjects balked at his attitude and demeanor so he seldom obtained a confession.

Floyd seemed surprised to see his sergeant. He made no attempt to shake hands or congratulate him. He eyed him carefully before speaking. "Are you back already? Did you finish school or were you kicked out?"

"Guess I passed," Luke replied half-halfheartedly. "At least they gave me a certificate of completion."

Simmons' eyes lit up and a wry smile crossed his lips. "Well, some people are just not cut out to do this kind of work. You…"

"He'll be fine," Merle interjected. "We'll see to it that he'll be fine. Let him sit in with you for a few tests so he gets used to sitting behind the desk. Then he can sit in with me for a few. I don't think he'll need much more than that. We'll start him out on pre-employments. I'll initially select some for him to do and we'll take it from there."

As a civilian, Merle was in charge of non-police functions of the polygraph section, and would be until Luke became proficient. Floyd didn't appreciate that, but Luke did. He was glad to relinquish all authority to Merle. He respected the man and trusted his judgment.

If only I trusted my own.

CHAPTER TWENTY-SEVEN

Luke was a silent observer, day after day, test after test, as Floyd and Merle conducted polygraphs. He tried to remember everything they did. He would soon be expected to conduct examinations, himself, and he had to be prepared.

Both polygraph rooms were similar to the ones at the Diogenes Polygraph Institute: nine by twelve, with one door, but no observation windows. The walls were bare and painted off-white to prevent the subject from concentrating on anything but the truth. The examiner sat behind the polygraph desk with his back against the far wall. The subject's chair sat parallel to the front of the desk, facing the wall to the examiner's right. During the test, the subject would be directed to keep his eyes to the front. In that position, he would be unable to see the instrument or the examiner without turning his head sharply to the right.

Luke didn't like the setup because the subject was always between him and the door. Officer safety was an issue. He was taught to always leave himself an avenue of escape. In addition, the left end of the desk butted against the wall, so he was forced to pass in front of the subject in order to leave the room or to get behind him to hook up and remove the attachments.

Monday morning, the second week back from polygraph school, Luke got to work before seven, grabbed his usual cup of coffee, dumped in some creamer, and settled down to review the day's scheduled polygraphs. The first one was an internal that Simmons was scheduled to conduct.

Luke carefully read the detailed report. He learned through experience that what *wasn't* in the official report was often as important as what *was*. So it was with this one. There were too many unanswered questions.

Officer Roland Riter was known as one of those people who were always on the edge. On the edge of following the rules. On the edge of doing the wrong thing–even when the right thing would be the normal thing to do–and on the edge of mental stability. If he didn't feel like doing something, he wouldn't do it. He knew from personal experience that with government employment, once they were in, it was hard to get them out.

During his nine years with the Police Department, Riter had received at least a dozen disciplinary measures, including one for

"Neglect of Duty" by failing to adequately assist an individual who had suffered a heart attack. His refusal to perform CPR had contributed to the man's death.

When questioned, his excuse had been, "I didn't want to catch anything by giving the man mouth-to-mouth. I figured maybe his time was up anyway, otherwise he wouldn't have had a heart attack."

He was initially fired, but the Civil Service Board overturned the chief's decision and reduced his penalty to a thirty-day suspension.

Officers had received family fight calls to Riter's house on several occasions. He wanted a divorce, but his wife refused unless he agreed to share his pension. He wouldn't go along with that arrangement so they stayed married.

Two months prior to his scheduled polygraph examination, Officer Riter called 9-1-1 and reported his wife unconscious. She was pronounced dead at the hospital. An autopsy determined she died from an insect bite. Although death was rare, she was allergic to the toxin of a black widow spider.

An examination of the body revealed a circle around the bite mark that conveniently fit the mouth of a drinking glass from the kitchen. It was suspected, but couldn't be proven, that a glass containing the spider was held against his wife's body until it bit her. An excessive amount of sleep medication was also found in her system, but she was known to take a lot of sleeping pills so that was a non-factor.

The deaths of his two children, however, a boy and girl, ages seven and nine respectively, were a different story. They died in a storage shed fire less than a month after the death of their mother. Riter became a focus of the investigation when it was determined the shed was locked from the outside.

When the investigators couldn't come up with solid evidence for or against him, Riter was ordered to take a polygraph. It would have fallen to Merle, but he was on sick leave with stomach ulcers.

Floyd Simmons strode through the door as Canfield finished reading the report. Without a word of greeting, Floyd poured himself a cup of coffee and settled down in Merle's chair, swinging his feet around to face his sergeant. He took a sip of coffee and set his cup on the desk.

Luke resisted the urge to tell him to get his cup off Merle's desk and his ass out of Merle's chair. He couldn't explain why it bothered him that Floyd was seated at Merle's desk, but it did. It bothered the hell out of him. It was like a peasant brazenly occupying the king's throne while the monarch was away. It wasn't right.

Simmons cast a glance at Canfield and then at the file the sergeant was holding. "Well, are *you* going to do that one or are you going to let me read it so I can?" His tone was rife with sarcasm.

"It's all yours," Luke said as he handed Simmons the file.

Simmons didn't comment. He took the file and started reading. After a few minutes and a few more sips of coffee, he got to his feet, leafing through the file as he headed to the waiting room. "Well, are you coming or have you learned enough?" he asked as he turned back to face Luke, a thin smile breaking the corners of his dour mouth.

"I'll be in the polygraph room," Luke said. He took a gulp of coffee, placed his cup on the desk, and got to his feet. He was seated against the wall, left of the examiner's chair, when Simmons led Officer Riter through the door.

Luke would never have pegged Riter for a Phoenix police officer. He might have been an inch or so over the 5' 9" minimum, but he lacked the command presence and clean-cut appearance that was prevalent in most Phoenix officers. A wrinkled shirt hung loosely over his narrow shoulders, and his curly black hair needed a trim. Even with his narrow body, his head looked too small. His thin lips were covered by an even thinner mustache that looked as if it had been painted on.

Floyd directed Riter to the subject's chair before closing the door and easing into his seat beside Luke. "This is my associate," he said as he nodded toward the sergeant. "He'll be sitting in with me this morning." Riter never acknowledged the introduction. He barely glanced in Luke's direction.

Simmons completed the preliminary requirements–name, age, medication–before concentrating on the reason for the test. "Why are you here to take a polygraph?" he asked.

Officer Riter glanced around the room and up at the ceiling before turning to face Floyd. "Don't you know?" he chuckled.

Floyd's face turned red. "I'll ask the questions. You're supposed to provide the answers." His steely tone and clipped words didn't seem to faze the subject.

"What's the question?" Riter countered, a smile still on his lips.

"Why are you here to take a polygraph?"

"To prove I didn't kill my family." His raised eyebrows and tone of voice gave every indication that he thought it was a dumb question.

Floyd leaned back in his chair. "Tell me what happened."

Riter shifted his body as though trying to gain a more comfortable position. "Well, somehow, my wife got bitten by a spider and died. A few weeks later, my kids died in a fire," he replied as calmly as if explaining what he'd had for breakfast.

The smile he had sported a few seconds earlier turned to a frown. He shot Canfield a quick glance. "I don't have any idea how the two incidents happened. They're trying to pin this on me because I won't take any of their crap. Otherwise, I wouldn't be here."

Luke had been hit with a bad feeling about Riter the minute he'd walked through the door. A knot started in his stomach and worked its way upward until it stuck in his throat. He coughed, trying to dislodge it. Neither Simmons nor Riter seemed to notice. Luke choked it back and remained silent. After all, Simmons was the veteran examiner. It was up to him to determine the subject's truthfulness. It wasn't Luke's place to offer an opinion, especially since the test hadn't even begun. Besides, protocol dictated that the subject's focus of attention must be on the examiner. The observer was to remain silent unless asked to comment by the person conducting the examination.

After obtaining no useful information from the subject, and going over the questions he was going to ask, Floyd placed the attachments and ran a test, not bothering to explain the function of each as Luke was taught to do.

The erratic tracings appeared unreadable. He tore off a length of chart and placed it on the desk, eying it intently. Riter remained silent, appearing unfazed by the whole affair.

"It looks like you know more than you're telling," Floyd said as he glanced back and forth between the chart and the subject.

"Oh really?" Riter leaned toward the examiner, eyebrows arched, and a thin smile on his lips. "You wouldn't be trying to bluff me now, would you?" He leaned back in his chair and crossed his legs.

"I'm giving you a chance to come clean about the death of your family so you can maybe avoid the *chair.*" Floyd's mouth was grim, his head thrust forward in a confrontational stance. "I don't think you'll be so cavalier with fifty thousand volts zapping through your body."

Riter smiled as he mentally stood toe-to-toe with Floyd. "If you have evidence, bring it on. If you only have an opinion, then we have nothing more to discuss. Besides, I believe the method of execution in Arizona is by gas, so you might want to get your facts straight before you speak." He turned his head to the front and faced the wall. It was obvious to Luke that the conversation was over.

Simmons' threats bounced off Roland Riter like rain drops off a sidewalk. Riter was a cop. He knew, as long as he made no admissions, there was nothing anyone could do. The circumstantial evidence was insufficient to indict him.

Luke was surprised when Simmons questioned the subject about deceptive reactions. The tracings were too erratic to call one way or the other. Luke had only a gut feeling that Riter wasn't truthful. He waited for Simmons to ask him for his thoughts, but to his chagrin, Simmons got to his feet and unhooked the subject without giving his sergeant a chance to comment. Riter hurriedly left without a handshake or a backward glance.

"There's something mentally wrong with that guy," Luke said. "I think it would be a good idea to get a psychological evaluation and then retest him. We should have questioned him further."

"I've tested people like him before," Simmons replied. "They'll never tell you the truth, and you'll never get an accurate reading, no matter how many psychological evaluations they've had. Further questioning would have been a waste of time." Simmons gathered his charts and walked out.

Luke sat staring at the polygraph, thinking he should have said something to Simmons before the subject left. But what? If the polygraph results were insufficient to show deception, what was Luke going to say? That he knew the subject was guilty? How did he know? It was something he couldn't explain, even to himself. How could he expect anyone else to understand?

Simmons was sitting in Merle's chair, sipping coffee, when Luke entered. Neither acknowledged the others presence. Luke had to get out of there. He needed a few minutes to cool off. He went to the restroom and washed his face. He resisted the urge to go back in the office, grab Simmons by the throat, and strangle him for his incompetence, but mostly because he was seated in Merle's chair.

CHAPTER TWENTY-EIGHT

On Friday, the second week of Luke's return from polygraph school, Merle picked up a file and thrust it toward him. "I think you're ready to get your feet wet. "What do you think?" It was worded as a question, but the tone left no room for refusal.

"I guess I'm ready as I'll ever be." Luke reluctantly took the file.

"Floyd will sit in with you, but you'll run the test. Is that OK with you, Floyd?"

Simmons nodded toward the door. "Go get your first victim. He's in the waiting room."

The word "victim" wasn't lost on Luke. He knew Floyd was labeling the applicant a "victim" because Luke would be conducting the examination.

Luke reluctantly walked out and called the applicant's name.

Delbert Dixon stood and shook Luke's outstretched hand. He was tall and thin. His long blond hair hung past his shoulders and a brief smile revealed tobacco-stained teeth. Luke stifled a grin as he remembered that his own dad and a couple of his brothers chewed tobacco. Their teeth looked similar. The applicant's faded blue jeans, long-sleeved shirt, and worn cowboy boots gave the appearance of a real cowboy. Luke liked him.

"Come on back." Luke tried to sound like he was in charge even though he didn't feel that way. "How's it going today?"

"OK," the applicant replied.

Luke led him to the polygraph room and motioned to the subject's chair. "This is my associate. He'll be assisting me," he said as he introduced Floyd, seated to his left.

Dixon acknowledged the introduction with a nod of his head and slowly settled into the chair.

Luke pulled out the standard applicant waiver form, filled in the name and date, and slid it across the desk, along with a pen. "Read this and if it's agreeable, sign at the bottom," he directed.

The applicant barely glanced at the form before signing. As he handed it back, Floyd interjected, his voice sharp and brows arched. "Don't you think you'd better read something before you sign it? You could be signing your life away and wouldn't even know it."

The applicant picked up the form, glanced at it briefly

and pushed it over to Luke. "I read enough to know I couldn't understand it anyway."

Floyd took immediate offense to what he obviously perceived as the subject's flippant response. He leaned across Luke's lap, his voice heavy with restrained impatience. "The form you signed, basically says you voluntarily agree to take a polygraph examination and any information obtained as a result of this test will be used to determine your eligibility for employment."

Luke had all he could do to keep from lashing out at Simmons for taking over.

So much for protocol. I wonder what he would have said if I had butted in when he tested the officer suspected of killing his wife and kids.

When the subject failed to respond and Luke was certain Floyd was finished, he took the waiver and placed it in a folder on the desk. He understood what the subject meant. He did the same thing when he took his polygraph. He guessed this was true with most documents people signed. They were either too confused or too overwhelmed by their environment to fully understand what they'd read. Most often it was legalese jargon, unintelligible to the average person, so why bother? Just sign and be done with it.

Luke rattled off a standard list of questions similar to what he'd experienced during his polygraph at the Diogenes Polygraph Institute. He tried to act as though he'd been running tests for years, while all the while his heart raced almost as fast as when *he'd* been the subject sitting in a chair similar to the one in which the applicant was now seated. He managed to verbally review the subject's application without any significant slips. The subject admitted nothing of consequence as Luke ran through the list of questions.

Luke mentally retraced his steps to make sure he'd covered everything. "Is there anything on your application that you want to change before we do the actual test?" he asked as he glanced back and forth between the application and the young man.

"No," the subject replied.

Luke turned to Floyd. "Do you have any questions?"

Floyd shook his head.

Luke got up from his chair and walked around the subject. "Lean forward," he said as he placed one of the pneumatic tubes around the lower waist. "This one goes low to accommodate the belly breathers." He pulled the slack out of the tube and hooked the chain that kept it snug. "And this one goes high for the chest breathers," he said as he tightened the second pneumo. "Both tubes measure relative changes in your breathing," he added.

He picked up the blood pressure cuff with the pneumatic tube attached and stepped to the left side of the subject's chair. "This is a standard medical blood pressure cuff," he explained as he placed it on the subject's upper left arm, squeezing the wrinkles out of the cuff as he pulled it snug.

"These last two attachments measure your skin's resistance to electricity." He placed the two galvanic skin response attachments on the first and third finger of the subject's left hand.

After hooking up the attachments, he took his seat behind the desk, inflated the blood pressure cuff and flipped the switch that started the chart to scroll. He marked the chart with beginning test time and cuff pressure before attempting to adjust the pens.

It took him a few seconds to get the pens adjusted to the right area of the chart. Now, he understood why the examiner at the school seemed to take so long before she started asking questions. She needed time to write all that stuff down and get the instrument adjusted. He finally finished and began asking questions.

Luke was nervous. He was taking too long. He knew from personal experience that the blood pressure cuff would be causing some serious hurt.

He concluded the first chart and released the cuff pressure.

The subject moved his arm up and down and then around to the front of his body, all the while looking at it as though trying to see through the long sleeve.

"Man! That was miserable. I couldn't feel my arm. All I could feel was pain. It still doesn't feel right. Has anyone ever had their arm seriously damaged from this?" Concern was in his eyes and an edge in his voice.

"There'll be no harm to your arm or anything else," Luke assured him. "It's no different than having your blood pressure taken at a doctor's office. Everything will be fine."

Luke didn't see any significant changes in the chart to indicate deception, but he needed to fill some time to permit the subject's arm to return to normal. He slid the chart over to Floyd.

"Do you have any questions?"

Floyd barely glanced at the chart before shaking his head.

Luke needed more time. It would take another minute or two before the subject's arm returned to normal. He decided to act as though he was still studying the chart, although it was pretty clear, even to him, that the subject was being truthful.

"Is there anything on your application that is incorrect?" he asked while pretending to study the chart intently.

"Everything on my application is accurate to the best of my knowledge," the subject answered dryly. "Why? Does that thing say it isn't?" He nodded toward the instrument that was deciding whether he would remain in the selection process.

"It just indicates a little reaction to the question." Luke suddenly found himself on the defensive. "Sometimes, something comes to a person's mind they had forgotten about until they respond during the actual test."

"Nothing except the pain in my arm. That's the only thing

that came to mind," the subject said as he briefly turned to face Luke, before turning back so he was again sitting straight in the chair. He obviously wanted to get the ordeal over and wasn't in the mood for unnecessary delays.

"This next test will be shorter and I'll reduce the pressure as much as I can, so just remain still and we'll get through faster," Luke said, as he prepared for the next test.

He completed the examination and determined the applicant was truthful and would remain in the selection process. Floyd agreed with his findings.

He shook hands with the subject and ushered him out the door. He'd conducted his first polygraph examination without things going too terribly wrong, but he was drained physically as well as emotionally. It was even more stressful than he'd imagined. He needed a cup of coffee.

Luke presented the charts to Merle, who scrutinized them carefully. Floyd stood by until Merle completed his review of the charts and agreed with Luke's conclusion that the subject was truthful.

"He passed the test all right, but he'll probably never be hired," Floyd smirked. "He'll need to have his arm amputated because Luke cut the blood flow off too long."

Merle busted out in a brief laugh before turning to Luke. "You're probably going to have to reduce your test time from four minutes to two or three. But that will come with practice. In the meantime, if you find you're taking too long, just run more charts with fewer questions."

Luke never thought of that. There were generally three charts run for pre-employment examinations. He made up his mind that from now on, he'd run four, with fewer questions.

"You should have told him that," Merle chastised Floyd as he fixed a stare on his colleague that visually implied what Luke was thinking: *I can't believe what an asshole you are.*

Floyd didn't respond. He went to get another cup of coffee.

Luke had always known that Floyd resented being replaced. It was one of the perks of working administration. He'd been privy to all of the scuttlebutt going on in the ranks.

Floyd tried to get the department to pay him more money. He didn't want to retire, but he'd backed himself into a corner by voicing an ultimatum: either increase his pay or he'd retire. He was angry when the chief called his bluff and wished him well in his retirement. Luke knew all that. Hell, everybody knew it. It was all over the department. It wasn't specifically Luke who Simmons disliked, it was anyone designated to replace him.

***

By Wednesday of the third week, Luke was no longer

afforded the luxury of sitting by while Floyd or Merle conducted a polygraph. They were the ones sitting in with him. By Friday, he was testing solo.

The days passed swiftly. As the workload increased, he found himself too busy to worry about having made a mistake on the last one as another would be waiting. He often started work at seven in the morning and didn't finish until seven at night.

Because of his supervisory and other administrative duties, it was nine or ten before he got home. Sheer volume significantly reduced his apprehension about conducting polygraphs, and he became more confident each day. But there was a toll to pay. Exhaustion became his constant companion.

CHAPTER TWENTY-NINE

The four months since Luke returned from polygraph school seemed like four years. The volume of tests never slacked off. Only three percent of applicants who applied were actually hired. Many never made it past the polygraph.

It was a hot Friday afternoon in late July. One more applicant and Luke would clean the pens and go home. It was after five o'clock and he was tired. He'd make short work of this one.

Fillmore Rosewood was a thirty-eight year-old white male, a little old for the rigors of the police academy. But he'd passed all the preliminaries, so the polygraph was next. He was just shy of 6 feet, and looked every bit of his 200 pounds. His belly was bulging under the short-sleeved shirt draped over his pants. Large flabby arms filled the sleeves. An open collar exposed a fat neck that supported a large head with curly brown hair. He was leafing through a magazine in the waiting room as Luke approached.

"You Rosewood?"

The man put down the magazine. "That's me," he said excitedly as he bounced up from his chair, an ear-to-ear grin spread across his wide mouth.

Most people about to take a polygraph were more subdued, almost to the point of depression, but this guy seemed elated, like his name had been called at a raffle.

"I'm Sergeant Canfield. Come on back." He led the applicant to the polygraph room and motioned for him to have a seat. "How's it going today?" he asked.

"If things were any better, I couldn't stand it," Rosewood said with a laugh. He lowered himself in the subject's chair and turned to scrutinize the instrument, leaning over the desk until half his body was out of the chair.

Luke hoped the guy wasn't another nut case. He'd had a couple of those in the past month. Both applicants seemed rational at first, but became unstable as the interview progressed. Rosewood didn't give that impression. His demeanor indicated a serious character flaw, rather than an emotional problem. No one who came in for a polygraph was that jovial.

After personal information was obtained and the pretest interview was concluded, Luke hooked up the attachments. He directed the applicant to look straight ahead as he gave his standard *beginning of test* speech.

Throughout the process, Luke had kept one eye on the subject while trying to determine why he had a bad feeling about him when nothing in the pretest interview supported his suspicions. People generally admitted something. It was rare that a subject was completely truthful or completely deceptive. There was always a little truth and a little deception in nearly everything that was said. "Liars all." The words Doctor Hardison had uttered in polygraph school rang crystal clear in Luke's head.

From the very first question, the chart showed erratic markings. Something very serious was on Rosewood's mind. Luke needed to find out what it was as soon as possible so he could get the hell out of there and go home. He was dog tired. If the first chart showed sufficient grounds for rejection of employment, he would discontinue the test and kick the guy out the door. He didn't want to spend a minute longer with this applicant than necessary.

He decided to cut to the chase and reverse the order of questions. He'd ask drug questions first. The subject acted strangely enough to be on drugs.

"Have you ever used drugs or narcotics that were not prescribed for you?" Luke asked.

"No," the subject replied.

No reaction. Well, hell, Luke thought. That blows that theory.

If it's not alcohol or narcotics it must be sex. He's probably some kind of pervert.

"Did you ever engage in an abnormal sex act?"

"No."

There were slight reactions, but not enough to warrant the bad feelings he had about the guy. He concluded the first chart and told the subject to relax.

Rosewood moved his arms and legs around and eased back in his chair before starting to chuckle, his gaze fixed on the wall to his front. No one ever thought anything was funny while in the polygraph chair. Jack Benny could have told jokes in the nude and no one would have laughed while hooked up to that infernal machine.

What the hell have I gotten myself into this time? Luke asked himself as he studied the face of the subject. If he concentrated hard enough, maybe he could get a better read on him, or...maybe he was wrong from the start and the subject was actually of good character. That was it. He must have read him wrong. He'd do another chart and clear things up. It was getting late. He wanted to go home.

"What's so funny?" Luke asked as he glanced at the wall to the subject's front in an effort to determine what triggered the laugh.

"Huh? Oh, there's a small hole in the wall at eye level. I was just thinking that someone in this chair must have been so scared, they burned a hole in the wall with their eyeballs." Rosewood was still grinning when Luke flipped the switch and announced the test was about to begin.

The only category not covered in the previous test was the commission of a serious undetected crime. That question would ordinarily have been in the first set of questions. Luke had taken them out of order because he was tired and wanted to get through as fast as he could. Had he obtained sufficient admissions, he could have terminated the test and gone home. But nothing significant was uncovered, so here he was, asking questions on the last chart that should have been asked on the first.

"Have you ever committed a serious crime for which you weren't caught?" He realized the question was a bit unorthodox, but it worked for him in the past. People seemed to understand it better than the formal, "Have you ever committed a serious undetected crime?"

The subject hesitated. He seemed to be preparing himself for the answer. Luke glanced back and forth between the subject's face and the markings on the chart. Rosewood remained physically still as directed when the test began, but Luke could feel his mind churning as he struggled to come up with a suitable answer.

"No." His voice was strained.

There was some reaction to the question. Luke decided to

follow up with another question, one that wasn't on the standard list of applicant questions. "Are you attempting to withhold any derogatory information about your true character?"

"No," the subject hurriedly answered.

If things hadn't been so serious, Luke would have laughed. Others had tried that–answer quickly and try to get their mind past the question before the pens catch up. It never worked.

That was the reaction he was looking for. The cardio, and both pneumo pens scribbled their dramatic message across the chart. The subject had lied.

Luke gave his end-of-test speech, slowly and deliberately flipped the switch that stopped the chart scroll, and turned the knob that released pressure from the cuff. He tore off a length of chart and spread it out before him. Each step was slow and deliberate. Then he leaned back and fixed his gaze on police applicant Fillmore Rosewood.

The subject turned to face the examiner. A slit of a smile crossed his lips. His eyes narrowed, but he said nothing.

He knows that I know, Luke thought as he continued to stare at the subject.

Rosewood sat quietly for a few minutes before straightening his legs and bringing them back to the chair. He swung his attention to his left hand, appearing to stare at the electrodes on his fingers before turning back to Luke. The smile was gone. A stone face had replaced it.

The air was heavy with anticipation. Each waited for the other to make a move. To call the steps. To begin the dance that each intended to control. Was it going to be a waltz? A fox trot? Maybe a two-step. Two steps forward and one step back. That's the way it was with interrogations. But this wasn't a criminal test. It was merely a portion of the applicant screening process. Rosewood wasn't there to determine his involvement in a crime. He was applying for a job.

After only a few months of conducting polygraphs, Luke felt like a veteran. He'd seen a lot in a short span of time. People had cried, pleaded, vomited, and even passed out, while in that chair. No other chair evoked such a range of emotions, except maybe the electric chair. There were some, however, who acted as if they were about to receive a death sentence. Being employed was the most important thing in their lives, so in their minds, they *were* facing their doom.

Fatigue screamed through every muscle in Luke's body. It was difficult to sit up straight, and even more difficult to keep his thoughts straight. He needed time to think. He leaned back in his chair, hoisted his legs over the edge of the desk, laced his hands behind his head, and closed his eyes. It was heavenly to relax, to let all of the muscles in his body become limp and loose as a warm, wet washcloth.

The smart thing to do is unhook this dip-shit and send him on his way. Just call him deceptive and blackball him from the hiring process. That would be the smart thing to do, but...whoever said I was smart?

He dropped his feet to the floor with a bang and thrust his body towards the subject. Rosewood reared back, wide eyed at the examiner's aggressive action.

Luke's face was grim as he eyeballed the subject who no longer appeared jovial. He acted more like an applicant now, a little scared and a lot apprehensive.

"Fillmore," The examiner's tone was stern, intimidating, "you are carrying a heavy load. I'm surprised your head doesn't fall off with all the stuff you're hauling around up there. Do you know it can make you crazy? Do you know that?"

Rosewood said nothing. His eyes darted back and forth, first at the chart that was spread out on the desk and then at the aggressive examiner who, a minute earlier, appeared to be falling asleep.

"Do you have a lot of physical problems?" Luke asked inquisitively. "I'd be surprised if you didn't."

The subject remained silent. He turned his head, his eyes fixed on the electrodes clinging to the fingers of his left hand. He raised his hand a few inches before gently returning it to the arm of the chair.

"Fillmore Rosewood." The name rolled off Luke's tongue as though he was calling roll. "You lying bastard."

The subject's body jerked backward as the sudden outburst seemed to startle him. It startled Luke too. It was his voice. But the words weren't something he would say to anyone, especially an applicant. He glanced around for Nathan Hardison. It was something *he* might say. But there were only two people in the room, and the words certainly didn't come from the mouth of the applicant. Luke reluctantly accepted ownership.

The subject's face turned red, but he remained silent. He looked confused. His wild gaze darted back and forth between the examiner and the wall to his front. Luke had seen the same look on a cornered rabbit unable to decide which way to run.

He's probably wondering what the hell he's gotten himself into. Welcome to the club, buddy. I keep asking myself the same question.

In a calm, clear voice, Luke said, "Fillmore, I know why you're here. You need someone to lean on. The job had nothing to do with your coming in for a polygraph." He kept a steady gaze on the applicant while he paused to let his words sink in.

Luke continued in a voice so low, the subject was forced to lean closer to hear what was being said. "You may not consciously understand why you're here. But your subconscious mind knows damn well why you're here. You're pretty close to being declared a nut case. If you're not aware of that fact by now, it may already be

227

too late. You have a chance here today–and don't ask me why I'm giving you that chance because I don't even know myself–to clear your mind."

Luke slowly shook his head, all the while keeping his eyes glued to the troubled face of the subject. "OK, here's the deal," he said in a cold, dramatic tone. "I'm going to give you an opportunity to get all of that vile stuff out of your mind and unload it on me. I can see into your head. You have a load of garbage in there. It's a rotting, stinking mass that a blind man can see. Hell, I can even smell it."

It wasn't an overstatement. A sickening stench emanated from Fillmore Rosewood. Luke was becoming nauseous. He'd been told about *flop sweat* in polygraph school. The term was coined during the early days of vaudeville when the entertainers became so fearful of a poor performance they would sweat profusely. It wasn't the normal "drops rolling down your face" sweat. This was mind numbing, gut clenching, terror driven sweat. It seeped out of every pore in the body and saturated clothing, hair, furniture, everything. The odor didn't quite match the intensity of a cadaver after a few days in the Arizona heat, but it was a close second. It was overwhelming.

Luke had been taught that the normal procedure during an interrogation was to close in on the subject, physically as well as mentally. That's why the polygraph room was small. You were to confine the person physically, as well as emotionally. Make him believe he was trapped, with no way out except telling the truth. In this case, Luke shied away from getting any closer than necessary. He had all he could do to keep from running to the bathroom and giving up his last meal and several others before it.

His eyes watered. He had to get out of there. He'd given it his best shot and Rosewood wasn't budging. He'd already spent way more time than required. The subject was concealing something serious, of that Luke was sure. But the examiner was tired, his head ached, his mouth tasted like dirty socks...and it was late.

Luke slowly rose and made his way around the subject. He'd unhook this walking garbage heap and get him the hell out of there so he'd be able to breathe some clean air again. No one would fault him for calling it a day.

He lifted the subject's hand and unfastened the galvos, then came the cuff, and lastly, the pneumos. All the while, he told himself he was completely justified in calling the subject deceptive and kicking him out the door.

But another voice clamored for attention. It was the voice that cautioned him to always do the right thing. He couldn't let the subject go without resolving his suspicions. That wouldn't be living up to his obligations. He was a police supervisor for the city of Phoenix, responsible for the welfare of its citizens.

He returned to his seat.

Damn it. Why am I compelled to take responsibility for the whole damn world?

A heavy sigh escaped his lips as he resigned himself to the fact that Fillmore Rosewood wasn't going anywhere until he purged his mind of all its secrets, even if it took all night.

"Fillmore, do you believe in God, or a divine power of some kind?" Without giving the applicant a chance to answer, Luke continued. "You know, I can see inside your head, and now we both realize the harm you've done to yourself by keeping such deep, dark secrets. Unless you shed some light on that darkness within you, you're going to evolve into a psychopath and end up in a mental institution or...dead...in the gutter." He ground out the words, slowly, deliberately. His voice low, ominous.

The subject's eyes opened wide as they jerked back and forth between the examiner and the wall to his front.

Luke leaned closer, his eyes boring into the subject. "How many people have you murdered?" Rosewood reeled away, leaning sideways in his chair as if to avoid a punch. His eyes jolted wide. The question obviously shocked him.

It shocked Luke too. He hadn't planned to be so direct. He normally chose subtlety, but the words just slipped out as they often had in the past. He didn't need to consciously consider what to say. Someone or something always seemed to take over when he was in interrogation mode. Funny, he couldn't even smell the putrid stench anymore.

"Six? Eight? More?" he asked as though it was no more important than any other question. "Did you shoot them? Stab them? Strangle them? How did you do it? I'm curious to hear how you did it. Or...did you just sit and stare at them until they died of boredom?"

Luke chuckled at the last question. He couldn't help it. Sometimes he was forced to laugh at the most inappropriate times. The subject never changed expressions, but he did cock his head away from the examiner, so that was a positive sign.

"OK, so we've determined that you've killed people. You must know you're going to hell. You do know that don't you? Or are you too far gone to realize it?"

"I didn–"

"I know that," Luke blurted as he glanced over his right shoulder. "You don't need to remind me." *Don't let them deny. Never let them deny.* Hardison's gravelly voice had come through, mockingly reminding the examiner of one of the tenets of interrogation.

Rosewood squirmed. His eyes had that scary look people get when startled. His knuckles turned white as his hands clamped vise-like around the arms of his chair.

Damn, he must think I'm the one who's nuts. The thought entered Luke's head as he watched the subject shrink back.

"Do you have any idea what you're doing to your soul by keeping that garbage bottled up inside your head?" he cautioned.

He slipped out of his chair and dropped to his knees at the end of his desk, all the while, keeping his eyes locked on the subject's face. "I can help you save your soul. Get down on your knees. We're going to pray that you have enough soul left to save. Get down here," he commanded. His authoritative voice rose as he again ordered the subject to the floor.

After a few seconds, Fillmore Rosewood slowly lowered himself to his knees, facing the examiner, his hands spread wide on the floor, his head hanging.

"Say this with me," Canfield directed as he bowed his head. "Lord..."

"Lord..." the subject mimicked, his voice barely audible.

"Give me strength..."

"Give me strength..." Rosewood barely got the words out. He raised his head enough for Canfield to see his shaggy eyebrows before dropping it again.

"To tell the truth..." Canfield's voice rose.

"To tell the truth..." Rosewood spoke a little louder.

"And clear my mind..."

"And clear my mind..." He was responding more quickly now, his voice a little stronger.

"You take it from there," Canfield said quietly. "Say aloud

everything that's in your mind...but only speak the truth. God will bless you for it."

Rosewood raised his head and closed his eyes before lowering it again. His lips moved several times but no words came. When he found his voice, he spoke like he was reading a story.

"When I was seventeen...I met a couple at a house party. They took a liking to me and invited me with them to Lake Pleasant. They had a picnic lunch and some booze and we were off by ourselves at the far end of the lake..." Rosewood stopped talking. His fingers dug into the carpet. His head hung within inches of the floor. A low moan escaped his lips as he swayed from side to side.

Luke raised his body a few inches to take some strain off his arms. He wished the subject would spit it out. His knees were getting sore and his arms ached. He didn't know how long he could keep this up. But confessions couldn't be rushed. He remained silent.

After a short while, the subject continued. "We all had quite a bit to drink and the woman started coming on to me. I guess I didn't try to discourage her any. I was flattered that a good-looking woman would think a seventeen year-old boy was attractive. Afterward, I realized it was probably the booze and not me."

Rosewood had been facing the floor while he was talking, but suddenly his head shot up. Both men were face-to-face, not more than twenty inches apart, their eyeballs locked. Canfield thought the confession was over. His little charade had failed. He was about to rise to his feet and call it a draw when the subject once again lowered his head and continued with his story.

"The woman had her arms around my neck and had just kissed me when her husband hit me in the back with his fist. It really hurt. I turned just in time to miss being hit in the head with nearly a full bottle of whiskey. The bottle slipped out of his hand so I grabbed it and hit him. He went down and I hit him in the head with the bottle about two or three times. His wife jumped on my back and I hit her until she quit moving. I left them and drove their car back to Phoenix. I heard they both died."

Luke's knees were painful. His arms hurt and his back ached. He stood up and helped Rosewood to his chair. Both men sat rubbing their knees.

Rosewood's face was white, his eyes watery. Between quivering lips, he haltingly asked, "What's...going to happen to me...now? I was only seventeen when that happened. I was drunk. And besides...I was just defending myself. What do you think they will do to me? Do you think I'll still go to hell?"

The subject was talking so fast, Luke couldn't remember all the questions. "You're going to have to speak to the detectives about that," he said.

He was glad the ordeal was over. His whole body felt like he'd just gone a few rounds in a cement mixer. He would think twice before he pulled that one again. "Just tell them what you told me. There's nothing anyone can do that would be as bad as what you've done to yourself by keeping all that crap bottled up in your head."

Rosewood nodded slowly as Canfield led him out of the polygraph room and to the elevator that would take them to the second floor and the Detective Bureau.

Luke explained the nature of their visit to the desk sergeant and returned to the elevator. He noticed the sadness in Rosewood's eyes as a detective led him to a holding room.

I guess I should feel sorry for him, but he had no pity for his victims. If he hadn't applied for a job and taken a polygraph, no one would have ever known. I wonder if they can scrape up enough evidence to charge him.

Luke drove slowly home. His mind was filled with thoughts of the day. He had satisfied the voice in his head to always do the right thing. Now it was up to someone else.

He should have felt good about solving two murders, but he didn't. The victims were dead. Nothing he could do would bring them back. He felt empty. It wasn't for lack of food. It was a lonely kind of empty, like the barn when the cattle were out to pasture, or the haymow when the hay was gone. It seemed he always did something after it was too late. Why couldn't he be pro-active and prevent something bad from happening? If he had only latched the gate, his little sister would be alive today.

No matter what other thoughts he had, the ones of his little sister's near drowning always creeped in. A lone tear trickled slowly down his cheek as he pulled into his driveway. He brushed it away. Sanctuary was only a few steps away.

He managed a thin smile as he walked into the house and closed the door. The haunting, *woulda, coulda, shoulda* ghosts were locked out. He would pick them up again in the morning. But for tonight, he was home...and life was good.

CHAPTER THIRTY

Two weeks had passed since Fillmore Rosewood admitted to murdering two people. Luke had heard that the applicant was booked later that night, but released from custody the following day. The county attorney wasn't comfortable charging him with murder without physical evidence.

The subject's confession, while applying for a job and without a Miranda warning, was a sticking point. An indictment, therefore, could not include information uncovered during the polygraph examination.

It appeared doubtful that the investigators could obtain sufficient independent physical evidence to make a murder charge stick. But it wasn't a total loss. The examiner's diligence had solved a major crime and prevented a murderer from becoming a Phoenix police officer.

Luke poured every ounce of strength and ability into his job. He felt good about screening out murderers, robbers, rapists, thieves and other undesirables who would have undoubtedly been hired if not for the polygraph.

In the four-and-a-half months since he started testing by himself, he'd become a human chameleon, just as Doctor Hardison said was necessary for an effective polygraph examiner.

It was hard not to laugh at some admissions, and harder still not to cry at others. But he was getting better at keeping his emotions in check. He was also getting more adept at reading people.

Earl Jamison was sitting in the waiting room when Luke called his name. He was a typical police applicant: white male, twenty four, six feet tall, 180 pounds. His short brown hair indicated a recent haircut.

Jamison immediately got up and shook Luke's outstretched hand. He seemed a little nervous, but no more than most who were faced with revealing their innermost secrets just to be in the running for a job. He breezed through the pre-test interview and appeared to be just what the department was looking for.

From their initial meeting, Luke had gotten that weird feeling again: an electrical impulse that started somewhere around his eyes and wound through his body until it settled like a sinker in his gut.

What's the matter with me? This guy looks like the type of person we're looking for. Why do I feel there's something wrong? Damn! I wish I didn't keep getting these strange feelings about people. They wear me out. I need to rely solely on chart interpretation and ignore everything else.

After the attachments were snugly in place, Luke inflated the blood pressure cuff and flipped the switch that started the chart to scroll. The pens left their trails of red ink as the questions were asked and answered.

No reactions indicative of deception were noted on the first chart.

Luke breathed a sigh of relief as he examined the response to questions concerning truthfulness on the questionnaire, as well as thefts from employers. He forced his initial uneasiness to the back of his mind.

He ran another chart. No reactions indicative of deception were noted to excessive drinking or use of illegal drugs.

By this time, Luke had eliminated most of his concern that the young man was concealing something vital about his character.

Luke prepared to run a third and final chart as he berated himself for developing preconceived notions. Maybe now he'd quit peering into people's minds and rely solely on the instrument.

As chart three began to roll, Luke was a little more relaxed.

He hadn't seen anything deceptive yet, and he didn't expect to see it during the last few questions. The subject looked too clean-cut to have done anything too bad. The last chart consisted of sex questions. In applicant screening, the final chart nearly always consisted of sex questions.

"Have you ever forced anyone to have sex with you?"

"No." The voice was firm. Confident.

"Have you ever engaged in a sex act with anyone under the age of eighteen?"

"No."

The two tough questions were over. No indication of deception. Luke was breathing easier. His gut instinct was obviously wrong.

"Do you drink coffee?"

"Yes."

"Do you drink beer?"

"Yes."

"Have you ever engaged in an abnormal sex act?"

"No." The subject's tone of voice lowered. All previous answers were bold and confident. The last one was subdued and doubtful.

For a few seconds, the pens followed their normal up and down movements prevalent throughout the first two charts. Then, some drastic changes occurred. The cardio pen pegged out at the top of its parameter, and the pneumo pens contracted from their normal up and down movements to nearly a straight line. The autonomic nervous system had contradicted what the mouth had said. Reactions indicative of deception were noted as the pens spewed red ink that marked forever the fact that the subject had lied.

Luke gave his standard end of test speech, marked the chart, and turned the knob that released pressure on the cuff. He flipped the switch that stopped the scroll, tore off a length of chart, and spread it out before him. Each step was slow and deliberate, meant to heighten the tension. Like the warning rattle of a Western diamondback slithering through the Arizona desert before sinking its fangs into its prey.

He glanced first at the chart and then at the subject. "Do you want to tell me about it?" Luke leaned back in his chair. He didn't want to appear aggressive. He wanted the subject to voluntarily explain the reactions.

"Tell you about what?" Jamison glanced at the examiner and quickly turned away.

"About why you reacted so drastically to the question about abnormal sex," Luke calmly replied as he continued to examine the chart.

The subject remained silent. Looking first at the examiner and then at the floor. His face turned pale. He licked his lips.

The silence grew. The subject was obviously not going to volunteer anything. Luke found it slightly amusing. It reminded him of the hand pump that sat over the cistern on the farm. It had to be primed before it would pull up any water. Earl Jamison needed a similar incentive.

"Some people believe the only person who was perfect had holes in His hands. I haven't had anyone in here like that, and you certainly don't see any in mine." Luke displayed his hands, turning them back and forth to show both sides. "I'm far from perfect, and I was hired after the same test you're going through."

When the subject still didn't take the bait, Luke decided to break out his secret weapon. He held up an almost new pencil with barely a portion of eraser showing. "Everyone makes mistakes," he said. "That's why they put erasers on pencils." He pointed out the well-worn eraser he had deliberately rubbed down to a nub. "You can see how many mistakes I make every day. This is practically a new pencil with hardly any eraser left."

He found the prop most helpful. Not only did it demonstrate mistakes the user had made, but there was also a psychological advantage. Using a pencil to write down admissions and confessions was less threatening than a pen. It implied a temporary, rather than a permanent record. Luke had learned more than he wanted from Doctor Nathan Hardison. With each examination, he found himself becoming more and more like the man he disliked.

Subterfuge and inference. Anything to get the confession.

The subject stared at the pencil with wide eyes and a grim mouth. Luke remained silent, unmoving, his gaze fixed on the face of the subject, waiting for a telltale sign. Was he going to become defensive? Contrite? Angry? The examiner must be prepared to counter any emotion.

Jamison was the first to show the strain. He shifted his body, sat upright, and swung his head to face the door, the only exit out of the little room. It was just to his left. Easy access.

A minute went by. Then two. The subject faced the front and lowered his head to his chest. His shoulders sagged. Another minute passed. Two minutes. Three. He lifted his head and turned to face the examiner. A forced smile teased the corners of his mouth as he began to speak. His voice was low as he struggled to say the words.

"I...wasn't sure...what...abnormal was...but...maybe I did do something once that wasn't the...normal thing to do...I never done anything like that before, and never will again...I can't really explain why I did it when I did."

The subject's face turned from pale to pink to red, all in a few seconds. "Several years ago," he began, "I was deer hunting in the Kaibab. I walked around for half a day before finally spotting a deer. Each time I got ready to shoot, the deer ran off. I was really getting frustrated. It was like the animal was just playing games with me. It would give me a clear sight, and then suddenly disappear before I could get a bead on it." His speech was slow and methodical. His eyes drifted around the room. "I trailed it most of the day. It was a weird feeling when I finally got off a shot. I was happy and pissed at the same time. The deer was hit, but managed to run off through the woods."

The subject turned his head toward the door. Luke saw his muscles tense. It looked like he was going to bolt for the exit, attachments and all.

Luke rose from his chair. He needed to stop the subject before he tore the instrument up trying to get out.

Luke resumed his seat, pretending to shift his position as the subject eased back and relaxed his shoulders. The threat was over.

After a few moments, the subject fixed his gaze on the floor and continued with his explanation. His words were coming faster now, as though he was trying to get them out before he changed his mind. "I trailed the wounded deer for over an hour, and finally came upon the animal in a small clearing. It was laying on its side in the process of dying. As I got closer, I saw it was a doe."

Jamison hesitated, appearing to relive the adventure he was trying to explain. His face turned an angry red and his eyes narrowed as he spit the words through clenched teeth. "That really pissed me off. The deer was acting just like a female. Just like women I've known. They tease and tease and then kick you in the nuts when you least expect it."

The subject drew quiet. He raised his left hand a few inches, appearing to visually examine the metal tips of the galvanograph attached to his fingers. Luke had noticed early on that subjects often did that when they had a burden to unload. He figured it gave them something to concentrate on while trying to get their story straight.

After a few moments, the subject continued in a quiet, calm and reflective tone. "I guess my thinking like that about women–the thrill of the hunt and then the shot–got me all worked up. I just lost it. I...stripped off my clothes and had sex with the deer as it was dying." He turned his head to face Luke. His eyes pleaded for understanding as much as his tone of voice. "It wasn't that I was sexually excited. I was mad at anything female and that was the only thing I could think to do."

Luke didn't know what to say. Maybe the applicant was telling him a story. Floyd–or maybe even Merle–had set him up. Well, he'd play their game.

He managed to conceal his surprise and act like he'd heard that one before. A few months ago, he would have been so shocked that he wouldn't have been able to maintain his composure. But he had heard a lot since becoming a polygraph examiner. People did weird things. This admission was just a little weirder than most.

Luke slowly shook his head. "You mean you had sex without even a kiss first? That doesn't sound very romantic. That reindeer didn't have a red nose by any chance? I hope you didn't shoot Rudolph. Regardless of which one it was, it might have been one of Santa's reindeer. Santa isn't going to be very happy with you. He's liable to leave a chunk of coal in your stocking come Christmas. That's what all naughty little boys get–a chunk of coal."

Luke waited for the laughter, and the admission that it was all a prank, but the applicant's face revealed nothing but a blank stare. The man must be serious.

"Is that the only thing that came to your mind about that question? There was quite a strong response for something as trivial as that," Luke managed to say with a straight face.

The subject heaved a sigh. His eyes sparkled. "That was it," he hurriedly said.

"Have you ever forced a human to have sex with you?" Luke asked.

"No, of course not," the subject replied.

Luke ran another chart and the area cleared up. He discounted his earlier suspicions that he'd been set up. It appeared to be a legitimate admission. He unhooked the subject from the instrument, thanked him for his cooperation, and ushered him out of the office.

Luke needed a few minutes to recuperate after hearing that one. He sat down, draped his legs over the corner of the desk, clasped his hands behind his head, leaned back and closed his eyes.

Sometimes, I feel like the whole world is just one big cesspool, and we're all swimming around bumping into each other trying to keep our heads above it all. Each day, a little more crap gets dumped on my head and I sink a little deeper. It's only a matter of time before I go under.

CHAPTER THIRTY-ONE

As he became more successful in obtaining confessions, Luke was given more work. Simmons had retired and Merle was off sick a good deal of the time, so Luke was working overtime and Saturdays in an attempt to keep up with demand. He requested another examiner, but his request was always "being considered."

After talking so much at work, he was reluctant to discuss anything at home. All he wanted to do was have a glass of Scotch, watch television, and go to bed. He was emotionally and physically incapable of carrying on a conversation with his wife.

As getting home late became the norm, there were fewer instances when the family was there to greet him. The kids were at a school activity or off with their friends, and Emily was either with them or visiting her mother who lived less than five miles away. Even the family dog seldom acknowledged his arrival.

Luke realized he was becoming so absorbed with his work that he was neglecting the most important aspect of his life–his family–the sole reason for going to work. He knew that a successful marriage required daily maintenance. If effort was lacking by one or both, it was doomed to failure. He also knew that the breakdown was usually so insidious, irreparable damage was done before one or the other realized it.

He knew all of that, and yet the demands of the job kept increasing. He was like a drowning man, flailing his arms as hard as he could and still being dragged under. His marriage was sinking right before his eyes and he couldn't swim well enough to save it.

They had argued so many times about his coming home late, and her failure to understand his situation, that there was nothing new to say. Each one regurgitated the same lines they had used a dozen times before. They always started in a normal tone and ended up in a shouting match. He could quote every word by heart:

"I'm going to buy you a watch."

"I have a watch."

"Well then, maybe I'd better teach you how to tell time."

"What the hell are you talking about?"

"I'm talking about your promise to be home at a decent hour so we can go out to dinner or a movie, or just go anywhere *together.* I don't care if it's to the grocery store. Go somewhere *together.* Do something *together.* Anything t*ogether.* Like a real husband and wife. *Together.* Like a family. Is that so hard for you to understand?"

"I'm alone down there and I'm up to my eyeballs in requests for polygraphs. Every day my mind is bombarded with confessions that make my stomach turn. You think I like hearing that shit ten hours a day, six days a week? You think I'd rather be down there, stuck in that little room with people puking on me, and stinking so bad it makes *me* puke? You think I like that? Hell no! I would *much* rather be sitting at home, reading a book, going places with my mother...*anywhere* else. But I was hired to do a job. It's my responsibility to do the best job I can. I—"

"I, I, I. Me, me, me. Do you ever think of anyone but yourself? What about me? Don't you think some of that responsibility that you keep harping about should include your *wife*, your *kids,* your *family*? You have your priorities screwed up. A person works in order to *live.* You don't *live* so you can work. Whoops! Lost my head for a minute. I should have prefaced that with, a *normal* person doesn't live so he can work. You haven't been normal since you got back from that damn polygraph school."

Uneasy silence before the final statement: "I'm going to bed."

Television news–the last voice heard.

CHAPTER THIRTY-TWO

It was a Friday morning, five months to the day since Luke had graduated from polygraph school. He checked his schedule book: four applicants, two criminals, and an internal. He saw an increase in requests for criminals and internals as he became more proficient. He mentioned his observation to Merle.

"Hell yes, there's an increase in requests for those type of tests," Merle exploded. "You have some lazy investigators who figure they can save time and decrease their workload by heaping it on us. Why spend days or weeks investigating something when they can find out everything they need to know in an hour or two? The better you get, the more they'll want you to do." He removed his glasses and rubbed his eyes. Luke had noticed that Merle often went through the same ritual when he was agitated.

"So what do we do? Tell them we're not going to do it?" Luke asked dejectedly.

The scowl on Merle's face reminded Luke of when he asked a stupid question of his father, like "Why can't we take the weekend off like city folks?"

His father always smiled as he gave a much longer answer than Luke thought necessary. "When you have the best things in life, you have to take care of them. City folks aren't as fortunate. They don't have a ready supply of milk, meat, vegetables and other things that are always within our reach. They don't have the clean air and the sunshine and the hard work that keeps us strong and healthy. They weren't blessed with the life of a farmer."

Merle's answer to Luke's question was equally thorough. "What, and have a higher up order us to do it anyway?" Merle's voice was full of disgust, his eyes wide and his brow wrinkled as though in competition with his craggy face. "No, the only way to slow things down is to schedule them a week or two in advance. Most are not willing to wait that long so they'll conduct the investigation the way they should have in the first place."

"Not a bad idea," Luke agreed. "We have enough applicants scheduled to fill each day anyway. I see the first one this morning is an internal."

He opened the file and read the contents. Detective Alfred Jones was suspected of providing police information to known criminals. An anonymous caller had reported seeing Jones in the company of theft-ring suspects who hung out in a bar on Buckeye Road, an area of housing projects for the low income. Each time one of them was served with a search warrant, nothing of a criminal nature was found.

"The Road," as it was known throughout the department, was a hotbed of criminal activity. Bars that lined the street were a regular source of calls.

Luke picked up the file and walked out to the waiting room. Alfred Jones was a black man of middle age, tall and thin, in the usual detective garb. He remained seated, eying the sergeant intently as he approached.

"Morning, Al," Luke said. "You ready for your polygraph?"

"Not really," Jones sighed as he slowly got up and followed Luke back to the polygraph room, "but I guess I'll have to do it anyway."

After the preliminary information was obtained, Luke asked the detective to explain his involvement in the group that he was accused of helping.

A faraway look came into the detective's eyes as he searched for the right answer. "Some are relatives, and some are friends I've known all my life. I've never given them information. I just never tried to get any out of them either."

Luke sensed this officer had a lot on his mind, but he brushed the thought aside. He had those feelings with certain individuals, but he fought hard to discount them, especially with internals.

He had tried to describe the feelings to himself. Maybe his subconscious picked up body language that the conscious mind was unable to decipher. Maybe he had some strange sense of smell, like a dog that knows when a person is afraid. It was hard to explain.

It started visually, but seemed to flow through his entire body like an electric current plugged into the subject. That was the best explanation he could come up with. He forced himself to suppress those feelings. It wasn't right to have preconceived notions. He would let the instrument decide.

After obtaining no admission of wrong-doing during the pretest interview, and going over the questions he was going to ask, Luke placed the attachments on Jones and ran the first chart. Reactions indicative of deception were noted to all of the relevant questions.

Luke tore off the chart and laid it out before him. He studied it for a few minutes before focusing his attention on the subject.

"It appears that we need to clarify some of your answers," he said, softly. "From what I can see, it looks like you're basically an honest man. If you weren't, you wouldn't be reacting so drastically. And I hear you're a good detective. Sometimes we have a mental slip and do things we wouldn't ordinarily do."

Luke glanced at the chart and then at the subject. Detective

Jones was a fellow officer and worthy of a direct approach. "There are reactions to every relevant question. What can you tell me about those?"

Jones didn't say anything for several minutes. He looked away and then suddenly turned his head, locking eye contact with the examiner. His mouth tightened and his eyes narrowed. "I don't know what you're talking about," he spat. "I don't have anything to tell you. My captain knows me. I clear more cases than anyone. I'm the one who keeps his performance rating up. You can talk to him about my performance."

Jones shifted his position and turned his attention to the wall in front, his fingers clasped tightly around the cupped arms of the chair.

"I don't doubt what you're saying," Luke said. "I believe you're a good cop. But that has nothing to do with what we're here to discuss. It appears you warned people that a search warrant was going to be served. And it also looks like you accepted payment for the information. I don't intend to interrogate you. I don't do that with employees."

Luke leaned towards the subject, his voice low and calm. "I'm calling on your oath as a Phoenix police officer to tell the truth. I'm sure you don't want to go back to your captain and tell him you failed the polygraph. I wouldn't want to tell *my* boss that."

After more cajoling and no admissions, Luke released the

reticent officer and wished him a good day. The polygraph did what it was designed to do involving internal matters–confirm or refute suspicions. All he could do at this point was to write up a report that the subject was deceptive. It would be up to management to launch a more in-depth investigation: obtain specific information from the person who reported the incident, and talk to witnesses. All they presently had were some unconfirmed suspicions.

Luke watched with disappointment as the officer walked to the elevator and punched the button for the second floor, detective bureau. A disquieting thought plagued his mind. *I wonder if we have any more like him.*

CHAPTER THIRTY-THREE

It was late afternoon and Luke was still bothered by the test he'd conducted that morning on Detective Jones. His decision to let the subject go without resolving deceptive responses nagged him.

He tried to put it out of his mind. The case required further investigation. There was nothing else he could do. There were other tests to run and he couldn't let his mind be bogged down with the past. He got a cup of coffee and sat down at his desk. He needed a few minutes to quiet his mind before taking on the next challenge.

"Damn. Every time I come in here, yer drinkin' coffee and takin' it easy. Well, yer prob'ly wise ta save yer energy. Yer gonna need it fer the one I'm bringin' in."

Luke hadn't heard Detective Jasper Julian come in. He liked the big detective even though he kept pestering the unit for polygraphs. He reminded Luke of a stuffed bear that was too big to carry around. Or a Saint Bernard puppy that stepped on your feet and slobbered all over you without intending to do so.

"Yeah, we got it pretty easy here," Luke replied as he took another sip of hot coffee. "What the hell do you want now, Julian? Haven't you ever heard of something the department refers to as an *investigation*? That's where you actually go out and question people and determine if they did it or not."

Detective Julian chuckled as he flopped down at Merle's desk. His huge body overflowed the chair that normally seated a much smaller man. "Wait 'tell ya meet Miss Wacko," he said, grinning ear to ear. "Then ya can tell me how ta go about investigatin' her. Her name is June, but everyone calls her "Junebug." I guess because she's crazy as one."

"Well, if she's nuts, how do you expect me to get anything out of her? She probably doesn't even know she's lying," Luke caustically replied.

"Hell, I thought you lie detector people could do anything," the detective said as his smile flickered away. "From what I hear, ya don't need the polygraph ta tell if someone's lyin'. Ya can see right inta their head."

Luke mentally kicked himself for ever telling anyone that he could sometimes determine what was going on in a subject's mind just by looking at him. He'd mentioned it to Merle over one of their morning coffees, and while Merle never missed an opportunity to rag him about it, Luke doubted he'd spread it around. No, it must have come from Fillmore Rosewood, the police applicant who turned out to be a murderer. Or maybe it was some other applicant, or even a criminal suspect who spread the news. Well, it was too late now. If he denied it, the ribbing would never end. He'd just have to contend with it.

Luke took a few sips of coffee before turning to the detective. "Yeah, that's right," he said as he eyed Julian intently. "I can see right through your head, and there's nothing in there to obstruct the view."

The puzzled look on Julian's face was an obvious sign he was unaware he'd been insulted. A few seconds later, he apparently realized he had. He let out a laugh, throwing his head back and slapping his huge thigh with his baseball mitt of a hand before turning a more serious face to the examiner.

"The woman yer about ta test is suspected of killin' at least one man and possibly two...or maybe even more. We can't git enough evidence ta charge her, and the polygraph is our last resort. She won't talk ta me. Maybe she'll talk ta you."

Luke opened the file on June "Junebug" Hillman. He'd already gone over the report, but it was always good to speak with the assigned investigator before a test. He liked the fact that Julian was always there without being asked, even if he was a pest.

"Can you tell me anything that isn't in the report?" Luke asked as he leafed through the file.

"Everything is in there except my suspicions," Julian said. "She was livin' with a man in the Deuce."

Luke had a sudden flash of what was going on in Julian's mind. He knew what the detective was about to say. He remembered the Deuce well. So named after the lowest card in the deck. It was four square blocks in the heart of downtown Phoenix that once boasted high-end department stores and upper-crust hotels. But as the city expanded, the area deteriorated into seedy bars and flophouses, teeming nights with the down and out, the drunks and the druggies, the whores and the pimps. He'd ridden the wagon down there during his early years.

Flashback to his days on the street was interrupted by Julian's continued explanation of the case.

"The manager found the victim dead after Hillman moved out. No sign of anything suspicious until the autopsy. Seems he was stabbed through the ear with what may have been an ice pick. It damned near come out his other ear. Now where the hell does anyone git an ice pick? I doubt if most people know what the hell...what the hell...they...are."

Luke looked up from the file to find the big detective staring trance-like at nothing in particular. He looked like he'd seen a ghost. His eyes were glazed and his face was chalky-white with little beads of sweat popping out on his huge forehead.

Luke kicked the leg of Julian's chair. He didn't want to take a chance on touching him. Anyone that big could knock a person out by reflex alone, and he wasn't taking any chances.

"Hey, are you all right? Julian, are you OK? Do you need a drink of water?"

Detective Julian lowered his head and stared at the sergeant before pulling out a well-used handkerchief and mopping his face. He slowly stood up and ambled to the door. "I gotta git outta here. This place is too damned spooky. I gotta git outta here."

He hesitated in the doorway, looking back at Luke, who was still seated, puzzled by the detective's comments. "Hillman used ta live with another man who died under similar circumstances," he said. "Stabbed through the head with a sharp instrument. Insufficient evidence on that one also."

The detective slowly closed the door, but suddenly opened it again and shot a quick glance at Luke. "I think I need a vacation," he whispered. "I could have sworn there were two of you in the room, and it felt like one of you was tromping around inside my head. I think I need a vacation."

"Wait a minute," Luke hurriedly said. "Aren't you going to be here during the test?"

"I'll be back," Julian said as he closed the door.

Luke slowly surveyed the room, wondering what the hell the

detective could have seen. There was nothing but typical office furniture: desks, chairs and file cabinets. He did catch a glimpse inside Julian's mind, but he discounted that as something he'd imagined. "Maybe he does need a vacation," he said aloud. "But who the hell doesn't?"

***

June Hillman was a typical flophouse tenant, too poor, emotionally as well as financially, to practice good hygiene. A flowered dress that reminded Luke of the ones his mother used to make from empty flour sacks, hung from her tall, skinny frame. Two large pockets looked like an afterthought. Wisps of straggly brown hair fell across her bloodless face. She reminded him of a wild animal–a hyena. She looked downright scary.

I understand what Jasper meant when he called her a wacko. Well, I'm half-nuts too, so we should get along fine.

The thought brought a smile to his face. It was quickly wiped away by a glare from "Junebug" Hillman.

"June Hillman?" Luke asked.

Their eyes met. The examiner and the adversary, an aggressor and a defender, locked in a temporary relationship that neither wanted to have. At this point, it was anybody's guess as to who would come out on top.

"Will you come with me please?"

The woman slowly rose from a chair that she'd apparently squeezed into a corner of the waiting room, and accompanied Luke to the polygraph room.

"Have a seat," Luke said as he motioned to the subject's chair. "Have you ever taken a polygraph before?"

She shook her head. Several strands of matted hair swung with the movement, but failed to return to their original position. They stuck to her face, but she made no attempt to pull them free.

Luke settled down in the examiner's chair, careful not to let his attention stray too far from the woman he was about to test, alert to the possibility that anything could happen with a mentally unstable person.

He vividly recalled the night he and three other officers tried to take a ninety-pound woman to the mental hospital. She'd thrown them around like rag dolls. They finally overpowered her, but not before she beat the hell out of all four officers.

"Do you know why you're here to take a polygraph?" he asked.

Hillman glanced wildly around the room, twisting her head back and forth as if trying to wrench it from her body. Luke half expected her head to keep spinning like in the movie *The Exorcist*, but her strange antics stopped as suddenly as they began.

Her wild eyes locked with his for just an instant. She looked away before answering. "Because some people are crazy," she croaked.

"Who's crazy?" he asked.

She turned to face him, staring with dull-gray eyes as cold and lifeless as a corpse. "For all I know, you are." Her words were flat.

She suddenly looked past him to the upper corner of the room, a blank expression on her bloodless face.

Luke glanced in the direction of her stare, but saw nothing unusual. "Sometimes, I wonder about that myself," he said. "But let's talk about the man you were living with. The one who died. What can you tell me about the way he died?"

Hillman shifted her attention to the wall at her front. "He just up and died. It was his turn to go, and he just up and died. When it's your turn to go...you go."

Luke was getting more concerned. People always used voice inflection when offering an explanation, but the words coming from "Junebug" were flat. Monotone. Without emotion.

Nearly everyone who took a polygraph was nervous and had to be calmed down. But not this one. She was devoid of emotion. That wouldn't do either. He needed to jack her up. She needed to show some emotion if he was going to get a proper response during the test. No need for euphemisms here. Maybe harsher language would spark a sense of urgency in her.

"That may be," Luke countered, "but in this case, someone

helped him along. Did you help him along because it was his turn to go? Did you kill him? Did you stab him in the head?"

He eased back in his chair, waiting for a sign that would tell him in what direction to proceed. All he saw was a face as blank as the walls of the polygraph room.

Luke had scribbled out some euphemistic questions, but revised them after the subject showed no signs of emotion during the pretest interview. Unless she was completely nuts, harsher language with direct questions were certain to produce physiological reactions.

Well, hell, I might as well give it a shot and see what I get.

He got up and moved slowly toward her. "I need to place some attachments on your body," he said as he crossed in front of her and edged his way behind.

"Don't touch me. I don't like to be touched," Hillman screeched as she leaned forward and turned in her chair, her eyes following the examiner's movements.

The strands of hair that were stuck to her face came loose when she tossed her head and now hung down with the rest. It did nothing to soften her appearance.

And I sure as hell don't want to touch you.

Luke managed to control the thought before it became audible.

The body odor drifting through the room stifled his breath.

He hoped he could keep from *throwing* up long enough to get her *hooked* up. This wasn't *flop sweat*. It wasn't even that wet-dog smell that the homeless get from sleeping on the ground. No, this was plain, old-fashioned body odor.

He had gotten good at ducking Lieutenant Sloan's cigarette smoke because he could see it coming. But the odor from "Junebug" Hillman hung everywhere, like an invisible fog. There was no escaping it.

"I'm going to have to touch you in order to place the attachments. Nothing will harm you. I'll explain each one before I do. Is that OK?" he asked.

She didn't answer.

He asked again, "Is that OK?"

Hillman slowly nodded. Her body was rigid. Her bony fingers clamped tightly around the arms of the chair.

Luke kept his head turned and took shallow breaths in an attempt to escape the stench while he slowly placed the attachments on her body, explaining each component as he did so. He could feel her muscles tense each time he placed one of the attachments.

He was relieved when that part was over and he could get back on the other side of the desk. She bothered him more than anyone he'd tested so far. It wasn't just the odor. She was obviously mentally unstable. *He* felt like the one being tested. He had to be on guard.

He flipped the switch that started the chart to scroll, inflated the blood pressure cuff, and adjusted the pens to their proper position before giving his standard "beginning of test" speech.

"Is your first name June?"

"Yes."

"Are you forty-two years old?"

"Yes." She sat rock still, her body–as well as her voice–void of emotion.

"Do you know how Joseph Butler died?"

"No."

"Do you know who caused Joseph Butler to die?"

"No." Her voice sounded hollow. Like an echo. Without soul.

The pens moved across the chart as if on a fixed trajectory. The amplitude hadn't varied. That wasn't right. Normal breathing produced fluctuations. He moved the pens up and down manually to make sure they weren't stuck. They moved freely.

"Did you stab Joseph Butler?"

"No."

"Did you murder Joseph Butler?"

"No."

Luke completed the end of test procedure, tore off a length of chart, and spread it out before him. The tracings were different than any he had previously encountered. There were no reactions to anything. Hillman had maintained the same monotone voice level throughout the test. She seemed detached from reality.

He took out his ruler and laid it along the apex of the respiratory indicator. It produced nearly a straight line. The cardio tracing looked similar. A normal person never produced a straight line.

The chart was nothing like the one Floyd Simmons had gotten when he tested the officer suspected of killing his wife and children. Roland Riter was nuts too, but there were reactions all over the place. Too many to determine truth from deception.

Luke was still upset with Simmons for his incompetence, but he was equally angry with himself for not insisting they question the officer further. He'd heard that Roland Riter was arrested a few weeks later for forging prescriptions. He was fired and eventually sentenced to prison, so that was some consolation. But that situation was over and done. He couldn't afford to let his mind wander. He had to stay focused. What was he going to do with this one?

He had to make June Hillman understand that she was suspected of murder. He needed to provoke a reaction. "The detective believes you murdered Joseph Butler. Not only that, he believes you murdered another man you used to live with."

The subject never acknowledged his comment. Her trance-like stare never varied. He was getting nowhere. He needed a new approach.

He ran another test with the same questions, but when it came to the relevant ones, he used his pen to push the cardio pen to its highest parameter. He held it there for several seconds before letting it return to its normal trajectory.

After the test was over, he tore off the length of chart and laid it out before him. He appeared to study it for a while, then held it up so the subject could see. He pointed to the drastic reaction in the cardio tracing following the questions pertaining to murder. "Do you see this reaction? That's where you lied. Now, I know you killed that man and soon the detective will know. Then the judge will know, and *then*...you will go to prison. Locked up. Confined to a cell day and night. But...worst of all...you'll have to take a shower."

Where did that comment come from? What the hell difference did that make in a murder investigation? Maybe he's as nuts as she. Once again, his thoughts had propelled themselves into words.

The subject sat motionless. Suddenly her head jerked to face him. Her hollow eyes peered first at the chart and then at the person who had accused her of murder. She tried to stand, pulling the attachments along with her. Her scrawny arms flailed about as if to shake loose from both the instrument and the threatening comments of the examiner.

"Just a minute." Luke jumped to his feet. "Sit down and I'll get you out of those. Just give me a minute."

She eased back to a sitting position while he unhooked the attachments and hung them on their hooks behind her chair. He returned to his seat, all the while keeping a wary eye on her.

The subject gave him a cold, hard stare. Her eyes drilled into him and made him uneasy. She started fooling with her clothes, running her hands in and out of her floppy pockets and over her body as if doing a law enforcement pat-down. He followed her movements. He'd seen aggressive behavior many times in the past and this was a classic start.

He rose to his feet, quickly slipped past her and threw open the door. Where the hell was that big oaf of a detective when he needed him? He stepped through the door to see just the man he needed. Jasper Julian lumbered toward him.

Luke didn't see the extended arm as much as he sensed it. He ducked and stepped aside as Hillman's hand, clenched tightly around the handle of a gleaming-silver ice pick, brushed past his ear.

He had no idea such a large man could move so fast, but Julian was suddenly there. Before the woman could rear back for another blow, the detective's big arm shoved him aside and wrapped itself around the waist of the woman who had just tried to stab him. The other hand wrested the weapon from her clenched fist.

It was over as quickly as it began. "Junebug" Hillman was in cuffs, face down on the floor, the weapon safely out of reach. Detective Jasper Julian was standing over her with a big toothy grin.

"Another satisfied customer, I see," he said, as he looked the sergeant up and down. "Did she git ya anywhere?"

"No, I don't think so," Luke said as he continued to examine his body. "But she came damn close. Thanks."

"No problem. I'm a public servant. That's my job. I protect the public," Julian grinned. He hoisted June Hillman to her feet and walked her out of the office.

Luke straggled to the break room. He desperately needed coffee. With shaky hands he poured a cup and took a sip. The hot liquid slid down his throat, warmed his stomach, and temporarily placated the nerve endings that minutes earlier had relayed their emergency message to the brain–the body was in imminent danger. The fight or flight part of his autonomic nervous system had kicked in.

He drank half a cup of black coffee before realizing he'd neglected to add creamer. He poured some in and flopped into a chair. The danger had passed. The brain was taking a time out.

It took a cup of coffee and several minutes for Luke to recuperate and get his heart back in his chest and his lungs operating to the point where he could breathe normally again.

He returned to the polygraph room and gathered up his charts. He marked the drastic rise in the cardio tracing as manually induced, folded the charts and slipped them in the file.

He would hate to have to explain why there was no reaction on the first chart and a dramatic one on the second, when the exact same questions were asked. Another examiner could spot it immediately, and if it ever came up, he would have to admit that he manually created the reaction. But a defense attorney would have a field day if it ever went to court. If he rigged that reaction, what other coercive shenanigans has he pulled to get a person to confess? He would cross that bridge when he came to it. Right now, he was running behind. An applicant was waiting.

CHAPTER THIRTY-FOUR

Monday morning, Luke got his usual cup of coffee and picked up the top file from a stack of applicants scheduled for polygraph. He had sufficiently recovered from his near-death experience with "Junebug" Hillman on Friday.

He never mentioned the ordeal to Emily. He doubted she could emotionally handle something as serious as him almost getting killed. He shuddered at the thought of how close he'd come to getting stabbed in the head with an ice pick. He reminded himself to be more careful, and to speak more kindly to Detective Jasper Julian.

With file in hand, Luke walked to the waiting room to find the twenty-two year old applicant sitting by himself.

"Are you Emil Bitner?"

"That's me," the young man said.

As Bitner got to his feet, Luke noticed he was thin to the point of appearing emaciated. He looked shorter than the five-foot-nine minimum required for employment, and a military-style haircut made his head appear too small for his body. But Luke had made it a point not to judge a person by appearance. He would wait until after the test to offer an opinion.

"Are you ready for your polygraph?" he asked as he extended his hand.

"I guess," Bitner said as he timidly took the examiner's hand and quickly released it.

"Come on back," Luke said as he led the man to the polygraph room.

As they walked, a rustling sound came from beneath the applicant's clothing, but a visual examination revealed nothing unusual. As they entered the room, the sergeant motioned to the subject's chair. Bitner stood rooted to the floor, staring at the instrument that would determine his fate.

Luke took his seat and waited. The subject's actions were unusual. Seldom had anyone ever shown the least bit of hesitation before sitting down. Eventually the applicant slowly turned and lowered himself into the chair.

As the examiner ran through the standard list of questions, the subject frequently shifted positions, crossing one leg for a few minutes before repeating the motion with the other leg. Each movement created a distinct crackling sound.

Luke could hardly keep from busting out laughing. He was pretty sure he knew what was causing the unusual noise. Others had tried to beat the polygraph. They had some ridiculous notion that if they wrapped their legs and body in aluminum foil or plastic wrap, a lie couldn't be detected. They seemed to think the machine sent out radio waves that penetrated their mind and recorded their thoughts. Wrapping portions of their body would throw off the recording. But the wrappings made them uncomfortable and they had a difficult time sitting still. He suspected that the man sitting before him was one of those.

Subjects had tried a variety of measures intended to beat the test. In the past two months, Luke had obtained admissions from three applicants who had put tacks in their shoes. When they lied, they pressed their feet down and caused themselves pain.

One applicant tightened his sphincter muscle when he lied, while another held his breath. Each believed their actions would make the chart unreadable. None of the methods worked. In fact, they produced a more dramatic response with each lie.

Luke never felt anger or disgust with any of them, and he didn't feel that way with the man seated before him. He felt empathy. He knew what the subject was going through.

As the test began, he put aside any thought of amusement and automatically became the "Examiner." The person in the chair was the "Subject." There was no room for levity. This was serious business.

After going through the questions normally asked on the first chart, he asked one more that wasn't standard. "Do you have any kind of material on any part of your body in an attempt to beat this test?"

The cardio pen pegged out at the top of its parameter, indicating a rise in blood pressure, while the pneumo pens marked a straight line, an apnea, an involuntary cessation of breathing.

It was eight seconds before the subject offered a weak, "Yes."

Luke concluded the test, released the air in the cuff, and tore off the length of chart that told the story of the conflict going on between the subject's mind and body.

"So, what's going on with the foil?" he asked as if he didn't know.

"I'd heard that if I wore aluminum foil, the polygraph wouldn't work," the subject said dejectedly. "I guess I was wrong."

"Have you done things that would get you disqualified? Is that why you tried to beat the test?" Luke glanced first at the chart and then at the subject.

"No sir. I've never done anything," Bitner replied. "I don't know why I used the foil. I really didn't have reason to. I'm sorry I did. Will that be held against me?"

"Yes, I'm afraid it will." Luke stood up and began unhooking the polygraph attachments. "We have to be able to trust our employees, and you've already demonstrated a reason for us to distrust you. You might want to tell others that nothing works except telling the truth."

He removed all of the attachments and opened the door before turning to address the young man with the foil-wrapped legs. "Now, I'm not suggesting that just because a person is truthful, they're going to be hired. I'm saying that if a person is *not* truthful, they will be automatically rejected. So a person has nothing to lose by being honest."

As with all test subjects, Luke shook his hand and wished him a good life.

The rest of the day has to get better. I doubt things can get any more weird.

Luke returned to his office to find Captain Dennis Berk pacing aggressively. Berk was a detective captain with nearly thirty years on the job. His short, misshapen body, coincided with his surly attitude. And his closely cropped graying hair made his ears look larger than normal. A wide mouth and fat lips below a bushy mustache reminded Luke of a walrus he'd seen at Sea World in San Diego.

"Good morning Captain," Luke said. "What can I do for you?"

"You can quit accusing my detective of being dirty," Berk shot back. He quickly approached Luke, his jaw tightly clenched.

The words caught Luke by surprise. "What are you talking about?"

Captain Berk's face turned beet-red, and for a minute, it appeared as though he might bust a blood vessel or start swinging his fists. Luke backed up a step and took a seat. He learned a long time ago that the best way to diffuse an escalating situation is to remain calm and give the other person some room. He towered over the captain when standing, and he didn't want to appear confrontational.

Berk continued to rant. "Alfred Jones is one of my best detectives," he growled as he glared at Luke. "And you and that damned machine accuse him of being crooked. If he's crooked, then I'm crooked. What the hell do you think you're doing in there? You people get a little power and you let it go to your head. I want a retraction on the report where you said he was lying." Berk jabbed a finger in Luke's direction, his head thrust forward like a turtle poking out of its shell.

"There were reactions indicative of deception and in my opinion, Alfred Jones is not telling the truth. That was my opinion yesterday, it's the same today, and it will be the same tomorrow. I can't change the results," Luke countered, his voice more calm than the emotion he was feeling.

"I'm going to the chief with this," Berk growled as he stormed out. "We'll see who changes what."

"Berk the jerk," Luke said softly as he repeated the title some subordinates had bestowed on their captain. He'd never put much stock in it, figuring it had been coined by some disgruntled employees. But now, he agreed with them.

Maybe if I threw Mr. Walrus a fish, he'd be easier to get along with.

Luke had to smile at his observation. He considered reporting the incident to his boss, but Lieutenant Sloan was out of the office again all day so he decided to let it pass. He'd never gone to his boss with a complaint about another supervisor. He could stand on his own two feet and didn't need someone intervening on his behalf. Besides, he didn't have time for the distraction. He still had some applicants and a criminal test to do.

Merle walked in as Luke downed his last gulp of coffee and was preparing for another applicant test.

"You should have been here earlier," Luke said as Merle took a seat and rolled a sheet of paper into his typewriter. "Captain Berk wants me to quit accusing his ace detective of being dirty, and to change the results of a test I did last Friday. He thinks I don't know what I'm doing. I have to agree with him there...I don't." Luke said. He pulled the file of Detective Alfred Jones and showed Merle the charts.

The veteran examiner studied the charts for a few minutes

before throwing them on the desk in Luke's direction. "That man belongs in jail," he said. "And if his boss is covering for him, he belongs there with him."

"I don't think Berk is covering for him. I think he's just incompetent, and this detective is his bread and butter." Luke folded the charts and slipped them back in the file.

"Well, I've known Dennis Berk a few years," Merle said, a look of scorn on his craggy face. "He's a classic example of someone with the Napoleon complex. He tries to make up for his short stature by talking big. You can't let people sway your opinion. Go by what's on the chart, not by what someone thinks who has no knowledge of the polygraph." The last sentence was barely out of his mouth before he began hammering away on his typewriter.

Luke was always amazed at Merle's typing skills. He typed faster with two fingers than many secretaries who used both hands. He nodded in agreement with Merle's assessment, and strolled to the lobby to get his next "victim."

CHAPTER THIRTY-FIVE

The following morning, while the examiners chatted over their morning coffee, the phone rang. It was Assistant Chief Reginald Parker.

"Sergeant Canfield, I read your report on Detective Alfred Jones. I have Captain Berk in my office. He thinks Jones didn't get a fair test. We'll be right over to discuss the matter with you."

"Yes, sir," Luke replied, as he slowly cradled the phone. He glanced at Merle, then back at the phone. "Gee. Can you believe that someone is unhappy with one of my tests?" he asked facetiously. "Chief Parker and Captain Berk are coming over to correct the problem. Hey, maybe they'll determine I'm too incompetent to run polygraphs and send me back to the field."

Merle looked at his protégé and smirked. "That's one of the problems of having the polygraph section on the same floor as the chief's office. It's too easy for them to walk over anytime they like. So, Napoleon, himself, is coming over to mingle with us peasants? Well, you'd better get used to it. You're going to be second-guessed nearly every day. The opinions we render are always unpopular to someone. It all depends on whose ox is being gored. If they didn't have a horse in the race, they wouldn't care who won."

Luke noticed Merle didn't address his comment about being sent back to the field.

***

"Good morning," Assistant Chief Parker said cheerfully as he and Captain Berk entered the polygraph office. "How's it going this morning?"

Parker was a tall man, neat and trim, with white hair that made him look more like a grandfather than a police officer. He spoke in a low tone, and commanded respect just by his demeanor.

Before Luke could respond, Merle broke in. "Well, it was going fine until you two showed up. We were sitting here having a cup of coffee and wondering what we were going to do with all the free time on our hands." He mockingly waved his coffee cup in the direction of the pair as he continued with his sarcastic comments. "I don't know how we'd have the nerve to collect our paychecks without the brass coming in and giving us something to do once in a while."

Chief Parker chuckled. "Well, I'm glad you're so pleased to see us. I'll have to drop by more often. Anyway, it's good to see you too, Merle, but we have business with your sergeant. We'd better get to it so you can get back to your coffee. I never like to keep a man from his mission."

Luke pulled the file of Alfred Jones and ushered the two men into his office. After they were seated, he spread the polygraph charts across his desk and went over the questions he'd asked Jones.

He pointed out the reactions as he was speaking. "I'm convinced that he was deceptive to…"

"Those are not good questions," Captain Berk snorted. "Hell, *I'd* react to those questions myself, the way they were worded. You didn't give him a chance to explain what he was thinking. He probably could have explained it."

Luke had to bite his tongue to keep from blurting out what *he* was thinking. *I don't doubt you'd react to the questions. Maybe you ought to be tested too.* Instead, he calmly said, "I questioned him about the reactions and he denied everything. I don't usually interrogate employees on internal matters, but maybe I should have with this one."

"Do you have a problem with retesting him?" Parker asked.

"But this time, I'll make up the questions and I'll sit in to make sure the test is handled right," Berk interjected.

"I'll be happy to formulate the questions with your input, but no one sits in who isn't a polygraph examiner," Luke said as he pulled out a legal pad.

If pushed, he'd refuse to do the test and take his punishment for insubordination rather than give in to Berk's demands.

He turned to Chief Parker who had stepped aside during the heated exchange between the captain and sergeant.

"Here's what we'll do," Parker said with a tone of finality. "The three of us will formulate some questions. I agree that only polygraph examiners should be present during a test. Sergeant Canfield will retest Jones, using the questions that we come up with, and we'll see how it goes from there."

After the questions were constructed and agreed upon, Parker turned to Luke. "When can you do the retest?"

"The first thing tomorrow morning," came the reply.

Captain Berk nodded approval and the two men walked out. Luke had won the battle of wills and kept Berk out of the polygraph room. Having to retest Jones was of no consequence.

Hell, I'd have done it anyway, even if Jones himself had asked me.

***

When Alfred Jones came in for his retest, Luke decided not to ask him why he'd told his boss that he hadn't been given an opportunity to explain his deceptive reactions. He didn't want the subject too worked up. He made up his mind, however, that his policy of not interrogating employees was no longer in force. This time, Jones wasn't leaving the polygraph room without a confession.

After going over the questions with Detective Jones, Luke tried small talk to put the subject more at ease, but the detective wasn't interested in carrying on a conversation. He'd been on the other side of the desk too long to fall for that. Luke smiled at the thought. It was alright with him. He wasn't much for small talk either, unless it would get him the truth.

Swish. Swish. Swish. Swish. The pens sang their cadence as the chart paper rolled. It had insidiously become the signal for Luke to leave the down-to-earth every day aspect of his being and become the *Examiner*. Jones was the *Subject*.

Just as in the previous encounter, and just as expected, reactions indicative of deception were noted to all of the relevant questions.

Luke gave his "end of test" speech and turned the knob that released pressure in the cuff. He tore off the length of chart and spread it out on the desk, glancing down at the chart before fixing his attention on the subject. It was a ritual: slow; methodical. Each deliberate movement was designed to provoke apprehension, and even fear, in the subject.

"Al," he said in a soft, calm voice, "You could take a hundred of these tests and unless you're completely truthful, they will all come out the same."

Jones stared at him. "I don't..."

Luke cut him off with a wave of his hand. "Don't say anything unless you're prepared to tell the truth," Luke said quietly. He continued to talk non-stop, explaining how the body reacts when a lie is told, and how physical, as well as emotional problems develop from the stress associated with lying.

He was following procedure drummed into his head during polygraph school. *During an interrogation, it is important to never let the subject say anything unless it is a confession. Always shut him up, either verbally or with a wave of your hand. Never let him deny. No matter what, never let him deny.*

He could still hear Hardison's gravelly voice echoing through his mind, could see his sallow face and thin lips mouthing the words. *Never let the subject deny.*

After nearly five minutes of constant talking and getting no acceptable response, Luke leaned back in his chair, hoisted his legs to the top edge of the desk and laced his hands behind his head. He needed to think.

Two minutes passed. Then three. Out of the corner of his eye, he noticed Jones had relaxed his body and slouched in his chair. That was the signal he was looking for, an unintended gesture that the will, as well as the body, was weakening.

Luke slowly and deliberately lowered his feet to the floor and moved his chair around the end of the desk so that his knee was within inches of the subject. Every move made from this point on must be slow and deliberate, the voice in his head dictated.

Luke realized Jones knew what was coming. Hell, he'd probably followed the same procedure himself during interrogations. His body language explained his feelings. He physically tried to escape the psychological danger by shifting his body back in his chair. He moved his leg to avoid touching, but he didn't jerk it away.

He's tiring. The thought entered Luke's head without conscious effort. He placed his hand closer to Jones's right arm and looked into his eyes. The subject slowly lowered his gaze.

"Al," Luke said. "I've given you two tests and they both came out the same. You're a smart man. You know that I know what you've been doing. I'm sure you didn't hire on with the intention of dishonoring the badge. I can tell more about you in one test than you know about yourself. You are an honorable man, Al, but you have done a dishonorable thing."

Luke sat quietly to give Jones time to process the fact that the game was up and he could no longer hide the betrayal of his oath.

When there was no reply, the examiner continued. "Nothing is free. It may appear to be for a while, but then, down the road there's a tollbooth. You can't turn back. You pay your money and you take your chances that there won't be another and another down the line."

Luke again hesitated, but all the while he was talking, he kept inching closer until there was no longer room for the subject to pull away. "You're a responsible adult, Al. If you don't face your responsibilities now and start over with a clean slate, you'll be dogged with this issue the rest of your life. Get it over with. Take your punishment and move on. Hell, with what Captain Berk thinks about you, you could probably commit murder and he'd still think you were the greatest thing since the cream separator." Luke immediately regretted using the cream separator as an example. *He probably doesn't even know what the hell it is.*

Detective Jones glanced around the room and up at the ceiling before responding. His voice was dry, cracked. "The only reason Captain Berk would come to my defense, is because I... and Dennis Creech...and maybe a couple others...are keeping his performance rating up that his pay raise is based on. If it wasn't for that, he wouldn't give me the time of day."

Luke remained silent for a few minutes. *Dennis Creech.* He hadn't heard that name mentioned since his transfer to Personnel.

They were on the same patrol squad in Sunnyslope when Luke was a probationer. And even though it was years ago, it still rankled him that Creech had always called him rookie.

Creech seemed smart enough. It was no surprise that he was tapped for detectives, but it was surprising that he'd never gotten promoted. There was always a thought in the back of Luke's mind that his former squad member was far more capable then he let on, and would one day be his boss. That was always the way things seemed to work out.

Luke grimaced as he tried to dismiss the name from his mind. He had more important things to think about than Dennis Creech. He had a suspected dirty cop to confront, and he wasn't quite sure how to go about it.

Then, a detached feeling came over him. It started in his head and continued down his chest, through his shoulders and into his arms. He was like the instrument embedded in the top of the desk–without feelings–neither tired nor energetic, hungry nor full, thirsty nor hydrated. He didn't need it and he didn't want it, but it was taking over nonetheless. He was in interrogation mode.

"Sometimes, we get caught up in things that we are unable to control." Luke could hear what he was saying, but the words seemed to come from his whole body instead of his mouth. "It's like we are trapped in a whirlpool. At first, we are on the edge and the water is swirling slowly. We could step out at that point, but something draws us in to the swirling mass from which there is no escape. We reach out for help. Maybe there is someone who will give us a hand...and maybe there is not."

He hesitated as he eyed the face of the subject in an attempt to determine if his words were hitting their mark. Jones remained solemn-faced; unresponsive.

Luke continued. "Others witness our struggle. There is someone with a pole who we thought was giving us a helping hand, but in reality, is pushing us deeper into the swirling water. So...is it our fault that we got swept in? Yes, to begin with. But are we totally to blame? No, we are not. All those people who did nothing to save us are equally to blame."

His cadence increased. The words spilled out of his mouth like oats from a threshing machine. "But wait a minute. We can barely see, but someone is standing at the edge of the swirling mass, throwing us a lifeline, trying to help us so we don't go down forever. That person cares about our welfare. Now, it is up to us whether we choose to grab the line and save ourselves. It is up to us. That person cannot save us if we do not grab the line."

Luke stopped talking. The silence in the room was stifling. The tension was palpable. Neither man seemed to breathe. Both appeared to be in a hypnotic trance that transcended the reason for their presence.

The examiner had called upon his own experience without

conscious awareness. He seemed to always be in a situation he couldn't get out of. And so far, no one has thrown him a lifeline.

"Anyway," Luke continued, as he reverted to normal presence. "Has this been going on a long time, you giving information on a search warrant, or did it just start recently?"

Detective Alfred Jones didn't respond. He kept staring straight ahead. His body was as rigid as the marble statues that graced the halls of the city library.

Luke was about to continue with the interrogation process when Jones looked down at the floor and began to speak, his voice hoarse, barely audible. Luke had to lean forward and strain to catch what he was saying.

"My cousin has been in trouble before. He's trying to support his mother. She pleaded with me to keep him out of trouble. He said he was going to quit dealing in stolen property. I wanted to give him a chance to go straight...so...I told him they were going to search his place."

"How many times did you tell him?" Luke asked.

"Twice," the Detective responded. "The idiot still continued buying and selling stolen property. I thought I would give him another chance. He isn't a bad kid. He's just screwed up."

"What did he give you for helping him?" Luke asked.

"He brought a pair of stereo speakers over. I told him I didn't want them, but he left them anyway." Jones said.

"Where are the speakers now?"

"They were laying around for a long time and I finally hooked them up to a stereo in my living room."

"Did he give you anything else?"

Jones turned to face the examiner, his eyes moist. He opened his mouth as if to reply, but quickly closed it. He turned back to the front and shifted his position. He sat quietly for a minute. "I don't think I want to say anything more," he said.

"One last question. Did you give anyone besides your cousin information about a search warrant?" Luke gave it one last shot to gain as much information as he could.

"I don't want to say anything more. Unhook me," Jones said as he raised his arm with the cuff attached.

Luke unhooked the attachments and extended his hand. Jones ignored the gesture.

"Good luck Al. You might want to talk with internal affairs, or at least with Captain Berk, and get this situation straightened out. Tell the whole truth. Start over and don't let yourself get caught up with friends and relatives who are bad influences."

Alfred Jones shuffled out of the polygraph room and headed for the elevator. Luke watched as the detective punched the button for the second floor.

Guess he thinks his best chance is with the captain. Luke gathered his charts and stood looking at the instrument that had just determined the fate of another human being. It had been a life changing moment for an employee who would soon be just another statistic.

Since being a detective was merely an assignment, rather than a promotion, Jones could easily be transferred back to uniformed patrol. But Luke suspected that the detective would be facing termination, and maybe even arrest. All because the polygraph indicated deception.

All because Hardison calibrated me like he calibrated his instrument. The truth matters above all else. Regardless of the consequence, always seek the truth.

CHAPTER THIRTY-SIX

Nearly a year had passed since polygraph school, and Luke continued working more and more and interacting with his family less and less. His mind was filled with applicant admissions and criminal confessions. There wasn't room for anything else.

"I'm going to try to get through at a reasonable hour tonight," he kept telling himself. He'd made that promise before, but something always got in the way. But this day was different. It was Thursday, and Thursdays had always been lucky for him. His horoscope said so. Sagittarians were born lucky.

The day went well. So well in fact that he finished ahead of schedule. He wrapped up his last test around four-thirty, so he had plenty of time to run over to the office supply store and back before end of shift. He'd make it home before six. He called his wife to tell her the good news.

Emily responded as she usually did when discussing his work. "Don't tell me they're letting you come home at a decent hour. What happened? Did the world suddenly become truthful or did you just run out of ink?" Without waiting for a response, she continued. "I don't care why you're getting off early. I'm just glad you are, and I'm especially glad I won't have to cook anything. Let's go to Manuel's. I'm dying for some Mexican food."

"That sounds good to me. Mexican food it is," Luke replied. "If you can round up the kids, they can go along. I'll be leaving here shortly after five. See you soon."

Luke got his needed supplies and hurried back to the office. He'd put them away tomorrow when he had more time. Tonight, it was home early and out to dinner.

As he was preparing to leave the office, his phone rang. He hesitated before picking it up. He knew it couldn't be good news, and he didn't want anything to interfere with him getting home early. But the ingrained attitude of always acting responsibly surpassed personal desire. It always had, ever since that day in the barn.

He picked up the phone. "Polygraph, Sergeant Canfield."

"This is Chief Tucker. Is Merle there?"

Luke was surprised to hear the chief's voice. He never called anyone directly. His secretary placed the call and got the person on the phone before the chief came on.

"Hi Chief," Luke responded. "Merle has gone home. Is there anything I can do for you?" He hoped the chief would say there wasn't.

"Yes, stand by. I'll be right over. I need a polygraph on one of my staff and it can't wait."

The room suddenly became very warm. Beads of sweat popped out on Luke's forehead. He pulled out his handkerchief and wiped his face before trying to make his voice sound calmer than his body was feeling. "I can call Merle at home and he can be back here in half an hour," he said, hoping the chief would agree.

"That won't be necessary. You can do the test. We'll be right there." The chief's voice sounded serious, matter of fact.

"Yes sir. I'll be here."

Luke hadn't conducted an internal examination of a superior officer before and he was worried about making a mistake. He made sure the ink bottles were full and the pens were operational. He'd failed to thoroughly rinse the pens on a previous occasion, and the ink dried and plugged them solid. He had to take them home and boil them out before they would work again.

He got out the proper forms: a felt pen to mark his chart, and his famous pencil with the worn eraser. He realized that being a staff officer meant it would be a veteran he was about to test. He undoubtedly knew all the tricks of the trade. But that was his routine, regardless of whom he tested. He sat down to wait for the chief, praying that by some miracle, Merle Broone would walk through the door.

***

It was a little after five-thirty when Chief Tucker walked in, accompanied by Major Lymon Garrison.

Alvin Tucker was a man of about sixty who looked like he could still fill his old college linebacker position. A scar across his face just below his right eye, was a reminder of an opponent's cleat that had caught him when his helmet rolled off. Luke had witnessed him speak at various functions and the chief frequently turned his head so the scar would show. He seemed to wear it like a badge of courage.

Luke greeted both officers and offered them seats. He hadn't spoken with Major Garrison since transferring out of the major's command. It was good to see him again, even though he was the one who had practically forced Luke into the polygraph business.

After the initial greetings, Chief Tucker asked Garrison to wait outside. After the major left the room, Tucker sat for a minute, giving Luke the once over. "I want you to polygraph Major Garrison," he said.

Luke was at a loss for words. He didn't know what to say. The relentless ringing in his ears drowned out the drumbeat of his pounding heart. He knew the chief was talking, but the words didn't register. His mind went blank. He was being set up.

This has got to be a test for me. It's too much of a coincidence that Merle would go home early, and then the chief would call and want one of his staff polygraphed. Not only that, but the person I'm supposed to test is the same one who sent me to polygraph school. This is just too damned weird to be legitimate.

"Is that all the information you need to conduct a polygraph?"

Somewhere in his mental haze, Luke suddenly realized the chief was asking him something.

"I'm sorry chief. I guess I was thinking too far ahead. Would you repeat what you were telling me? I want to make sure I understand everything so I can conduct an accurate examination."

The chief remained silent for a minute. Luke had seen Tucker's face turn red when he was about to lose his temper. It was a deep crimson now. His eyes narrowed and his lips tightened to the point where it looked like his mouth was sewn shut. Luke wished it were. The chief wasn't used to repeating himself, especially to a sergeant.

Luke braced for a torrent of words best kept on the football field, but instead, the chief calmly repeated the reason for the test.

"Major Garrison is accused of tipping off a couple of prostitutes on East Van Buren that some vice officers were about to arrest. The officers reported to their supervisor that the major was seen talking with the women a few minutes prior to their approach. The women seemed to know that the supposed clients were vice officers. The officers were certain Major Garrison tipped the women off."

Luke was having trouble accepting the information. But the chief was dead serious, and the story sounded credible.

"What do you think about the possibility of Major Garrison having done what the vice officers suspect?" Luke asked.

"I have no pre-conceived notions. I'm treating this like any other complaint, and I'm relying on a polygraph test to determine if the investigation should proceed."

The chief got up to leave. "Is there anything else you need?"

"No, sir," Luke replied.

"I'll be in my office," the chief said as he walked to the door. "Call me with the results of the test?"

Luke took a deep breath, and while he still wasn't fully convinced that it wasn't a setup, he invited Major Garrison in, motioning to the subject's chair as he did so.

"How are you doing, Sergeant?" the major asked as he took his seat. "I hear you've been busy. Am I your first internal?"

"No, I'm afraid not," Luke replied. "These tests happen more often than I like, but a test is a test. It doesn't matter who is tested or what type it is."

Luke wished he could believe that, but an internal test was always more intense and more difficult, especially when it involved a person as respected as Major Garrison.

Luke sat quietly for a minute, trying to get his mind to accept the situation. "When you sent me to polygraph school, you probably didn't expect that one day I'd be giving *you* a polygraph. There's a bit of irony in that don't you think?"

The major smiled. "Yes, I guess there is."

After obtaining the necessary preliminary information–name, birthdate and medication history, Luke said, "Tell me why you're here to take a polygraph."

"Didn't the chief explain it to you?" asked the major with raised eyebrows.

"Yes," said Luke, "but I need your version. I still have to do things by the book. I have to follow protocol in order to make sure I get everything right. I'm required to ask for your understanding of the reason for the test as well as your version of events prior to the actual examination."

"A couple of vice officers reported to their supervisor that I tipped off two prostitutes they were trying to set up for arrest," Garrison said. "I knew the two women were hookers. I'd busted both of them years before, but I hadn't bothered them for some time because they were supplying me with information about other criminal activity going on in the area. I was unaware that the undercover officers were about to entice them to make an offer and arrest them for prostitution."

Luke knew he should be writing all of this down, but he'd already heard it from the chief, and the major had repeated basically what the chief had already told him.

"Had I known," the major continued, "I would have told the vice guys to hold off for a while. Both women have been in the business a long time and they can spot an undercover a mile away. The officers never asked me why I was talking with the prostitutes, they just assumed I was tipping them off."

"Why do you think they reported the incident instead of discussing it with you?" Luke asked.

"I suspect it was because they weren't having much luck in their undercover capacity and saw an opportunity to blame their poor police work on a supervisor. But that's only my assumption," the major added.

The major's explanation made sense. It was readily believed by many supervisors that some employees were always on the lookout for an "I gotcha." It made the employee look better in the eyes of their peers if they could get a supervisor in trouble.

It was usually the incompetent employees who tried to shift the blame on a supervisor for their own shortcomings. Once they reported a supervisor infraction, the reporting employee could skate for a long time because no supervisor wanted to take a chance on being accused of retaliation.

There were also incidents, however, in which nothing was done with an incompetent supervisor, no matter how many complaints came in from subordinates. In fact, some of the worst seemed to gain a faster track to promotion. Luke had worked for at least two who fit that distinction. But Major Garrison certainly wasn't one of those.

Luke slowly and carefully developed a list of questions and discussed them with Garrison to make sure he understood and approved of each one. After a few minor adjustments, the major agreed that the questions were specific, fair, and appropriate.

Luke was still uneasy about conducting the polygraph, but he had stalled long enough. It was time "to put up or shut up," as he had often heard people say.

He hooked up the attachments, explaining each as he placed them in the proper location on Garrison's body.

He resumed his position behind the desk and flipped the switch that set the chart paper in motion. He inflated the blood pressure cuff just enough to get an accurate reading. There was no need to cause any more discomfort to the major than he had already endured.

The pens were set to their proper locations and the red ink trailed their up and down movements in cadence with the subject's vital functions.

Once the chart began to roll, paranoid thoughts of being set up, and any apprehension Luke felt when he was first called by the chief, faded away. He had no feelings, either good or bad. He was totally neutral, just like the instrument. *Just like Doctor Nathan Hardison.*

Luke spoke in a calm, even tone, as he delivered the stock statement that he used for every test, regardless of the type. He enunciated each word carefully so there would be no doubt as to its meaning. "I am going to begin. I am going to be asking you some questions. Just answer the questions by yes or by no. Don't do any other talking. Do not move throughout the test, and... don't shake your head when you answer."

He immediately noticed irregularities in the cardio tracing. The amplitude was subdued in its upward movements while the downward tracing fell faster than normal. He knew something was wrong. He just didn't know what. Maybe the major had taken something to reduce a reaction. No, not him. Someone else maybe, but not Garrison. Maybe Luke didn't smooth the cuff out well enough after wrapping it around the major's arm. It would eventually correct itself. He continued.

"Is your first name Lymon?"

"Yes." Garrison's tone was resigned.

Luke heard an octave lower in voice inflection than the major used during the pretest interview. The question was obviously troubling, but the chart failed to register a change. It was no secret that Major Garrison didn't like his first name and preferred being called by his rank.

"Do you live in Phoenix?"

"Yes."

"Do you intend to try to lie during this test?"

"No."

"Have you told me the whole truth about this matter?"

"Yes."

What the hell is happening? Luke asked himself. *What am I doing wrong? I'm getting nothing readable.*

"Do you drink coffee?"

"Yes."

"Do you drink beer?"

"Yes."

"Did you speak with the two prostitutes in question, solely for the purpose of obtaining information from them?"

"Yes."

"Did you tell the women in question that the undercover officers were cops?"

"No."

"Are you attempting to withhold any information about this matter?"

"No."

"Remain still. I'll release the pressure on your arm in just a few seconds."

Luke made the necessary markings, stopped the chart from moving, and tore off a section. He studied it carefully. After getting past the question about his name, the major's tone of voice never varied. His answers were emphatic, but not overly so. He demonstrated no more concern than before the test began.

Luke couldn't figure out why the tracings lacked a sharper contrast. The changes were minimal. He mentally reviewed the procedure.

With any polygraph examination, there were always some reactions, even when a subject was truthful. The mere fact that the subject was *suspected* of wrong-doing caused reactions to one or more questions. Sometimes the biggest reaction was to an irrelevant question, such as "Do you smoke," or "Have you ever been drunk?"

It was the duty of the examiner to determine truthfulness or deception based on total chart evaluation, including reactions to irrelevant questions. Sometimes, voice inflection was sufficient to require a more careful examination of the chart.

On Garrison's test, the only change in voice inflection occurred when asked if his name was Lymon. Luke would have to go with that. After all, Major Garrison was one of the most respected members of the department, and Luke liked him.

If you like him, he's probably lying to you. Luke jerked his head up and scanned the room. Doctor Hardison's haunting voice came through as clearly as it had the first time Luke heard his cautionary words. He tried to ignore it. He knew how to tell if someone was lying. He didn't have to be reminded.

But the warning wouldn't go away. He had to shake it. "There was some reaction to your name. Why is that?" Luke asked, knowing full well why the major reacted to the question. He needed all the psychological advantage he could get, and he wanted to prove to the subject early on that the polygraph worked, even though he wasn't sure at the moment.

Garrison slowly turned to face the sergeant, a smile flickered at the corners of his mouth. "Well...I never really cared for the name my mother gave me."

Luke usually ran two charts when testing for a specific issue. Sometimes he asked the same questions on the second chart and compared reactions. He followed that procedure since the questions adequately covered the situation.

The second test proved as unreliable as the first. He'd exhausted his list of questions with no significant reactions. Without proof that Garrison was capable of reacting, he'd be forced to call the examination inconclusive. Even the thought was unacceptable.

He gave his end of test speech, but he didn't stop the chart or release pressure on the cuff.

"I'm going to ask you one more question. You don't have to answer if you don't want to." Luke made his tone of voice sound as suspenseful as a creaky door. It didn't matter if the subject answered verbally or not. All he was interested in was a physiological response that would show the subject was capable of reacting.

"Have you ever deliberately violated departmental policy?" His tone was sharp, accusing.

Garrison hesitated before answering. "Yes."

That question always produced a considerable reaction regardless of whether the subject answered truthfully or not. This time, it barely registered. What was he going to do now? He had to call the test inconclusive. He released the air from the cuff and flipped the switch that stopped the chart scroll.

"That last question is not included in my report. It's called a control question. You weren't reacting much to any of the questions and it was thrown in to prove you were capable of reacting," Luke hurriedly explained. He didn't want the major upset with him for asking a question they hadn't gone over beforehand. "I don't know of anyone who hasn't violated department policy, so it makes a good control question."

Anyone except my old lieutenant.

He thought about Lieutenant Jerry Harvy, his boss when he

was a squad sergeant in Maryvale. The "Book," everyone called him, because of his ability to quote chapter and verse of the policy manual, and his unbending insistence to follow its guidelines.

"That's OK," Garrison said, as he turned to face Luke with the same reluctant smile teasing the corners of his mouth. "I'll tell you about it anyway so you won't wonder what I might have done. You can report it if you need to, but I'd do the same thing again."

Garrison shifted his position and lifted his left hand. He appeared to study the electrodes wrapped around his fingers before tapping them lightly on the wooden arm of the chair. Many subjects had gazed questionably at the galvo attachments, but this was the first time anyone had made a tapping sound. Was the major nervous? He didn't act like it. Maybe he just needed time to get his thoughts together like others before him.

The examiner's silent inquiry would have to wait. Garrison was back on track. His voice was clear, matter-of-fact, self-assured. "Some years back, when I was a lieutenant, I juggled an officer's time sheet. It wasn't an actual falsification of public records, but it was probably pretty close."

The major stopped talking and stared directly at Luke as if trying to read his thoughts. Luke stared back, trying hard not to show approval or disapproval. He couldn't believe what he was hearing. Never in a million years would he think the major was even capable of such a thing.

Luke glanced at the chart. He didn't want the major to see the disappointment he was feeling. When he again looked up, Garrison was no longer looking his way. Luke was relieved.

"I had a sergeant working for me who had terminal cancer," Garrison slowly continued. "He'd used up all of his sick leave and vacation leave. When he was unable to return to work, I was ordered by my captain to terminate his employment. But the man had a wife and two little kids. His wife had to quit her job to care for the family, and I couldn't just cut them off with no income. I told my boss I would take care of it, but instead of firing the man, I carried him present for a few more months until his death."

"What about his squad?" Luke asked. "Didn't they question the absence of their sergeant?"

"I, along with one of the other squad sergeants, covered his duties," Garrison replied. "I told the squad that their sergeant was on light duty and working from home. I sent some "make work" over to his house, and convinced myself that he was still doing a day's work. He was just doing it at home instead of at the station."

The major became silent as he turned to face the wall to his front. Luke also remained silent as he tried to determine if the major was thinking about the situation he'd just explained, or about the possible repercussions of his decision to violate a direct order.

Luke thought it a shame that there wasn't something legitimate the department could do for employees who found themselves in similar situations.

"I know my opinion doesn't count for much," Luke said, "but I see no other way than what you did. And since that last question is not considered relevant to the issue for which you were tested, neither are your comments. None of that will be reported."

Luke unhooked the major and thanked him for his cooperation. Garrison nodded his head and walked out the door, never asking if he had passed the test or not. Most people asked. The only ones who didn't were those who were sure of their truthfulness. They didn't care what the instrument registered.

Neither did the major question whether or not Luke would honor his commitment to keep their conversation about the dying sergeant confidential. Did he trust Luke that much, or did he even care if the information got out?

A smile came to Luke's face as he wondered what control question he would ask if he ever tested Lieutenant Jerry Harvy. He doubted his former lieutenant would ever commit a policy violation, no matter what the circumstance.

Luke heaved a sigh as he slumped into his chair, his body as limp as an old rag. He badly needed a cup of coffee, but he didn't have the strength to get one. He sat with eyes closed, resting his head on leaden arms that he somehow managed to raise high enough to reach the top of the desk. How was he going to call this one? What was he going to tell the chief?

***

Emily slipped on a clean blouse and a hip-hugging pair of slacks. She checked herself in the bathroom mirror, ran a brush through her curly blonde hair and stopped mid-stroke. A frightening site met her eyes. A gray hair. She had a gray hair. She pulled it closer. How had that happened? She wasn't old enough to have gray hair.

She cringed as she jerked it loose and peered closer. Sure enough. It was gray. She quickly examined the rest, pulling section after section around to the front. No others were found. She breathed a sigh of relief. "I guess I shouldn't be surprised," she murmured. "Luke is frustrating enough to give any woman gray hair." But he was getting home early tonight. The family would be having dinner together, and for the present, all was forgiven.

"Do you think dad will make it home early like he said?" Amy put into words what everyone was obviously thinking.

"Well, he said he would. It sounded like he was through for the day so maybe this time he will." Although it was often difficult, Emily spoke in a positive tone when discussing their father's late hours with the kids.

"It'll be nice to all go out together again," Becky said as she twirled the long strands of brown hair gracing her shoulders. "And it's super nice that I got out of class early. Dad sure works a lot. I wish there was some way I could help him. He always looks tired."

"He's always late when we have plans," Michael whined. "He needs to just tell them he's not going to work more than eight hours a day. I don't think he ever complains. I don't know what he's afraid of. He doesn't like the job anyway, so why doesn't he just do something else? He..."

"Michael, I'm sure your father didn't plan on being late. He must have a good reason. Be a little more considerate, please." Emily was struggling to keep her emotions in check. She was much more successful in doing so with the children than when she and Luke were alone. "I know you and Steve planned to shoot some pool, but your friend will just have to wait, along with the rest of us."

Emily grimaced. Maybe she should have let him go to his friend's house. He was like his dad. If he didn't get his own way, he'd sulk until everyone around him was miserable too.

Emily glanced at the clock. A little after six. If Luke got home by six-thirty and they went to Manuel's, they should be home no later than eight. Plenty of time for a shower and a little television before bed.

Seven o'clock and still no sign of her husband. Maybe the

traffic was bad and he was on his way.

Seven-thirty. Then eight. Nothing. Not even a phone call. At first she was anxious, then angry. But now she was worried. He would have called if he could. He always had. Maybe he'd had an accident and couldn't get to a phone. No, she would have heard by now. Bad news always travels fast.

She pretended to be on her way to the bathroom, lingering near the window that overlooked the carport, the one she often peered through to see the passion vine. Her Buick Electra looked lonely out there by itself. She missed the old Chevy pickup that Luke drove.

"Mom, looking out the window a dozen times in the past half-hour isn't going to make him get here any faster." Becky's tone was impatient.

Emily flashed a brief smile. Her daughter was right of course, but it was funny, because all three kids made the same trip nearly as many times. "I guess you're right. He's going to get here when he gets here. I'm sure something came up at the last minute. He'd be here if he could."

Michael didn't attempt to hide his displeasure. "I could have played a dozen rounds of pool by now. Why do I have to stay home just because Dad can't get here on time?" He splayed himself on the couch, his arm hanging to the floor, his head propped on Amy's lap.

"Don't lay your big Charlie Brown head on me," Amy said as she hurriedly rose, letting his head drop to the cushion. She often referred to her brother by the Peanuts character when he did something displeasing, which, according to her, was most of the time.

***

Luke woke with a start. He wasn't sure how long he'd sat there. He must have gone to sleep. Or maybe he just passed out from exhaustion. "Damn! Seven-thirty," he muttered as he picked up the phone and dialed the chief's office.

"Chief Tucker." The voice sounded irritated.

"Hi Chief," Luke said in his best official sounding voice. "This is Sergeant Canfield. I finished the test on Major Garrison."

Luke took a deep breath. Something was wrong with the way the instrument responded. Maybe it was the instrument or maybe it was the major. He had to make a decision quickly; he was on the phone with the chief. "There was no indication of deception to any of the relevant questions."

"OK. Very good. Thanks," Chief Tucker's tone was much softer than when he answered the phone. "There was no doubt in my mind that he was truthful. I just wanted to satisfy any doubts in the minds of others."

Luke smiled. That's not what the chief had said earlier. "I'll type up the report and bring it right over," Luke said.

"Bring the complete report, along with any hand-written notes that you made, and bring the charts too. I'll keep the file here in my desk." The chief's authoritative tone of voice reminded Luke of his old army drill sergeant. "Keep this confidential. I don't want you discussing this test with anyone," he cautioned.

"Yes, sir. We keep all tests confidential," Luke replied. He didn't mention the control question, or the answer it had elicited. All the chief needed to know was that his staff officer was truthful concerning the issue in question.

After dropping the file off to the chief, Luke returned to the polygraph room and tried to figure out why the instrument was not responding correctly. Was the problem with the instrument, with the major, or with himself? Maybe he'd wished so hard for the major to be truthful that he subconsciously made it happen. He decided to calibrate the instrument first thing in the morning.

He glanced at his watch. Nearly eight-thirty. He'd been so wrapped up in testing the major, he'd forgotten to call Emily and tell her he wouldn't be home early after all. She was going to be madder than a wet hen. How could he explain this one after telling her he was through for the day and would soon be home?

***

Emily knew the kids were getting more impatient by the minute. They were tired of waiting for their father. It was up to her to do something about it. "I'll tell you what we'll do. Let's all chip in and cook up something to eat. If your dad gets here before it's done, we'll save it for tomorrow and go eat Mexican food. If he gets home later, he'll be too tired to go out anyway."

Michael turned up his nose. "I'm not hungry. I'd rather go to Steve's and shoot some pool. And even if we did go out, I'd just have to sit there while everyone else ate."

Emily didn't like to buckle under once she decided on something, but there was no need for the whole family to suffer because of Luke's short-sightedness. "OK. You can go to Steve's, but be home no later than ten. Is that clear?"

"Yes, mom. Ten it..." Michael was out the door before the last word cleared his mouth.

After eating and clearing the table, Becky and Amy retreated to their rooms. Emily finished tidying up and had just settled down in front of the television when headlights flashed through the kitchen window. She glanced at the clock. Nine-thirty. Their husband and father had finally made it home.

***

Luke hesitated before going through the door. He couldn't blame Emily for being mad. If he weren't so tired, he'd be mad too.

"Sorry I'm late," he said, apologetically as he plodded into the family room and collapsed into his favorite chair without stopping to pour his usual glass of Scotch. "I was just going out the door when the chief called and ordered me to do a polygraph. He said it couldn't wait 'til morning. I just got through. Does anyone still want to get something to eat?" He was dog-tired and really didn't want to go back out, but he would, just to keep the peace.

"Was the telephone busy too? Is that why you couldn't call and tell us you were going to be late again?" Emily's sarcastic tone matched her drawn mouth.

At least she wasn't yelling. *Maybe if she keeps it down, the kids won't know we're fighting.* A thought was all he could manage as Luke tried to get his fatigued mind to respond.

He was too slow. Emily wasn't through. "Tonight was one of the few times when we were all together. Becky got home early and Michael didn't have a game, so we were all here but you. If we'd known you weren't going to show up, we'd have gone without you."

"I'm sorry, I..."

"It's OK. It's my fault for believing you'd be home early. I always fall for the same line. Maybe one day I'll learn." She turned back to the television.

Luke had to catch himself from blurting out a response. He wanted to strike back at Emily's selfish attitude. He wanted to tell her that he didn't work ten or twelve hours a day, six days a week because he wanted to. He did it because he was obligated to take care of his family, and the only way he could do that was to take care of his job. He wanted to rant and rave and throw things and scream at the top of his lungs. But as usual, he kept his emotions in check.

It was getting harder to do with each discussion they had about his work. Maybe one day he'd let loose, but not tonight. Fatigue wouldn't let him. He gobbled down some leftovers, stumbled to the bathroom, took a quick shower and flopped into bed. He was asleep as soon as his head hit the pillow.

***

The man he was chasing kept drifting in and out of the shadows. At times, he was within arms-reach. But each time Luke grabbed an arm, the sleeve was empty. He finally got the man cornered. They tussled and came face-to-face. Funny. The man looked exactly like him. How could that be? It was impossible. But maybe it *was* him. Maybe he was two people. Two personalities. A normal person when he wasn't running a test, and a psychic with the ability to peer into the subject's mind while in the polygraph room. It was too ridiculous to even consider. There must be another explanation. But the man kept calling his name.

"Luke...Luke...Wake up." Luke thrust his body upright. Emily's hand grasped him by the arm, shaking it gently.

"What? What is it?" he asked, his voice groggy. He wasn't sure if he was awake, or if it was just another part of his dream.

"Wake up." Emily's voice was loud. Insistent. "You have a phone call. Some sergeant wants to speak with you. He says it's important."

Luke rubbed his eyes and glanced at the clock. Eleven-thirty. "Don't tell me they want a polygraph at this time of night," he groused as he slipped out of bed and reached for the phone.

"Michael isn't home yet." Emily sounded worried. "He was supposed to be home by ten."

Luke gave her a disapproving look as he picked up the phone. He would deal with Michael tomorrow. Right now he had more pressing matters. "This is Luke. What's going on?"

"Hey Luke, this is Jerry Witt, burglary detail. Sorry to bother you this time of night. Your wife said you were sleeping. Are you awake now?"

"Hell no. I'm still asleep." Luke couldn't help being sarcastic with some idiot who woke him up and then asks if he's awake.

"We have your son in custody," Witt said.

The burglary detective's words shot through Luke's brain like a bolt of lightning. The autonomic nervous system that he'd studied so diligently was in overdrive. The parasympathetic portion had slammed the brakes on too hard. It shut him down. He couldn't think. His breath caught in his throat.

"Hello? Hello? Luke, you there?"

"Yaa." Luke managed to make a noise that substituted for a verbal response. It wasn't a conscious decision. It just came out because it was supposed to. That's what people do when asked a question. They respond.

"What for?"

"Burglary." The voice sounded official.

It wasn't just a word. It was a stab through the heart. It painted a picture of a broken window or smashed door, of property damage, of goods hauled out by the truckload. Luke had seen the results of many burglaries over the years. They weren't pretty.

"What did he burgle?" Luke was more awake now. More in control.

"He and another kid broke into a pop machine and took a bunch of pop." Sergeant Witt's tone was somber, as though it was something *really* serious.

Luke could have busted out laughing. He didn't dare of course. It wouldn't have been appropriate. But he was so relieved that it wasn't something more serious, he wanted to celebrate. He wasn't even sleepy anymore.

He sighed deeply, leaving him almost as breathless as when Sergeant Witt first mentioned burglary. Breaking into a pop machine was bad enough. It was still a felony. But it wasn't as bad as robbery or drugs, or...worse. He couldn't even consider, *or worse.* "Where can we pick him up?"

"You can't. He has to spend the night in Juvenile Detention. You can check with them in the morning to see when he'll be released."

"OK. Thanks for calling. I appreciate it."

"No problem. Sorry to bring you the bad news."

Luke stood silently after he hung up the phone. He didn't know how he was going to break the news to Emily.

She'd overheard part of the conversation and had already run to the medicine cabinet to load up on God knows what. He hoped whatever she took was fast acting.

Tears were rolling down her cheeks as she stood trembling. "What? Tell me what?" she stammered through quivering lips.

"It's not as bad as it sounds. Michael and another boy were caught taking some pop that didn't belong to them. They're being held overnight in juvenile detention to teach them a lesson. We can pick Michael up tomorrow."

He took Emily by the shoulders and wrapped his arms

around her, drawing her close. "So, it's not something *real* serious, like drugs or armed robbery." He tried to soften the blow as much as possible without completely distorting the facts. Hard telling how she'd react if he told her the charge was burglary.

"Oh my God! Oh my God! Michael arrested for stealing? Why would he steal pop? We have the refrigerator full. There must be some mistake. There's no need for him to steal pop. You call them back and tell them there must be some mistake. I can show them we have plenty of pop." The flood gates had opened. Tears gushed down her cheeks and spilled onto her nightgown. The thirsty cotton material soaked them up as fast as they fell.

"What's the matter with mom? Are you guys fighting?" Becky stepped into the bedroom. Her concerned and bewildered expression matched her tone of voice. Both hands were clasped to her ashen face.

"What's going on? Why is mom crying?" Amy was standing in the doorway. Strands of silky brown hair hung over her sleepy eyes.

"It's OK girls. It's nothing real serious. We just got a phone call saying Michael and Steve were caught taking pop they hadn't paid for. Michael has to stay overnight in Juvenile Detention to teach him a lesson, but we can get him tomorrow. Your mom and I feel bad about it."

Luke's voice was calm. His role as head of the household

had surfaced. Outwardly, he appeared to be in control. Inwardly, he was a bowl of jelly. He never felt so helpless. His wife and daughters were frightened and upset, and there wasn't a hell of a lot he could do about it. And his son was in jail. Arrested for burglary.

CHAPTER THIRTY-SEVEN

Clang! Clang! The sound of steel doors slamming shut brought a new round of tears from Emily. Luke put his hand on her shoulder. He tried to convince her to stay at home while he picked Michael up from the detention center, but she insisted on going.

"Steve's mother went alone to get her son," was her reply.

Even as he watched his wife cringe with each slam of the steel doors, he couldn't help but admire her courage. He understood how difficult it was to do something she was afraid to do. He'd been down that road a few times himself.

It was late morning by the time the release papers and promise-to-appear were signed, and Michael walked silently through the door. Emily threw her arms around him. Her furrowed brow had relinquished its death-grip on sorrow and softened her features.

"I'm sorry, Mom. Dad, I'm sorry. It was a really dumb thing to do. I'm really sorry." Michael glanced up for an instant, but immediately dropped his gaze to the floor as he tried to shake loose from the grasp of his mother.

"I'm OK, Mom. Let up so I can breathe."

Emily loosened the bear-hug she had on her son and stepped back. She didn't let go completely. She clung to Michael's arm as if fearful he'd be taken away again.

Luke remained silent. He squeezed Michael's shoulder as they walked to the car. If he made too big a deal out of his son's arrest, it could prompt him to rebel even further. If he said too little, it could lead to something worse. This was no place to discuss the situation. He would wait until they got home.

The ride home was quiet except for the radio. Country music helped Luke relax. It gave him time to think. He was still mulling the situation over when they pulled into the driveway.

Michael hurried into the house and started for his bedroom, but abruptly turned to the kitchen and took his usual place at the table. Emily and Luke joined him. Michael's face was red. He placed both arms on the table, clasping and unclasping his hands in nervous repetition. He briefly made eye contact with his father before looking away.

"Do you want to tell us what happened last night?" Luke's

voice was somber, official sounding. He'd arrested juveniles for breaking into vending machines when he was on the street. If they had no priors, he wrote a referral and released them to their parents. He needed to find out exactly what his fifteen-year-old son had done to warrant being detained.

"Well," Michael began, his voice low, his eyes downcast. I went over to Steve's to play pool, but his mother had a headache and couldn't stand the noise so we decided to go to Circle K and get a soda. We spotted a pop machine in front of Greene's Nursery so we decided to get one there." Michael's eyes were getting watery. He pulled the corner of his lapel up to his eye and rubbed vigorously.

"Don't do that with your shirt. You'll get an eye infection," Emily cautioned as she handed her son a handful of tissue.

Luke wished she hadn't done that. Never break a subject's train of thought during a confession. He suddenly felt guilty. That was his son, sitting before him, not a *subject*. Maybe he was too screwed up in the head to tell the difference anymore.

Michael sat silently for a few minutes, drying his eyes with the tissue. "We put in our money, but no pop came out. We started shaking the machine and the door popped open. We didn't try to get it open or anything. It just popped open. We each took the pop we paid for, and then decided to each take an extra one. That's when a police car pulled up and arrested us." The words tumbled from his mouth without hesitation, like they do when a person tells the truth. No need to buy time to make up a lie. The truth is always easy to remember, always the same, no matter how many times it's repeated.

Luke was waiting for more. There had to be more to it than that. He searched his son's face. Funny. He couldn't tell a damned thing. He could tell when a stranger was lying. Hell, he could damn-near tell what they had for breakfast, but he couldn't tell a thing about his own family.

Why would they place the boys in detention if that was the whole story? Michael didn't appear to be lying. There was no voice inflection to indicate anything other than a truthful explanation. Why would Sergeant Witt authorize detention if that was all there was to it?

Luke wanted to believe his son, but he needed more details from the burglary sergeant before he committed himself.

He stood up and placed a hand on Michael's shoulder, much like his father did with him when he made a mistake. Like that day in the barn. The day his little sister nearly drowned because he neglected to latch the gate. It was decades ago, but it seemed like yesterday. Thank God Michael had only committed a burglary.

"I'm glad you're all right and no one got hurt, but what you did was unacceptable and disappointing to your mother and me. We expect better of you. Always do the right thing whether anyone is watching or not." The words his father often quoted had served Luke well over the years. Hopefully, it would do the same for his son.

Luke hesitated long enough to place his hands on Emily's shoulders. He kissed her lightly on top of the head and walked out to his car. He'd called Sloan to tell him he'd be a few hours late, but he had a full schedule and had to get to work.

***

It was noon when Luke walked into the station. He went directly to the Detective Bureau. He needed to speak with the burglary sergeant face-to-face and get the details.

Sergeant Witt was in his office munching on a sandwich when Luke strolled in.

"You got a minute?" Luke asked as he settled into a seat that fronted Witt's desk.

"Eating lunch," Witt mumbled as he took another bite.

"I need some details on my son's arrest." Luke said. He sat quietly, waiting for an explanation, but Witt continued chomping on his sandwich as he gazed out of the window.

"Maybe you didn't hear me. I want the details on why two fifteen-year-old boys were detained for taking a can of pop. I won't ask again." Luke had all he could do to keep from reaching across the desk and grabbing the beer-belly detective by the throat. His tone of voice and clamped jaws appeared to be as intimidating as he intended. Sergeant Witt stopped eating and put his sandwich down.

"Your son and his friend were caught breaking into a pop machine. The arresting offi..."

"Breaking into? They actually broke into the machine? How? Did they use a crowbar? A screwdriver? What kind of tool did they use to break into the machine?" Luke was out of his chair, his hands clamped tightly around the edge of Witt's desk.

"Once I read the report...it looked like they either pulled the door open or they found it open. They just helped themselves." Sergeant Witt scooted his chair back against the wall. His half-eaten sandwich out of reach.

Luke could see Witt was scared. His face was ashen. His grip on the arms of his chair had turned his knuckles white. Maybe it wasn't a bad idea after all to let it get around that Luke was different. That he had a special insight into a person's head. That he was a little bit nuts.

Luke slowly and deliberately inched around the end of the desk. "You got about three seconds to start talking, or you and that chair you're sitting in are going out the window. I hope you both can fly."

"Wait a minute. Wait a minute." Witt threw up his hands

in a defensive gesture. "It wasn't my idea to detain them. I voted against it. Captain Berk was the duty captain. He told me to do it. We didn't have all the facts at the time. Otherwise we would have just referred them."

"Berk the jerk. Where is that walrus-looking son of a bitch?" Luke backed off his aggressive stance. But the glare in his eyes was apparently sufficient to maintain the scared look on Sergeant Witt's face. "I ought to throw you out the window anyway, just for being a piss-poor police officer, let alone a supervisor. You better fix this. Next time we meet, this situation better be fixed. If it's not, I won't waste time with talk."

Luke strode down the hall and burst through the door of the Detective Bureau's administrative office. He wasn't sure what he was going to do, but he didn't care anymore. He'd witnessed enough incompetence to last a lifetime. He was going to put an end to it. He was no longer restrained by oath of office or superior rank. He'd had enough.

Christy Johnson, the captain's secretary, looked up when Luke stormed in and hurried past her into Berk's private office. It was empty. "Where's the walrus?" Luke asked. "Where's the jerk who masquerades as a captain?"

"If you're referring to Captain Berk, he's on vacation. He won't be back for another week." Johnson's face was white. A shaky hand rested on the phone, but she made no attempt to pick it up.

"Where did he go, to Sea World to visit his relatives?" Luke asked as he stomped out.

He glanced back to see if Berk's secretary had called for help, but her hand was no longer on the phone so maybe she'd just let it be. He was now convinced that Michael had told the truth. His detention was payback for Luke showing the captain up by proving his ace detective was a crook as well as a liar.

Luke went to his office. He needed to calibrate the instrument before he ran any more tests. But even if the instrument was working properly, the job required focus. He couldn't deliver that right now.

He left a note for Lieutenant Sloan who was out of the office, and he directed the secretary to reschedule all of his tests. He was in no mood to listen to someone else's troubles. He had enough of his own. Calibration of the instrument would have to wait too. He was going home.

His drive home was filled with guilt for spending so much time at work, and for not getting home earlier the night before.

He entered the house and walked softly to the bedroom. Emily was probably in bed. She'd had a tough night and an even tougher morning seeing her son behind bars. She was on top of the covers staring at the ceiling when Luke walked in.

"How are you feeling?" he asked, knowing full well that she

couldn't be feeling good.

Emily's normally blue eyes were watery and bloodshot. It was hard to tell what color they were. A half-box of tissue lay next to her.

"If I'd gotten home at a decent hour last night, none of this would have happened. I should have called, but I was nervous about testing a high-ranking officer and it completely slipped my mind." He thought if he got the jump on blaming himself, it wouldn't leave her much ammunition to throw at him.

Emily lay motionless as she continued to stare at the ceiling. Luke eased down beside her. She would talk when she was ready. He would wait.

"It all seems so futile." Emily's voice was low and calm, as though she was talking to herself. "You never seem to question anything that comes from the police department. I think they could tell you to jump off the roof of the Valley Bank building, and you would do it without hesitation. Your family is just an afterthought, like a hobby. If you happen to find time for us, OK. If not, that's OK too."

Her listless presentation bothered him more than if she'd screamed the words. It sounded like she had given up on him. In some respects, he couldn't blame her. There were times when he had pretty much given up on himself. He considered telling her that he'd stuck his neck out in Michael's defense, but it would sound too much like he was trying to excuse his own actions, so he let it be.

He turned towards her, his head resting on his elbow. "I'm sorry I didn't make it home on time last night. But regardless of whether I'm here or not, Michael's actions were unacceptable." His tone was somber. "I did check things out. He was truthful with us. I'm trying to get the charges dismissed." He didn't want to tell her more than that. If she knew some captain had it in for him, she'd worry even more.

Emily turned to face him. "Is that possible?" Her tone of voice matched the pleading in her eyes. "It would be terrible if this one mistake follows him the rest of his life. Promise me you'll do everything you can to make this go away."

"I promise," Luke whispered as he placed his arm around her and pulled a pillow under his head. He hadn't realized how tired he was. The warmth of Emily's body and the pleasant aroma of her skin melted the last bit of resistance to complete relaxation. Or maybe it was sheer exhaustion. It didn't matter. Sleep was the victor.

CHAPTER THIRTY-EIGHT

No polygraphs were scheduled for Saturday, so Luke had the weekend to contemplate his next move in getting Michael and Steve's burglary charge dismissed.

Emily had calmed down considerably since he promised her he'd do everything he could to make the matter go away. The whole family went to church on Sunday and to breakfast at IHOP afterwards. Emily liked the strawberry crepes at the pancake house.

Michael had also mellowed since his stay in juvenile detention. *Maybe some good can come out of the situation after all.* The thought crossed Luke's mind after his son held the door open for the family and several other patrons as they left the restaurant.

Amy must have noticed the change in Michael, too. She hadn't complained since he got home. Luke smiled. It was good to have everyone together, and everything in harmony. He wished it would last forever, but he knew better. That peaceful feeling never lasts that long, especially when he's married with children.

CHAPTER THIRTY-NINE

The following Monday, Luke was still fuming over the decision by Captain Berk to detain the two boys for stealing a can of pop, but there was nothing he could do about it now. He would give Sergeant Witt an opportunity to get the charge dismissed. He wasn't sure what he was going to do about Berk. Luke didn't lose his temper often, but when it came to his family, there were no limits to what he would do to protect them. But he didn't have the luxury of dwelling on family problems. He had work to do.

He was still haunted about the examination of Major Garrison, and why the polygraph failed to register a proper response. He was half-afraid to calibrate the instrument. What if it checked out OK? What was he going to do then?

No matter how early he got to work, Merle was already there. He always had coffee made and all of the tests laid out for the day.

Luke got a cup of coffee and eased into his chair. He sat

silently, sipping the hot coffee as he mulled over Friday's events.

"Well, spit it out. Something's eating you. What is it?" Merle's impatient tone brought Luke back to the present.

Luke decided to tell Merle about testing the major, even though the chief ordered him not to discuss the test with anyone. There was too much going on in his head. He had to let some of it out or he'd bust. Besides, he trusted Merle to keep it confidential.

"Michael got himself into a little trouble and I had to deal with that Friday, but I didn't get out of here soon enough Thursday," Luke said. "The chief called me about five-thirty and asked for you. When I told him you'd gone home, he told me to stand by, he wanted me to do an internal. I told him I hadn't been out of school very long and offered to call you back in, but he declined and directed me to do the test."

Merle wasn't acting the least bit sympathetic. He just sat there grinning, not saying a word. Luke appreciated a good joke as much as the next man, even when it was on him, but the sadistic smile that Merle displayed, prompted him to add another comment. "I told the chief you wouldn't mind coming back to work in order to compensate for all the days you left early, and then wasted time when you were here. But he insisted I do the test. I guess he wanted it done right."

Merle threw his head back with a loud guffaw. "So you finally got your feet wet and couldn't weasel out of an internal. I'm glad

I went home when I did. It's about time you're doing some of the high profile ones."

"I had to test Major Garrison," Luke reluctantly admitted. "Two vice cops accused him of tipping off some hookers they were about to arrest. I thought it was a setup. It seemed more than a coincidence that you left early and I was required to test the guy who sent me to polygraph school."

"Don't get paranoid on me," Merle said as he shot Luke a sideways glance. "This job will make you crazy enough without you adding to it."

Luke rose to his feet. "I need to calibrate the instrument. The tracings didn't look right."

"None of them look right if you don't know what you're doing," Merle heckled as he followed Luke to the polygraph room.

Luke picked up an empty coffee can and a ruler and sat down behind the polygraph desk. He wrapped the blood pressure cuff around the can and inflated the cuff. He held his breath as he flipped the switch and watched carefully as the chart paper began to roll. The cardio tracing began a steady drop.

"You got a leak in the cardio," Merle said. "It may be the hose. We'll change the hose first because that's the easiest. We may as well test the pneumos too."

Luke breathed a sigh of relief. He put the ruler down and stretched one pneumo tube to six inches and held it. The pen began a steady drop.

"Must be a leak in that tube also," Merle said. "That's highly unusual. Those tubes are relatively new and shouldn't be leaking yet. Let's try the other one."

Luke pulled the other tube to a six-inch length, and watched as it, too began to descend. He was euphoric. It was the instrument that was wrong. Luke had made the right call.

"Something is screwy," Merle said. "Three tubes never go bad at the same time. What's going on here?" He looked at Luke as though he could somehow explain the problem.

"Everything was working fine when I did my last pre-employment about three-thirty Thursday afternoon. I don't see how everything could go bad between then and five-thirty when I ran the internal," Luke explained.

Both examiners stared at each other. The questioning look in Merle's eyes matched the apprehension Luke was feeling. Luke finally broke the uneasy silence.

"I had to leave the office for about a half-hour or so before the test, but everything was working fine when I left. I didn't notice anything wrong until I tested the major. I'll ask Marilyn if she saw anyone messing around in here. Maybe Floyd came back to pay us a visit."

"That wouldn't do him any good now," Merle said. "He's been gone too long. Only another examiner would know enough about a polygraph to sabotage it like that. We'd better keep our ears open and our mouths shut and see if anyone mentions anything."

With the new hoses connected, the cuff was again inflated. Both examiners watched as the cardio pen delivered a straight path as hoped. The pneumos operated equally as well.

Merle glanced at the instrument and then at Luke before retreating to his office. Luke wondered what Merle was thinking. If he had an idea of who may have damaged the hoses, he wasn't saying. *Maybe he just doesn't want me to worry any more than I have to...or maybe he's just as dumbfounded as I am.*

Luke sat for a few minutes trying to figure out who the hell could have done such a thing. *Someone has it in for me. I'd better be on my guard.*

***

Luke's first test of the day was Roy Kraft. He had been scheduled for the first slot the Friday before, but had to be rescheduled when Luke took the morning off to get Michael from detention.

A couple of weeks prior, Tom Kraft, one of the background investigators, mentioned to Luke that his son, Roy, had applied for a police officer position. Tom loved police work. He was very happy and proud that his youngest son was choosing to follow in his father's footsteps. His other son had chosen a life of crime and was presently serving time for holding up a convenience store in Kingman. Tom was devastated by the news of his eldest son being involved in crime, but relieved when his youngest son decided to become a Phoenix police officer.

Luke knew Tom wasn't the type to seek favors. He would be very careful not to interfere with the hiring process of his son. Neither would he ask for information, regardless of the polygraph results.

During the pretest interview, Luke spent more time with Roy Kraft than he usually did with an applicant. He wanted to make sure Tom's son was completely at ease so there wouldn't be any problems with the test.

Luke always tried to remain detached from personal feelings about a subject, but by the time he completed the pretest interview, he found himself liking the applicant. He had many attributes of his father, and the makings of a good police officer.

As the examination began, Luke dismissed his feelings about the young man in the subject's chair, and conducted the test as he was trained to do, without emotion or consideration for the outcome. He was automatically transformed into a different person. Like a robot, without prejudice, without preconceived notions, without feelings.

After running the first test, Luke examined the chart very

carefully. He sensed, more than he visualized, that something was wrong, and while reactions to the questions were insignificant, Luke was certain he hadn't yet asked the specific question that would justify his feelings.

He ran another chart, and without advance warning, he asked, "Have you ever done anything that you wouldn't want your father to know about?"

The question provoked the response Luke believed was coming. He noted a rise in blood pressure and an involuntary cessation of breathing. After an eight-second apnea, the subject responded with a weak, "Yes."

Luke concluded the examination and pulled his chair around to the end of the desk as he often did when interrogating suspects. He sat quietly for a few minutes before speaking.

"Whatever you tell me here will be kept confidential. Your father will not have access to the information."

The subject hung his head and remained silent as Luke continued with his coaxing.

"Everyone has things they wouldn't want their parents to know. Hell, I wouldn't want my father to know about some of the things I've done."

He waited quietly and patiently before continuing. This was the son of a well-respected officer and friend. He remained patient. He owed his fellow worker that much.

"I think you'll feel better if you get things off your chest," Luke said softly as he put his hand on the subject's arm. "You have nothing to lose, except the burden that you're carrying. You need to unload that burden. You know how difficult it is to carry a pail of water uphill. Share it with me and I'll help you carry it."

Luke could relate to what he was saying. He'd carried buckets of water from the windmill to the henhouse twice a day when he was on the farm, and it would have been a whole lot easier if someone had shared the load.

He continued to talk in a quiet, gentle, understanding tone that had become an automatic part of his interrogation technique. He couldn't recall when he first acquired it. It was just there, as though it had always been that way. Outside of the polygraph room, he was a quiet person who never said much. It was difficult for him to carry on a meaningless conversation. But during an interview or an interrogation, he never ran out of things to say.

After nearly ten minutes of steady talking, the applicant responded to Luke's probes.

"My father and I never really got along." The words came slowly, softly. "In fact, my father never really got along with any of us. I'm not sure he ever really wanted us, even my mother," Roy continued, his voice low, his head bowed. "I blame him for the problems my brother got into. Dad drove him to it. Getting in trouble was the only way we could get his attention. We knew we would catch hell, but at least he would pay attention to us for a few minutes, even if it was to beat the hell out of us. We would rather have taken a beating than be ignored. I think most people would."

Roy Kraft sat silently for a few minutes. He gazed at the floor and then to the ceiling as if asking for divine guidance. He finally continued his story in the same resigned tone of voice that he'd started with. "Dad was always too busy with the police department, and with other interests to pay much attention to his family. He may be a good police officer, but he's a lousy father and husband."

Luke had heard comments like that before from sons and daughters of employees whom he'd polygraphed. Always, in the back of his mind, was the thought that he, too, was falling into the same rut. He was too busy with his job to find time for his family. Too busy taking care of strangers who didn't give a damn about him. And too busy worrying whether he'd made the correct decisions when calling someone truthful or deceptive. But just as he'd done in the past, he put those thoughts aside. He would do something about his personal life later. Right now, he had work to do.

"One night, about two or three years ago..."

Roy's voice jerked Luke out of his personal thoughts. He hadn't been listening; unacceptable during a polygraph examination. He resisted the urge to tell the subject to start over.

"Yes, you were saying?" Luke leaned forward as though he'd heard what was said, but didn't understand.

"One night, about two or three years ago," Roy picked up where he'd left off, "Mom and Dad went out for dinner as they often did. I wasn't invited. Not that I would have gone. It was never a fun evening with Dad. If any little kids were seated near us while we were eating, he'd get up and leave, regardless if we were through with our meal or not. Of course, if *he* left, we all had to leave."

Roy swiped a hand across his face, stopping to pull at his eye lash before continuing with his story.

"Once, when I was with them, we'd just ordered when a family with a couple of little kids was seated a few booths over. The kids were noisy, sure, but not that bad. We left the restaurant before they even brought our food." Roy slumped back and turned his head away.

Both men sat quietly and motionless for several minutes.

"What happened that night when your parents were out?" Luke asked. He couldn't let the silence linger too long. He had to keep the conversation going.

Roy turned to face the examiner. "They got home late as they usually did when they went to visit and out to eat. I was home alone as I've been on many occasions. This time though, I began tallying up all the times I'd been ignored and taken for granted because my father was too absorbed with being a cop. I guess my thoughts finally reached a boiling point."

Roy swallowed and licked his lips. Luke thought about getting him a drink of water, but he didn't want to disrupt the balance that was going on. The subject was willing to talk, and Luke was willing to listen.

"I took my father's favorite rifle that no one but him was allowed to touch...I...waited for him to come home." Roy continued.

A trance-like stare came over Roy, as though he was reliving what he was about to tell, and seeking some inward guidance. "I heard them pull into the driveway and I lined up the sights. I intended to shoot him as soon as he stepped through the door."

Roy stopped talking and dropped his head to his chest. After a few seconds, he raised his head and turned to Luke with a strained expression. His voice sounded hollow as he continued.

"My mother came through the door first. I almost shot her instead of my dad. It scared me. I put the gun away and went to my room. I never tried that again."

Luke was stunned by Roy Kraft's admission. It took him a while to regain his composure before responding. "I can understand your feeling of isolation and anger, but there's always a better way to resolve a situation than to resort to something that can't be undone. There are many people willing to listen to what you have to say, and people a whole lot smarter than me have answers to your problems...regardless of what they may be."

After Luke's comment, both men sat quietly. There was nothing more to add.

Luke finally broke the silence. "How is your relationship with your father now?" He hoped he wouldn't have to take immediate action to prevent Roy Kraft from carrying out the deed he'd contemplated years earlier.

"It's a lot better," Roy answered. "I don't know if it's because I'm older and can handle it better, or if Dad has mellowed, but I've never considered harming him again. I can't believe I did that. I wouldn't think of such a thing now." Roy shook his head and lowered his eyes to the floor as he finished his explanation.

Luke let him sit quietly before commenting. "I think the best thing for you to do is to withdraw your application for employment. That way, there's no chance that your father will find out about this. I also think you should get some professional help so that you can find acceptable ways to deal with your emotions. Even though things are better between you, talking with a professional will put your mind at ease."

Roy nodded. His face was red.

Luke discontinued further testing. He shook hands with the young man and wished him luck. "You can call me whenever you need to talk with someone. Everything will be kept confidential." He watched as Roy left the building without stopping to speak with his father.

Luke returned to the polygraph room. "What am I going to do with this piece of information?" he muttered. "What in the hell am I going to do with this?"

He slowly left the polygraph room and walked to the outer office where Merle was going through a file. Luke slowly lowered himself in his chair and sat quietly, struggling with the decision to pass the information up the chain or bury it somewhere. He finally realized Merle was staring at him.

"Well, Atlas? What is it?" Merle asked facetiously. "You look like you're carrying the weight of the world on your shoulders. You may as well spill it or you won't be worth a damn the rest of the day. What's eating you?"

Luke hesitated. If he wanted to keep the information confidential, he'd better keep it to himself. If more than one person knows a secret...But he had a pretty heavy load to carry alone. Just as he'd explained to Roy Kraft that it was easier if someone shared his burden, it would be a lot easier for him to carry if he told Merle the story.

"I need to talk with you in the polygraph room," Luke said as he rose to his feet and turned to go. He was seated behind the desk by the time Merle came in and shut the door. Merle showed no emotion as he settled into the subject's chair.

Luke repeated what Roy Kraft had told him. "I'm not quite sure what to do with the information" he said. "I'm inclined to keep it bottled up instead of passing it up the chain."

Merle thought for a bit before responding. "I understand your dilemma, and I agree that the information would have a devastating effect on Tom Kraft as well as on his son, if it was included in the general report. Do you think he's given up trying to harm his father?" He eyed Luke expectantly. His tone of voice required a definitive answer.

"I think he's through with that, but who knows?" Luke hesitated before continuing. "Who really knows what anybody will do? Hell, I might come in here some day and shoot this damn machine full of holes. Lord knows I've been tempted." He nodded his head toward the instrument embedded in the desk. "The incident with the kid's father happened more than two years ago, so if he was going to do it, he probably would have done it by now. I suggested that he withdraw his application and he agreed."

Merle removed his glasses and massaged his nose where the nose guides left indentations. He slowly replaced them, shoving the glasses up the bridge of his nose. "You'd better keep the file in your desk, and keep it locked," he said. "If we report it up the chain, all hell will break loose. Tom's son will be in trouble, Tom's career will be blemished, and so will the life of his whole family.

It's better for everyone if the information doesn't go any higher. If you tell Sloan, he'll be obligated to pass it on."

Luke nodded. "I'll write up the report, but I'll store the file in a separate location from the rest. I don't want Tom to find out that his son wanted to kill him.

"I'm sorry to get you involved in this," he added as he glanced at Merle. "I should have kept it to myself. If it's ever discovered that we covered this up, we'll either be fired or they'll make it so tough on us we'll wish we'd been fired.

"Roy probably wouldn't be charged with a crime. All we have is his word that it happened. There's no independent evidence. But I understand if you don't want to take that chance."

Merle gave Luke one of his patented looks of disgust. His normally soft-gray eyes looked harsh. "Let me get this straight. You could have kept this to yourself, but you chose to tell me about it so the decision falls on me whether to report it as we should, or accept the burden of keeping it hidden. Is that about right?"

When Luke failed to respond, Merle continued. "I'm surprised you haven't made chief by now, the way you manipulate people."

Luke understood Merle's disgust. "I guess you're right," he said. "I never really thought about it like that, but I guess you're right. Well, now that I've passed the information on to you, what is your decision? After all, you *are* the Chief Polygraph Examiner, so I guess it's up to you."

Luke grinned as he watched Merle study him before Merle managed a grin of his own. "You wear the stripes," Merle said. "I'm merely following your orders. So, I guess you're still on your own."

"Boy, no matter how hard I try, I can never get ahead of you, can I?" Luke chuckled. "OK. It's solely my decision to bury the file, and I order you not to tell anyone about it."

"Well! Finally you're making a major decision. You might make it in this business after all," Merle chided.

"Come on," Luke said as he got up and headed for the break room. "I'll buy you a cup of coffee. Consider it a bribe to keep your mouth shut."

"I'm cheap. I accept," Merle responded as he followed Luke to the break room.

CHAPTER FORTY

It had been six days since Michael's arrest, and Luke had heard nothing from Sergeant Witt, or anyone else, about the case. If it was going to court, he would surely have been notified by now. He decided to wait until the following week before confronting Witt again. Or maybe he would go directly to the county attorney and see if he intended to prosecute.

It was half-past eleven, and he'd already completed four polygraph examinations. That gave him plenty of time to have lunch and catch up on some paperwork before his one o'clock test. He was debating whether to eat first or wade through his in-basket when the phone rang.

"Polygraph. Sergeant Canfield."

"This is Chief Parker. Am I interrupting anything?"

Luke hadn't spoken with the assistant chief since their

meeting with Captain Berk. His voice was pleasant, as though it was a social call. "Hi Chief. No, you're not interrupting anything. What can I do for you?"

"Can you come to my office?"

"Yes sir. I'll be right there."

On the way down the hall, Luke tried to determine why Parker wanted to see him. Maybe Captain Berk's secretary complained about the way Luke barged into her office. Or maybe Sergeant Witt filed a complaint. Perhaps he wanted to know the details of Michael's arrest. Canfield was still running through a litany of reasons as he walked into Chief Parker's office.

The chief looked up from some papers he was leafing through. "Thanks for coming. Have a seat."

Luke settled into one of the chairs that fronted Parker's desk. The assistant chief's office didn't have the view or decor that Chief Tucker enjoyed, but it was still pretty "chiefly." The office furniture was a lot more elegant than most offices Luke had been in, and a hell of a lot better than any in Personnel.

"How are things going in personnel?" Chief Parker's tone was casual, as though making idle conversation.

"They're swishing right along," Luke said esoterically.

Parker smiled as he made eye contact with the sergeant. "I understand you had another little run-in with Captain Berk."

Luke's muscles tensed. The mention of Berk's name made

his blood pressure rise. He could feel his face getting hot. The secretary must have complained after all.

"Not really," Luke managed to say through clenched teeth. "It was probably lucky for both of us that he wasn't in when I went to see him."

Parker nodded. "Yes, I guess it was."

Both sat quietly. The calm, in control, assistant chief gazed at the sergeant, who appeared calm on the outside, but struggled with a raging volcano simmering just below the surface.

"I heard about your son and another boy being charged with burglary, and placed in detention for taking some pop. They should have been referred and released. It was a bad decision." The chief eyed Luke as if waiting for a comment, but Luke remained silent. He wasn't sure if the chief was siding with him, or preparing to make an excuse for Captain Berk.

Luke couldn't help but wonder if Parker had ever raised his voice or become angry. He was still mulling the thought over as the chief continued. "I spoke with Captain Berk about the matter. We couldn't come to an understanding, so...he decided it was best if he retired. He will remain on leave until retirement, so that should resolve the conflict you have with him."

Luke was glad he wouldn't have to deal with the "walrus" anymore, but he really didn't care about that. He was concerned about the charge against Michael. He was trying to get his thoughts organized enough to make an intelligent comment when Parker interrupted them.

"I spoke personally with the county attorney," Chief Parker said. "He agreed that the circumstance of the arrest doesn't rise to the level of burglary. His office has dropped all charges, but you'll have to petition the court to have the record expunged."

Luke couldn't believe his ears. That was the best news he could have heard. He didn't give a damn about Berk retiring. All he cared about was the fact that Michael and his friend Steve wouldn't have a burglary charge hanging over their heads. He owed a great deal to Assistant Chief Reginald Parker.

"That's the best news I've had in years," Luke said as he heaved a sigh. "That's...the best news ever. Thank you very much."

"Actually, it was a call from a detective who didn't leave his name that brought the matter to my attention. Seems he happened to run across the case and thought I should look into it. I didn't do much. Just made some phone calls. It was the least I could do. It was the least the *Department* could do," Parker said as he leaned over the desk, his hands clasped on top of the papers he'd been leafing through. "Have you considered taking a promotional exam?"

"Not really," Luke answered, surprised by the question. "I'm too busy to think about anything except the work I'm doing now. I'm not sure I'm cut out to be anything but a sergeant.

I don't have the gift of gab that seems to be a requirement for advancement."

Parker's grin prompted Luke to add a disclaimer. "I'm not saying that only talkers get promoted. I'm just saying that it certainly helps."

"I believe you're correct in your assessment about promotions," Parker said as the smile left his face. "Generally speaking, promotions are based on who can talk the longest without saying anything meaningful. It seems the least competent in their present position finds an easier pathway to higher rank. But that may be a good thing for the department. Move them on before they can do too much harm and make way for those who can actually do the work."

Parker swung his chair around and gazed out of the window. Luke sat quietly, unsure if the chief was through talking with him. Maybe he should get up and leave. No, that would be rude. He'd wait until he was dismissed.

The chief turned back to face Luke. A frown replaced the smile that had been present a short time ago. "If we didn't have some good sergeants and lieutenants, hard telling what would happen. By the time a person reaches the rank of captain, he's forgotten how to be a cop. His main concern is figuring out who he needs to impress in order to make himself look good. That's one of the things I admire about you. In the few contacts we've had, you don't seem to care about anything except getting the job done. People like you are rare. Don't change your attitude...but have more foresight. Take the promotional exam."

Luke nodded as he rose to his feet. "Thanks Chief," he said as he ambled to the door. "I'll take your advice."

He returned to his office and immediately called Emily.

"Hello," a soft voice answered.

"Hi, I've got good news," Luke hurriedly said. "I just spoke with Chief Parker. He told me the charges against Michael and Steve have been dismissed."

"That's wonderful." The relief in Emily's voice flowed through the receiver. "I knew you could do it if you put your mind to it. Michael and Steve will be so relieved. Thanks for calling. That was very good news."

"I thought it was too," Luke replied. "That's why I didn't want to wait until I got home to tell you. Well, I'd better go. I have to grab a quick bite before my next test. See you later."

He felt good when he hung up the phone. Better than he had in a long, long time. He wondered who the detective was that had made the call to Chief Parker. Either it was someone who had no love for Captain Berk and his sergeant, or else there was an underlying good guy hidden somewhere inside the detective bureau. Maybe it was *pain in the ass* Dennis Creech. He grinned at the thought. But yet, as his father had often said, "Stranger things have happened."

CHAPTER FORTY-ONE

Shortly before noon, a month after the polygraph of his son, Tom Kraft suddenly slumped over his desk, dead from an apparent heart attack. Luke's earlier vision of Tom's soul leaving his body while in the office had come true.

Luke was at the police academy teaching interrogation techniques to recruits when it happened. He was returning to his office as the ambulance was leaving.

The passing of his friend and fellow officer was difficult for Luke to accept, but he didn't have time to grieve. An applicant was waiting.

Almost immediately, the subject admitted excessive use of marijuana. He last smoked a "joint" the night before his test. He needed to get "mellowed out" so he wouldn't be nervous. There was no need to prolong the agony for either of them. The applicant was rejected for employment and sent on his way.

Luke remained in the polygraph room. He had gone from an emotional high, with the news of dismissed charges against Michael, to a tidal wave of depression over the loss of his friend and coworker.

He was lost in thought when the bureau secretary walked in and closed the door.

"If you came to confess, have a seat," Luke said. "It's still warm from the last confessor."

Marilyn plopped a file on his desk.

Luke gave it a quick glance. Roy Kraft. The name on the file shot a jolt of adrenalin through his body. "Where did you get that?" he asked accusingly. "That was locked in my desk. How did you get it?"

"It was lying on Tom's desk, under his body," she said, mocking the accusing tone in Luke's voice.

"Did you read the contents?" Luke asked.

"I read enough to know that Tom shouldn't have seen it." Marilyn replied. "What's going on? Why would Tom have the file of a police officer applicant–especially the file of his own son– when he works with civilians?"

Luke glared at Marilyn as he fought to control himself. "That's what I was about to ask you," he said in a steely tone. "Do you have a key to my desk?"

"No, you have the only key," Marilyn replied, irritation coloring her voice.

Luke repeated the story Roy Kraft had told him, and of Roy's decision to withdraw his application. "I locked the file in my desk, and the only other person who knew about it was Merle. I'm certain Merle would never disclose the file."

Luke checked his desk drawers. They were all locked. "Well, someone has a key. I never leave this desk unlocked. Who the hell could have done such a thing? Maybe Tom had a key. Did you notice if he was in my office this morning?"

Marilyn slowly shook her head. "I don't keep track of who goes in and out of other peoples' offices. Floyd Simmons was in here earlier looking for you. I told him you were out. He's always hanging around so I didn't pay much attention to him. But he doesn't have a key, and he wasn't here that long, so he couldn't have done it. He had some charts he wanted you to look at."

Luke tried to logically decipher the mystery of how Tom ended up with his son's file. Tom must have done it himself. He must have started wondering why his son withdrew his application and decided to find out. That's the only explanation.

"Wait a minute. Wait just a damn minute." Luke rose from his chair. "I think the mystery has been solved. In fact, there were *two* mysteries, and I think I've solved them both."

Marilyn shrunk back at Luke's sudden outburst. Her face

turned pale and her eyes teared up. She snatched a tissue from the box on Luke's desk and wiped her eyes.

Luke saw the look on her face and restrained himself from further jubilance for solving what had bugged him since he'd polygraphed Major Garrison. Someone had sabotaged the polygraph, and it was now pretty clear who the culprit was. He wanted to explain the situation to Marilyn, but he had already gone against the chief's orders when he told Merle about testing the major. He'd better not say anything more.

"Sorry to startle you," he said as he offered Marilyn another tissue. "Tom Kraft must have had a key to my desk and found the file. I never thought he would do such a thing, but who knows what people will do when they feel pressured?"

Marilyn sniffled and dabbed at her nose with the tissue. "You said *two* mysteries. What's the other one?"

He had to think quickly. What was he going to say? Marilyn was no dummy. He wanted to keep the information confidential about the polygraph being sabotaged until he was absolutely sure that Tom Kraft was the culprit. "Some things were moved around in here. Tom must have done that too when he was looking for his son's file."

Luke looked at Marilyn, trying to gauge her next move. He couldn't tell whether she believed his story about the mysteries, but it was the best he could come up with on the spur of the moment. Her knowledge of the file on Tom's son was more pressing though.

"What do you intend to do now?" Without waiting for a response, he continued. "What's done can't be undone. I felt it was better not to send this up the chain. The incident happened several years ago and I didn't want to cause Tom more headaches, especially since his other son is in prison. He and Roy are getting along now. I was concerned about causing the family more grief."

Marilyn nodded. "It wouldn't do anything but cause more harm to make it public. I'll keep it confidential. But if it was found once, it may be found again. The entire report should be destroyed, and the file say only that the applicant withdrew his application prior to the polygraph."

Luke was uncomfortable with her suggestion. He had never destroyed a file or falsified a report. He did withhold information, and he had to live with that decision. But destroy a file? Never.

"I'll take care of it," he said as he buried the file in another location in his desk and locked the drawer.

As uneasy as he was with Marilyn knowing about the incident, there was nothing he could do about it. He would have to trust her not to say anything. At least he had figured out who damaged the polygraph, and the culprit was dead, so that was a load off his mind.

Tom Kraft had been in the bureau a long time. He knew

how the polygraph worked. He stuck holes in the tubes in order to give his son an advantage. That was the only explanation. No need to be on guard anymore. Yet something still bothered him about the sabotage. He couldn't visualize Tom doing such a thing. It wasn't like him. He also had reservations about Marilyn's pledge of silence. *A secret is no longer a secret if more than one person knows about it.*

CHAPTER FORTY-TWO

Fernando Carrillo was an applicant who aspired to become a police officer like his father and uncle who were currently on the force. Fernando had barely turned twenty-one, eager to join the department and make his relatives proud.

Luke noticed him in the office on several occasions during the past few months. He seemed to spend a lot of time with Marilyn. The bureau secretary was a good ten years older than Fernando. Luke occasionally wondered what was going on between them, but since neither was married, it was none of his business.

Two months after Tom Kraft's death, Marilyn handed Luke the file on Fernando Carrillo.

"Your next applicant is waiting," she said as she offered him the file.

As Luke attempted to take it, Marilyn held on. "I really

want Fernando to pass the polygraph. He's a lot better than the ones with crappy backgrounds that the chief's office ordered us to hire."

Marilyn released the file, but continued talking as she placed her hand on Luke's arm. "No one is perfect. Not even you," she said, her eyes soft, her voice half pleading, half threatening. "I'd consider it a great favor if you took it easy on this one."

Luke remained silent, trying to grasp what Marilyn was saying. She had never intervened in a test, and had always treated applicants equally whether they were known or not. In this case, she was openly committed to seeing that this applicant receive favorable consideration.

"Let's run the test before we jump to conclusions, either good or bad," Luke said. "He'll get the same test as everyone else. The results will be evaluated and we'll take it from there. Do you know something about him that's not in the file? What's your personal interest in this man?"

Marilyn hesitated. "I...have to tell you that...well...I think a lot of Fernando and want to see him hired. He's never done anything bad. I just want to see him do well. He's passed everything up 'til now, so..." Her voice trailed off.

Luke turned to go when Marilyn said, "You've given others a break. All I'm asking is that...well...don't be too hard on him."

She turned away and strolled back to her desk. Luke watched

her go. He thought he knew her, but this attempt to intercede on behalf of an applicant, proved him wrong.

Does anyone ever really know anybody?

Luke escorted Fernando into the polygraph room and looked closely at him, trying to determine the meaning of the conversation with Marilyn. He was also trying to get a read on the young man. Had he asked Marilyn to intervene on his behalf? It was obvious that she wanted him to pass the polygraph, regardless of his background. It was also obvious that she was referring to the information Luke had concealed about Roy Kraft. She didn't come right out and threaten exposure of Luke's cover-up, but he got the message.

Fernando appeared unnerved by Luke's steady gaze, or maybe it was because he was seated in the polygraph chair. He shifted his position several times, but said nothing.

"Have you spoken with anyone about what to expect with your polygraph?" Luke asked.

"Yes," Fernando responded. "I asked my dad and my uncle about the test."

"What did they say?"

"They said to just be truthful and I wouldn't have any problems."

"Did you speak with anyone else about the test? Did you ask Marilyn or anyone else about the test?"

"No, just my dad and my uncle."

Luke had a feeling that the young man before him was telling the truth, but he dismissed that thought.

If you like them, they are probably lying to you. The words of Nathan Hardison echoed in his mind. He had to be on guard.

Luke went through the preliminary procedure of waiver signing and reviewing the standard questions. But all the while, he was bothered by Marilyn's obvious attempt to sway the test in favor of the applicant. Did she know something that would eliminate him from the selection process? The subject hadn't admitted anything derogatory, so Luke couldn't figure out what Marilyn was afraid of. *What am I missing? What didn't I ask?*

After hooking up the attachments and taking his seat behind the desk, Luke asked, "Is there anything else that you want to say before we begin?"

Fernando paused before turning to face the examiner.

"I was told what type of questions would be on the written test."

"Were you told the actual questions that would be asked?"

"I was told they would be multiple choice, but not what the actual questions were."

"Is that it, or is there something else you want to tell me?"

"Well, someone did help me study for the test. I was wondering if that was OK or not. I wanted to pass the test, but I didn't want to do anything that would keep me from being hired. Both my dad and my uncle told me to be sure and tell the truth because that guy that runs the polygraph can practically read your mind. So I thought I'd better say something." Fernando hung his head as he finished his explanation. "Is that going to hurt my chances?"

Luke had to smile at the apparent naïveté of the young man seated before him. People had admitted felonies with less conscience than Fernando was displaying, just because he received help in studying for the test.

"So...no one gave you the answers and you didn't cheat on the test. Is that what you're saying?" asked Luke.

"No one gave me the answers and I didn't cheat on *anything*," Fernando replied.

"OK, then. Don't worry about it," Luke said as he prepared to start the test.

He inflated the blood pressure cuff and flipped the switch that set the chart in motion. Once more, he became indifferent to the person in the chair. As far as he was concerned, this was just another subject and he would let the chips fall where they may. He never asked Fernando who had helped him study because he didn't care who it was. It didn't matter. He was pretty sure the helper was Marilyn, but so what if she led him in the right direction? Luke would give her that much. He owed her that. He would wait until the test was over to see if there was reason to question Fernando further.

Luke ran one chart with no more than the usual reactions. He ran another chart and then a third, wrapping up all of the standard questions. No significant reactions indicative of deception were noted on any of the charts. Luke breathed a sigh of relief.

He had never compromised his position with any examination, and he wasn't about to start now. There was Roy Kraft, of course, but that was totally different and necessary. He had gotten everything he needed to know from this applicant. Anything more was unimportant. Luke had maintained his integrity, and satisfied Marilyn's request to take it easy on her friend.

"Well, I don't see why you can't continue in the process," Luke said.

Fernando breathed a heavy sigh. "Boy, that's a relief. Thank you very much. My dad and my uncle were right. They told me to tell the complete truth and I would be alright. Thank you."

"Now, just because you passed the polygraph doesn't mean you're going to be hired," Luke reminded him. "It just means that your name will be added to an eligibility list with a whole bunch of other applicants. So you may be called and you may not. It depends on when and if there are vacancies."

"I understand," Fernando replied. "I'm just glad this part is over."

Luke unhooked the polygraph attachments and shook hands with Fernando before ushering him out the door. As often happened, a doubt flickered through his mind. Maybe he'd missed something with this young man. He quickly dismissed his concern. Another applicant was waiting.

"We could do worse," he murmured as he watched Fernando make his way to the elevator. He'd satisfied his ethics by not granting the applicant special consideration, and he'd satisfied Marilyn's request to pass her boyfriend. His secret about Tom Kraft's son was safe. At least for the time being.

CHAPTER FORTY-THREE

It was nearing 11 p.m. Luke had been asleep for little more than an hour when the incessant ringing of the telephone managed to pry him free from his fatigue induced slumber.

It was Wednesday, the one day of the week that no matter how hard he tried to do things right, they usually went to hell. He'd often wondered why Wednesdays were more difficult than other days of the week, but he couldn't come up with a rational explanation. They just were. Some, however, were worse than others, and today turned out to be one of the worst.

Luke prided himself on his punctuality. But this morning, an accident midblock had tied up traffic for nearly an hour. That made him late for work and set him behind on all of his scheduled polygraphs. Each one seemed to be more difficult and time consuming than the one before. He'd even skipped lunch in an attempt to catch up. A candy bar from the vending machine kept him going.

Then the ink bottle that fed the cardio pen ran dry in the middle of a criminal test. Stopping to fill it would have disrupted the emotional balance that he'd worked so hard to build during the pretest interview. It would also have put him further behind, so he kept the chart moving and used the subject's voice inflection as an indicator of deception.

That meant he couldn't use the chart to show the subject where he'd lied and prove to him that the polygraph worked. The subject eventually confessed to a series of burglaries, but only after a prolonged interrogation.

It was late afternoon, and Luke was worn out by the time his six o'clock appointment walked through the door. A pediatrician was accused of molesting his patients.

The doctor was a small man, clean shaven and immaculate in appearance. He handed Luke a thick folder as soon as he stepped into the polygraph room.

"Have a seat," Luke said as he motioned to the subject's chair.

While the doctor was being seated, Luke thumbed through the first few pages in the folder. It contained academic achievements and letters of commendation from peers and parents of patients. Luke suspected what the folder contained before he'd even opened it. Others had tried the same tactic in an attempt to sway the opinion of the examiner before the test had even begun.

Luke waited until he had the doctor's full attention before tossing the folder on the floor in a corner of the room. He wanted to set the ground rules early. Titles were meaningless in the polygraph room. The doctor said nothing.

After obtaining the standard personal information, and the doctor's explanation of the situation, Luke conducted the test and tore off the usual length of chart. He didn't have to study it. He knew the doctor was guilty as soon as he walked in. But he needed an admission.

He tried a number of avenues in order to break the subject down and make him give up his innermost secrets, but the doctor refused to admit any wrong doing. He did admit camping with some of the children, and occasionally one of the boys would sleep with him in his sleeping bag. He said he may have touched the boy in his sleep, but it was nothing deliberate.

As the interrogation became more intense, the subject turned to face the examiner with a strained look. He appeared to be holding his breath. His mouth opened and his tongue began to swell until it protruded from his mouth. He choked and motioned wildly at his throat and tongue.

Luke ran to the breakroom and returned with a cup of water. He poured water over the subject's tongue while speaking to him in a soft, gentle tone. The tongue slowly returned to normal and the subject began taking normal breaths.

Luke removed the attachments and quietly waited for the doctor to compose himself.

Without saying anything further, the doctor rose to his feet and gathered his folder from the floor where Luke had tossed it. He walked out and never looked back.

It was one of the strangest tests Luke had ever conducted. But then, it was Wednesday. Shit happened on Wednesdays.

But even shitty days finally end. Luke got home, ate a bite, took a shower, and flopped into bed. And now, the freaking telephone was adding the finishing touch.

"Hello," he growled.

"Luke, this is Sloan. I hate to wake you, but we need you at the office. Take a minute to wake up. I'll wait."

"I'm awake," Luke mumbled.

"A legislator has been murdered. We need a suspect polygraphed."

"Can't it wait until morning?"

"No. We have the suspect here in the office. The chief, the county attorney, and even the mayor is here in the office, waiting for you. They need this guy polygraphed right away."

"I'll be there as soon as I can," Luke muttered as he hung up the phone and reached for his pants.

"Are those people down there insane?" Emily fumed. "This is

getting ridiculous. You can't physically keep up this pace. You're going to become ill, and then they'll *have* to get along without you. That means I will too. Don't they realize you have a family and a life outside of that damned police department?"

"I don't believe they give a shit," Luke answered as he continued getting dressed.

He arrived at police headquarters in half the time it normally took. He wished traffic was that light all the time.

He parked in front of the building and hurried up to the 3rd floor. The office was filled with people when he walked in.

"This is probably the most important polygraph you will ever do," County Attorney Emmitt Bass said.

"Who's the lead detective?" Luke asked. He wasn't in the mood to listen to some politician. He needed to know what the hell happened so he could do the test and get back to bed.

"I am." Joe Pelton stepped up.

"Come with me," Luke said as he led him into the hallway. "Just give me the basics. What do you have for sure and what do you suspect?"

The detective thumbed through his notes as he described the situation. "Senator Alfred Rains' body was found in the desert by some hikers. He appeared to have been beaten in the head with what appeared to have been a rock. He was also shot a number of times. Several rocks with blood on them were recovered at the scene, but we didn't find a gun.

"The biker we have in custody was driving Rains' car when an officer stopped him for a traffic violation. The woman was in the passenger seat. The officer got suspicious when the driver handed him Rains' driver's license which didn't fit the description of the driver. Both were detained and found to have several hundred dollars, along with some personal property belonging to Senator Rains.

"The woman is Jillian Sands. She has a record for prostitution. She said she had a date with Rains. He loaned her the car and gave her the money.

"The biker, Christopher Cruse, said he was hitchhiking when the girl picked him up and asked him to drive. He continued to deny any knowledge or involvement in the murder, but he agreed to take a polygraph. We thought it best to give him one right away before he has time to change his mind."

"Where is the suspect now?" Luke asked.

"He's in the polygraph room," the detective replied.

"He's what? In the polygraph room? He shouldn't be in there until he comes in for a test. And he should never be in there without an examiner. Who the hell's idea was that?" Luke was pissed.

"I don't know," the detective said. "I guess they thought he would confess if they put him in the chair and showed him the machine. This all happened before I got here."

"How the hell do they expect me to get anything out of him after he's been hammered on by a dozen other people?" Without waiting for a response, Luke grabbed the detective's notes and walked through the office and into the polygraph room. He deliberately ignored the dignitaries he had to wade through in order to get there.

He wondered how the hell he was going to break down the psychological wall that the subject had undoubtedly built while being questioned by a bunch of amateurs. Every denial added another brick.

Christopher Cruse was a typical biker. He had a shaggy head of dark hair and a full beard. His huge body filled the subject's chair. His brawny arms were covered with tattoos. He looked and smelled like he'd been camping in the desert for a week or two.

Luke never even glanced at the subject as he brushed past and took his seat on the opposite side of the desk. He sat for a minute before hoisting his legs to the top of the desk and draping them over the corner. He laced his hands behind his head, leaned back and closed his eyes. It felt good to be relaxed. He considered letting the suspect and all the brass in the other room stew while he caught up on his sleep. But he had a job to do, and he'd better get at it so he could get back to bed.

He needed to come up with an avenue of approach that

would get the biker talking. He had to find a common ground. But what the hell did a police sergeant have in common with a biker?

After a few minutes, he lowered his feet to the floor and looked directly at the subject. "I sure as hell don't want to be here anymore than you do," he sighed. "I'd rather be sitting out in the barn with a cold beer, playing my Kay."

The biker remained silent for several minutes before turning to face the examiner. "You got a Kay?" he snorted. "I got a Gibson."

Luke gave him a quizzical look. "Are you shitting me? You have a Gibson? That is probably one of the finest guitars ever made. Who the hell did you steal that off from?"

"I actually bought it," Cruse replied. "A guy needed some money and I just happened to have some. Of course it probably helped that the guy was pretty shit-faced at the time," he chuckled.

Luke chuckled with him. He now had an in. A key to unlocking the subject's mind. A sledge hammer to break down the psychological wall of defense. Bikers spend a lot of time in bars. And bars play nothing but country music. Luke owned a Kay guitar and he loved country music. They did have something in common after all.

"How in the hell did you get yourself in such a shitty

situation?" Luke shook his head. "It had to involve a woman. You look smarter than that," he lied. The guy looked like a moron. But honey catches more flies than vinegar as his father had often said. "You have to realize that the woman spilled her guts."

The biker shot him a doubtful look before turning away.

"You know, I don't know about us men," Luke said. "Every one of us may be different. But no matter who we are, how smart we are, how wealthy we are, or how poor we are, we all lose what little sense we had when it comes to a woman. I don't care if it's freaking Einstein or some idiot who can't count the number of fingers on one hand. When it comes to women, our brains fly out the window."

The biker sat quietly, staring at the wall to his front.

"So how the hell did you get mixed up in this situation?" Luke asked again.

The subject shook his shaggy head and remained silent. After a while, he glanced over and said, "Well, like I told the first dozen guys who asked me, I was just hitchhiking and the woman picked me up. I guess I just got nervous when we got stopped. I handed the cop the wrong driver's license. He ended up haulin' us in."

"What about the money and the other items belonging to the guy whose car you were driving? How did you come by those?" Luke asked.

"She gave them to me," the subject replied.

Luke decided not to question the subject further until he ran a chart. He already knew the outcome. It was obvious to him that the subject was lying. But he'd let the instrument decide.

He ran the first test and watched the pens make their dramatic paintings of the subject's innermost thoughts. Reactions indicative of deception were noted to all relevant questions.

Slowly and deliberately, he tore off a length of chart and spread it out before him. Luke smiled broadly as the subject glanced over.

"Chris," Luke said. "You need to get into a different line of work. You are way too honorable to be a criminal. I bet your conscience plays hell with you every time you do something wrong. I bet the twins, *It's OK* and *don't do it*, play hell with your mind. I know they do with mine.

"You're like me. I can't get by with anything either. My conscience slaps hell out of me if I even think about doing something I know I shouldn't. But that's the lot we were given. You know what they say. What can't be cured, must be endured.

"Every one of the relevant questions bothered you. But it's up to you whether you want to take the whole rap for a woman who thinks nothing of throwing you to the wolves to save her own skin."

Without waiting for a reply, Luke continued. "This woman tells the detective that you put her up to forcing the man to withdraw money from the bank. That was all she wanted. She tried to talk you into letting him go, but you forced her to go with you to the desert, and made her watch while you beat and shot him. I figured she had more to do with it than that. In fact, I wouldn't doubt it was her idea. But the county attorney and nearly everyone else wants to just make a deal with her and hang you for the entire thing. They're ready to cut her a deal, and some didn't want you to take a polygraph. It might come out that the woman had more to do with it than what she said. The lead detective, however, is dragging his feet. You know, you are damned fortunate to have Joe Pelton working this case or you'd be heading for the chair. You did know the guy was a state senator, didn't you?" Luke waited for a reply but none came.

After more time had passed, and the subject refused to admit his involvement, Luke scooted to the edge of his chair and looked the subject full in the face. "Well, Chris," he said. "I hate to see a fellow country music guy bite the dust over a woman. But it's your choice. They already have enough to hang you. I was just trying to give you a chance to save your hide. But it's your hide, and if you choose to get gassed over some hooker, hey, that's up to you."

The subject's eyes darkened as he glared at the examiner for the first time.

"What? You didn't know she was a hooker?" Luke asked. "Not

that it matters," he added. "You must know she has a record for prostitution. But if you love someone, their past doesn't really matter. You can put up with other guys smirking because they only had to pay a few dollars to get what they wanted from her. You'll have to pay with your life. But as I said before. It's your life. Hey, maybe I'll write a country song about you two."

Luke laboriously rose and unhooked the attachments from the subject's body. "I guess we're done here," he said as he returned to his seat and gathered up his notes and the manila folder with the chart he had just run.

He sat quietly for a few minutes before speaking. "We may seem like two totally different people Chris, but we aren't that much different. I had a shitty childhood," he lied. "Maybe yours was the same. But I found that a guitar and a cold beer could work wonders with my sense of belonging, my sense of wellbeing. I don't know about you, but I can actually lose myself in a good country song."

Luke sat silently, staring at the wall, seemingly oblivious to the man in the subject's chair. "Maybe it's because we both like country music. I don't know. Not many people around here do. Or maybe it's because I hate to see a guy get taken for a ride by a woman who really doesn't give a damn about him personally, and is only out to get what she can."

Luke seemed to ignore the subject as he continued to talk as though he didn't care if anyone was listening or not. "You know, Chris, we all do things that later we wish to God we had never done. I haven't told anyone about the horrible mistake I made when I was young. I keep asking myself how I could have done such a stupid thing."

The polygraph room became eerily quiet as Luke stopped talking and appeared trancelike staring off into space. The subject turned his head to look at the examiner.

Luke pretended not to notice as he resumed speaking in a low monotone. "I was born and raised on a farm in the Midwest. We always had the radio on in the barn, and it was always tuned to a country music station. I spent a lot of time alone in the barn. I always felt a little different, like maybe I didn't belong. The barn was my sanctuary. The one place where I could be myself without having to put on a front to please others. The cows and horses accepted me as I was.

"Then, one day, I neglected to latch the gate between the house and the farmyard. My little sister got out and fell into the stock tank. I was in the barn helping my pet cow deliver a calf, but something told me Evy was in trouble. I got to her in time to save her from drowning, but she'd been under water too long and she died at an early age. Her death has haunted me every minute of every day.

"There's nothing I can do to bring her back, so I decided I

would live every day to help keep others from drowning. Maybe not literally, but in an emotional sense. We all make mistakes, and I made a doozy. But I made my peace with God, and I'm still working on making peace with myself. I fought it at first. I tried to tell myself it wasn't my fault."

Luke placed his left hand in his lap and crossed his fingers. He assured himself that his father wouldn't mind if he fudged the truth a little in order to solve a murder. "But one particularly bad day when I couldn't get the image of my little sister's lifeless body out of my mind, I finally confided to my dad that it was all my fault. The disappointment in his face was something I had never before witnessed.

"From that moment on, I promised myself to always tell the truth no matter what. It was like a light went off in my head. I accepted the blame. It was my fault. It was like the weight of the world had been lifted from my shoulders, Chris. I knew God had forgiven me, and equally important was the fact that I had forgiven myself. I don't know about you, but I would much rather take my punishment here on earth than in the afterlife. Eternity is a long time Chris. It never ends. Eternity goes on forever."

The subject's huge body seemed to shrink as he relaxed his shoulders and slumped in his chair. That was the unmistakable sign of surrender Luke had been waiting for. He edged his chair a little closer to the end of the desk.

Both men sat quietly for several minutes. It was as if the world had stopped turning and time stood still. Each man apparently lost in his own thoughts. Waiting for the other to make the first move. To end the stalemate that seemed to have no end.

The silence was eventually broken by the creaking of a chair as the burly biker turned his head toward the examiner. "Aw, what the hell," he said. "I know damned well they're not gonna let me go so I may as well get this over with." He turned to face the front.

Several minutes passed. Their conversation was at a delicate balance. A teeter-totter that could go either way. Pressing too soon could stop the flow of information. Waiting too long would give the subject time to think about the consequences of a confession.

With a snort and a shake of his head, the subject picked up where he'd left off. "It was her idea to pretend to be a hooker and rob the first guy who picked her up. From what you say, I guess she didn't have to pretend much. She'd pulled this same stunt before, and the men she'd robbed never reported it. I guess they didn't want to admit they'd picked up a prostitute. I was just going to be there in case the guy refused to pay her. We didn't know the guy was a senator until he said he would have us hunted down. He kept threatening to have the whole police department after us. He said no one would believe us if we told them he'd picked up a hooker. He would say he just gave the poor girl a ride and ended up getting robbed. So…"

Several minutes ticked by. That time balance was teetering in the wrong direction. Luke needed to correct it.

"I know exactly what you're talking about," Luke said. "I've known some legislators, and they can be real assholes. They get filled with their own self-importance. They're always bragging about what they're gonna do, but they seldom accomplish anything. So why take him to the desert once she's got the money?"

"He was gonna run to the nearest phone and have us picked up before we could get far enough away," the subject snorted. "We thought if we took him away from town and let him walk back, it would give us enough time to get away. But he didn't know when to keep his mouth shut. He kept screaming at us and saying he was going to see that we were put in prison for the rest of our lives for kidnapping.

"We never considered a kidnapping charge until he mentioned it. He was going nuts so I hit him once. He fell to the ground, but continued to scream about how he was a senator and he would see that we hung. Then he lunged at Jilly. She shot him and he fell to the ground, but he kept screaming about having us hunted down.

"I guess Jilly got tired of his mouth and hit him in the head with a rock. He lay there moaning so I took the gun from her and shot him again. I figured he was dying anyway and I didn't want to see him suffer. When he still continued to moan, Jilly shot him a couple more times. If the guy had just kept his mouth shut, he wouldn't have lost anything but a few dollars."

The subject's eyes seemed to plead for understanding as he looked at the examiner before resting his head on his burly chest.

"Whose gun was it?" Luke asked.

"It belonged to Jilly," Cruse replied.

"Where is it now?"

"I threw it out the window on our way out of the desert. I was pissed that she even had it. We wouldn't be in this mess if she hadn't shot the guy. I'd have just bounced him around some and left him there. But she had to bring a damn gun."

"I think you're right about the gun," Luke agreed. "I also think you're right about politicians. Some people get caught up in their own self-importance. But you're going to be OK, Chris. You have a psychological advantage over most people. Your conscience is clear. No matter what happens from now on, you won't have to try and cover anything up. You can tell the complete truth and feel good about it. Most of all, you will leave this world with a clean slate. And that…is a very good feeling. I know, because that's the way I feel."

The subject sat quietly, seeming to reflect on his confession and the consequences that awaits.

"I'm going to call the detective in," Luke said. "Just tell him what you told me. I'm sure he'll do everything he can to see that you're treated fairly."

The subject repeated his confession to Detective Pelton. He answered all of the detective's questions without hesitation, including a more detailed description of the gun and where it was tossed. Luke shook hands with the man before he was placed in handcuffs. "Thanks for your honesty Chris. Just keep in mind that regardless of what happens, your mind is free and clear."

All of the dignitaries in the outer office looked expectantly to Luke as he stepped out of the polygraph room. He brushed past them without a word and hurried out the door. He'd let Detective Pelton provide the news they'd been waiting for.

Luke glanced at his watch as he climbed into his truck. Nearly 2 a.m. His first polygraph examination was scheduled for 7 a.m. He wouldn't get much sleep this night. But there was one consolation. Wednesday was finally over.

CHAPTER FORTY-FOUR

A year had passed since Luke became a polygraph examiner. Merle was on sick leave, so Luke had been working overtime in order to keep up with demand.

It was Saturday night, and the last applicant didn't show for his polygraph so Luke knocked off early. He decided not to call Emily and tell her he was coming home. Since it wasn't a school day and no function was scheduled, he'd surprise everyone by showing up early and taking them out to dinner. The family hadn't gone anywhere together since breakfast at IHOP the Sunday after Michael's arrest. This would be a real treat.

It was a little after five o'clock when he pulled into his driveway. The Buick was parked in its usual spot. He got out of his truck, careful not to slam the door. Quietly, he opened the door leading from the carport and stepped inside.

"Surprise! I'm home and ready to go eat. Is anyone hungry?" His announcement was met with silence.

"Hey, is anybody home?" he yelled as he strode into the family room.

A quick survey of the house revealed no one there except Skippy.

"Where the hell is everyone, Skip? Have they all deserted us?"

Skippy wagged his tail a few times and retreated to the family room, leaving his master standing alone in the hall.

After wandering around the house for a few minutes, Luke spied a note on the kitchen table.

"Luke, my mother and I have gone to Celebrity Theater. The kids are eating out and going to the movies with their friends. I didn't know when you would be home so I didn't cook anything. I'll be home late so don't wait up. Love, Emily."

Luke kept reading the note over and over. He shook his head in disbelief. *The one time that I get home early and everyone is gone. They had other plans. Unbelievable! Well, I guess it serves me right for not calling ahead.*

He rummaged through the freezer, pulled out a TV dinner, and popped it into the oven. He poured a glass of Scotch and settled down in front of the television. It was always comforting to have a drink and a snack while watching television, but now that he had the place to himself, it wasn't nearly as enjoyable. He went to bed early, and was fast asleep before the rest of the family got home.

On Sunday, Luke accompanied the family to church. He couldn't remember the last time he'd gone to church. Working six days a week wore him out, and Sunday was the only day he could sleep-in. But for some reason he woke early and felt obligated to join them. They never asked him to go. In fact, they would have left without him if he hadn't stepped up and announced that he was going. He felt like an outsider, a distant and unpopular relative who had purposely shown up to disrupt family functions. Neither Emily nor the kids commented on his attendance.

The rest of the day was uneventful. No one deliberately ignored him. They just didn't go out of their way to acknowledge his presence. He wished the day would pass faster so he could get back to work.

What the hell is the matter with me? When I'm at work, I can't wait to get home, and when I'm home, I feel guilty about not being at work.

He slowly shook his head. He learned at an early age that life can flow smoothly until fate throws in a life-altering curve. The family would just have to adapt. They always had, no matter what obstacles they encountered. Their love for each other, and the family bond, was strong enough to withstand any outside force. Their present situation would just take some getting used to. But in the back of Luke's mind, a haunting question lingered.

Hardison, you son of a bitch. What have you done to me?

The End

L. D. Zingg

Made in the USA
San Bernardino, CA
16 June 2019